Dark Victory

TOR BOOKS BY MICHELE LANG

Lady Lazarus
Dark Victory

Dark Victory

Michele Lang

TOR®

A TOM DOHERTY ASSOCIATES BOOK
NEW YORK

DARK VICTORY

Copyright © 2012 by Michele Lang

Edited by James Frenkel

A Tor Book
Published by Tom Doherty Associates, LLC
175 Fifth Avenue
New York, NY 10010

www.tor-forge.com

Tor® is a registered trademark of Tom Doherty Associates, LLC.

Library of Congress Cataloging-in-Publication Data

Lang, Michele.
    Dark victory / Michele Lang.—1st ed.
      p. cm.
    "A Tom Doherty Associates Book."
    ISBN 978-0-7653-3045-1 (hardcover)
    ISBN 978-0-7653-2318-7 (trade paperback)
    1. Witches—Fiction.   2. Nazis—Fiction.   3. World War, 1939–1945—
Europe, Eastern—Fiction.   I. Title.
 PS3612.A5544D37 2012
 813'.6—dc22

                                       2011025172

First Edition: January 2012

Printed in the United States of America

0 9 8 7 6 5 4 3 2 1

In loving memory of my grandparents who died in the war:
Hendryk Landau, Tosca Landau, and Gyula Berger.

And with love and gratitude to the only grandfather I ever knew
growing up, my grandmother Irene's second husband,
Josef Weber.

Of blessed memory.

ACKNOWLEDGMENTS

In addition to all the usual writing suspects who know who they are, special thanks go to early readers Amy Lau, Beth Sherrard-Maurin, and Juliet Blackett, for their discerning eye and honesty. I also thank Louis Badolato for re-creating the Battle of Warsaw for me, and providing invaluable insight into the air battles of World War II. As usual, all historical inaccuracy and spiritual blasphemy is solely attributable to me.

Thank you to the production, sales, and marketing team at Tor, especially Alexis Saarela for her publicity smarts, Christina MacDonald for her eagle copyediting eye, and Steven Padnick and Leslie Matlin for their organizational skills.

My thanks once again to Lucienne Diver, my agent, for believing in my writing and in me. And much gratitude to my editor, James Frenkel, for all that he has done and continues to do.

And finally, and always, my deepest thanks to all of my family. And as for my husband and greatest inspiration, Steven, and my sons, Joshua, Gabriel, and Sam—you are pure magic.

Dark Victory

I

August 30, 1939: 11 a.m.
Dohány Street
Budapest, Hungary

My doom was trapped inside a tin of Hungarian paprika.

I rolled the thin metal canister between my fingers and almost dropped it; the tin was hot enough to burn my skin. In the silence of my dusty little kitchen on Dohány Street, in Budapest's Seventh District, my pulse pounded in my ears. I knew that if I could not control the demon I had captured, Hitler would invade Poland. And the world would explode.

The situation was just that simple and that difficult. I had captured Hitler's personal demon. But I didn't know how to use him.

We simply didn't have any time left. Hitler was going to invade Poland in two days, on September 1, 1939. I knew it. Gisi had seen this dark future in a vision more than a month ago. And knowing this, as a Jewish witch, I was in mortal danger.

But on this hot and over-bright August morning losing my own life was the least of my problems. My breath caught in my throat. I longed to put the tin down, curl up on my cot, and hide from the demon in dreams.

But I could not rest—not with war so close. I had warned the diplomats of the Polish embassy of the imminent war. I also had sent word to the Zionists through my best friend, Eva Farkas, who had joined their number. But now I had to put this demon, Asmodel, under my power, somehow.

I licked my lips and forced myself to breathe. It was time to call forth the bound and hidden Asmodel; only he could tell me what September first would truly bring. Only he could stop Hitler before he unleashed the war.

I had the strength to bind him, but I had to find out whether I had enough magic to compel him to my will.

My little sister Gisele had begged me not to take Asmodel out of the tin; my beloved Raziel, once an angel but now a mortal man for my sake, only shook his head and laughed when I told him I meant to challenge my captive spirit.

I sat in my chair at the kitchen table and cupped the paprika tin in my hands, my fingertips dancing over the hot metal. Raziel stood behind me, and I was grateful that I could not see the expression on his face. Only a day or two before, the demon had fought Raziel, an angel of the Lord, hand to hand, and Raziel stopped him, but at the cost of sacrificing his very place in Heaven.

Gisele, trembling like a wind-tossed leaf, sat next to me, her left arm trailing over my shoulder as we stared together at Asmodel's makeshift prison. The paprika tin Gisele had found proved a surprisingly sturdy prison for Asmodel's soul, with only a dusting of paprika left inside.

"Have a care," Gisele whispered, and her arm tightened around mine. Her sweet solicitude drew tears to my eyes. The cleverest part of me, the part that had seen Gisele and me through the hard years after my mother's death, wanted nothing more but to throw the tin in the Danube and run away to Paris, like my friend Robert Capa had done. I could save Gisele that way.

But Gisele, my little mouse, was also the one who had dared me to rise above my craving for self-preservation. In her quiet way, Gisele dared to resist. Some heroes, like my little sister, are born that way. Other people, like me, are forced by sheer desperation into daring.

I struggled to hold back the tears, and tried to paste a brave-looking, enigmatic smile onto my lips—bravado will carry a person surprisingly far in this world of illusions. The demon was well bound with the spells I had recently learned from an ancient and powerful witch in Amsterdam. But despite all these precautions, Asmodel was by far the stronger of the two of us, and we both knew it.

I flipped open the sifter with my thumb, and immediately I heard Asmodel's low, creepy laughter. Powdered paprika wafted out of the sifter like a pestilent little cloud, and I fought the sudden urge to sneeze. I ran my palm over the top of the sifter, made sure Asmodel wasn't trying to slip into the little cloud and away.

I took a deep breath and a sudden calm descended over me. "Peace, ancient one," I said. I recited the central verses of the Testament of Solomon, the ones that the king himself had used to bind Asmodel, to make sure the demon stayed put.

Somehow the great king had compelled this very demon to serve a larger good, long ago. I was a Lazarus, a witch of the blood, and I now had the power to cast spells. Could I too rule Asmodel?

The low, rumbling laughter stopped, and for that I was grateful.

"You disturb my peace, Jewish witch."

His peace? The creature locked inside the paprika tin disturbed my peace far more, as did his former host and master, the Führer of Germany. In fact, like Hitler, Asmodel disturbed the peace of all the world.

My voice trembled as I spoke, though my nerves stayed steady. "September first, Hitler invades Poland."

The demon scrabbled against the bottom of the tin like a trapped mouse, and the tin twisted ominously in my fingers. "Maybe, maybe not," he growled. "Who knows?"

Tension knotted the base of my skull. "You know, Asmodel. And you will tell me."

The laughter rose again, muffled but clearly intelligible from inside the tin. "How will you make me? You have the power to bind me, but not the power to compel my speech, witchling."

"And yet, a baby witch like me somehow bested and captured an ancient, cunning creature like you. How embarrassing. Your humiliation was witnessed by my own army of imps and demons, by other mortals. And by the Angel Raziel himself."

The laughter devolved into an inarticulate, furious roar. But I ignored Asmodel's outburst; he still resisted me. "I cannot summon the truth out of your soul, demon. But I can convince you to speak the truth of your own volition."

I began singing the Ninety-first Psalm to him in Hungarian, my favorite psalm for banishing and parrying evil spirits. I am not known for my melodious voice, so I am not sure whether it was the substance or my delivery that tormented him more.

After a minute or two, Gisele joined me in the tender serenade; Raziel's hard laughter from behind my shoulder fortified me even as Asmodel snarled.

Gisele and I started singing again, and tried harmony this time. The snarl rose to a shriek. "Stop it! For Lucifer's sake, shut up!"

I paused, took a deep breath to steady myself. I had won the first move in the deadly game we played. "So shut me up then, Asmodel. Tell us."

"Tell you of your death? Tell you of death? It is too late to avert the future, you hapless bitch. What more do you need to know besides the fact that you die?"

Gisele's fingers dug into my shoulder. I ignored her. "Tell me."

"You die at Ravensbruck. Tortured to death—the SS interrogators there are under orders to take their time. They break you, you betray your fellows, and you die in disgrace. Mortals warded from magic murder you—none of your spells and tricks will stop them."

I did not know what Ravensbruck was, but it did not sound good. I swallowed hard. "Go on."

"Your insipid little sister dies right here in Budapest, machine-gunned along the railroad tracks after the local commandant is done with raping her. A pity, he won't know what he has, the potential you have. A waste. Your entire life."

A tear dripped onto my forearm. "He sees, too," Gisele said. "The things that I see he knows."

Gisele was wrong. She had to be. Asmodel knew nothing except how to conjure fear and despair like demonic minions. Raziel and I had fought too hard, stirred up too much celestial mayhem, for his words to remain true.

I pushed forward. "It's too late for all that, Asmodel. Your prophecies are out of date. Raziel and I have turned them aside. Tell me something that is of use to me."

"Oh, I don't think I am wrong about you, witchling child. The world has a date with destiny on September first, and so do you on the day of your death."

"You lie. I have already had a date with death, a number of them in fact. And still I walk the Earth, quite alive."

The vehemence of his roar rattled me. I rocked back, clutching the tin to keep it from wriggling out of my grasp altogether. We wrestled for a few minutes and I stood up to brace the tin better against the table.

The white metal grew even hotter in my hands, and his low growl rose from between my fingers. "See if I speak right, bitch, then know your end is foreordained. Hitler will orchestrate a provocation. He is staging a supposed act of terrorism by Poles on the border, at the radio station in Gleiwitz. Every detail has been arranged. They will dress the corpses in partisan costumes, though the dead men are concentration camp prisoners. . . ."

The demon spoke faster and faster, a litany of overwhelming destruction and misery, echoing like gunshots. He unfolded a grim picture of the war to come, Hitler's plan to crush Poland, to buy time with guns and lies until he could turn his sights to further conquest, richer prizes to both the west and the east.

Asmodel finished his litany of curses and bellowed with laughter. "You little fool. It is too late for you to avert the destiny of the world. You struggle like a fish already on the hook. You are already caught. And every twist and turn only brings you closer to the fishermen's deck. You are already dead!"

My stomach churned, I tasted acid in my mouth. "Death is nothing new to me," I stammered out. "If the Nazis murder me at this Ravensbruck, so be it. I will only summon myself back."

"Oh no, you won't," he replied, the low rumble rising to a horrible bark of laughter. "This last death will be so agonizing, so dehumanizing, you will run toward death. You will embrace it. They will burn your body before you will even consider coming back again. And supreme evil will reign over all the Earth."

His words made me queasy. They hung like acrid smoke in the kitchen, as if Gisele had burned a cake made out of brimstone. I understood better now why Gisele had tried to stop me from speaking to the demon. "You never told me all that," I reproved her mildly.

She shrugged, even as the tears poured over her cheeks. "I told you what you needed to know. Like you said, the details don't really matter, do they?"

Unfortunately, they did. Though Asmodel's words sucked the very air out of the room, I took faint comfort in the fact that if he was right, at least I had nothing much left to lose.

But we were at an impasse, now. Asmodel and I both knew the only way I could control him for sure, force him to serve my purposes. Gisele must have caught the rebellious glint in my eye, for she shook my shoulder.

"No!" she cried, and I winced—her voice wasn't too loud in my ear, but the pain in it pierced my heart. "Please, Magduska. You overreach yourself. Close up the tin and rest."

I had a hard time replying; my jaw was clenched too tight. I kept my eyes on the tin, knowing that Asmodel was ready to pounce at the slightest evidence of weakening in my resolve. "My darling, of course I overreach. I must."

She knew what I was after; she wanted me to find it, too, as long as I didn't lose my soul in the hunt. *The Book of Raziel*: the ancient book of spells that Raziel himself had given to Eve when the world was young and human beings faced existential danger, as they did now. And everyone in that room, demon, fallen angel, and mortal, knew that Book was my rightful inheritance.

A version of it resided with Adolf Hitler in Berlin, but I could not let that fact stop me now. Perhaps I could find a way to force Asmodel to get it for me, somehow.

To find out, I needed to converse face-to-face with my nemesis. "Asmodel," I whispered. "Come forth, still bound by spell, but in your chosen guise."

Asmodel materialized on the splintery wooden surface of the round kitchen table, in the form of a breathtakingly beautiful youth, completely naked, curled up like a fern frond on the mossy, slippery banks of a hidden stream in Eden. Slowly he lifted his head, and his enormous almond eyes met my gaze. The breath caught in my throat.

"This is my true aspect, Magduska," he said, in a soft, warm baritone. So changed, so transformed, yet I recognized him in this guise.

His beauty threw me off balance, and I struggled to maintain my self-possession. "Don't say Magduska," I shot back. "Only those who love me may call me that."

His smile was gentle. "You invoke love? I know of love. Your

Raziel fell from Heaven the same way as did I, for love of a woman. Naamah was as beautiful as you, her kisses were as sweet as yours. We had many hours of bliss, lying together and knowing love when the world was young and such things were common."

My cheeks burned. About the ways of magic, I had few illusions left, but I was still a novice at the sorcery of the love a man and a woman might share.

Raziel drew closer to the back of my chair, and his mere presence cut through the confusion of Asmodel's words.

"You lie," Raziel said, and though he spoke bitter words, his voice remained kind. "Brother, you descend not to help humankind in their exile, but to grind them into the dust. You want the Earth and all its dominion for yourself."

The demon's honeyed smile grew jaded. "What of it? That is no secret, not like your blessed secrets, the secrets of your blasted Book with its elemental magic."

I gathered up my strength, leaned back in my chair, and looked directly into the demon's eyes for the first time. "Yes, the Book. We must talk about that Book. It is mine by birthright. I want it. You will help me. I am willing to go to Berlin to get it if I have to."

Asmodel stretched his arms over his head and smiled at me, the sleepy rapturous grin of a lover who wants more satisfaction. "Magduska, the copy of the Book in Berlin means little. Not even Hitler himself can use it without cracking open its magic and mastering it. His best wizards could not do it. He needs a witch like you."

The very thought of serving Hitler as a witch of the Reich made my skin crawl. "I will never serve Hitler, and you know it.

But the Book will serve him, if they can find a dark sorcery to enslave its magic. I won't let that happen, Asmodel. The Book is mine, in its every form."

"You can forget the Book in Berlin, little fool. You do not need it. The original of your Book still exists."

My body stiffened in shock, and only with a desperate effort was I able to keep my composure. All of us had fought a terrible battle over the mere reconstitution of the Book only a day or two before. If Asmodel spoke the truth, if the unsullied original could still be found . . .

I closed my hand over the now empty paprika tin, the sharp edges cutting into my palm. I tried to imagine what the original Book, in my power, could mean to the future that Asmodel had predicted.

"You are the prince of lies," I said.

His gaze locked onto mine, and my heart raced at the sight of him. I blinked hard to keep my focus despite the seduction of his words.

Asmodel's smile grew even wider. "But I tell the truth. It is your beautiful love, your own fine fallen one whom you tempted, your Raziel, who murders truth now with his silence."

I tore my gaze away and twisted around to look at Raziel, standing tall behind my chair. His face was as still as stone.

Asmodel's voice, soft now, snaked into my ears. "Tell her, brother, of the elemental nature of your Book. Tell her of the Sapphire Heaven. And of the power your girl may command with the gem in her hand."

Raziel said nothing.

I knew the ancient one sought to divide us with his honeyed, poisoned words, but I listened to him anyway, hoping for a slip of the tongue that would help my cause. I kept my eyes trained on Raziel even as I spoke to the demon. "Raziel is not talking. So go on. I am listening."

Raziel closed his eyes against me, and I noticed for the first time the all-too-human stubble now tracing the line of his jaw. Raziel was no longer an angel, but a man. And men make mistakes.

I turned to face Asmodel once more, and the demon leaned forward, his smile broadening, close enough to kiss me.

"You speak in riddles, demon," I said, and I could not keep the tremor out of my voice now. "*The Book of Raziel* is a book, not a gem. And why did we all chase the handwritten copy of the Book to Amsterdam last month if the original could still be found?"

His gaze exposed me where I sat, my heart pounding so hard my pulse roared in my ears. Asmodel's eyes narrowed. "You think so little of your angel, now that he is shorn of wings. Unlike you, I have not tasted the pleasures of my brother's flesh. But he is no better than I; he is fallen as am I. He has no more reason to keep the secrets of God, not now. Make Raziel tell you, tempt him as Naamah once tempted me."

A trembling worked its way from the base of my throat to my lips. Again I blinked back the sting of tears and kept my voice as level as I could. "You are a liar. I cannot trust a thing you say."

Asmodel shrugged. "That is true," he said, his oily voice now maddeningly mild. "But the truth is worth my speaking when it serves my purposes. And you said you wanted the truth."

I clutched at despair as to the side of a lifeboat. "It doesn't matter now, regardless," I said. "I've already lost everything. Without *The Book of Raziel,* gemstone or book of spells in Berlin, I cannot stop Hitler. You are right after all . . . I am too late."

"You don't understand me, mortal girl. You cannot stop Hitler—but more than this, you cannot stop death. Now Raziel will die. No longer an angel, he will face the Throne upon his death, the Lord's wrath. Like Naamah, he will die. He is no demon like me. No witch like you, with the power to return from the dead.

"Raziel is now only a man. You cannot stop his death, you know that. As much evil as he has done to save you, you have gained nothing. But you can still save him, Magduska. Vanquish death itself! Forget Hitler—do it for Raziel's sake."

Gasping, I turned to face Raziel. This time, Raziel smiled, a small, knowing smile, one that confirmed everything that Asmodel had said. It occurred to me that Asmodel had tempted him to fall many times before, in times long gone out of human memory—and now Raziel had succumbed, given up his place in Heaven, for no other reason but to stand with me. And he could only watch now as Asmodel similarly tempted me.

I turned back again to Asmodel, my heart cold, an extinguished candle flame. "What is it like to be so very old?" I said, allowing my thoughts to take flight into words. "Killing humans must be like swatting gnats."

Asmodel sighed in what looked like bliss and closed his eyes. "Entertaining and useful gnats; foolish gnats, with the power to choose the way of the world."

"Do we really? Choose anything?"

The demon's eyes opened and he pierced me with his gaze, speared me. "You could make this world a paradise with your choices, Magduska."

This time I let him get away with the endearment. It was my

turn to be silent and consider his words. I was listening, really listening.

"Come with me as I restore the Garden," he said, his voice low and beseeching. "You could be the one to do it. *The Book of Raziel* was first inscribed in the sapphire, its wisdom encased in the structure of the gem. The Book exists. It is a lost treasure, but it is real. We lost it when the Temple was destroyed, but we have our theories of its location, do we not, my brother Raziel?"

"Why do you need the Book, copy or sapphire?" I asked. "You seem to exert your dominion quite well without it."

"Nonsense. I am in chains, dear sorceress," he murmured. "My dominion has ended—I went from the great Führer to nothing, nobody, my prison an old tin of paprika."

"But how did you conquer Hitler in the first place?"

"I already told you before, Magduska, and I do not lie. He invited me in, to augment his puny mortal powers. Had we but preserved *The Book of Raziel* as it had been transcribed, retained the original geography of the gemstone, no one could have stopped me."

"Not even Hitler himself," I remarked, more to myself than to him.

Asmodel shrugged and, like a cat, relaxed bit by bit against my forearm, the stubble of his cheek scratching through my flimsy cotton blouse. Abruptly I remembered his nakedness, and my cheeks flushed with shame.

The demon pretended not to notice my mortification. "Hitler wanted me to own him. How could he live a thousand years otherwise?"

"Could you give him a thousand years, demon?" I asked. My

head throbbed and I was shrouded in weariness, dragged toward the grave by the hands of despair.

I sat perfectly still, unwilling to betray my weakness. But I feared that Asmodel somehow sensed it nonetheless.

"What does it matter? There is nothing more to say, my beautiful one," he murmured. "Let me in. Raziel and I will share you, and you will experience such pleasure as you cannot comprehend. Together we will find the gemstone; you will learn to call it from its hidden place. And you would vanquish both Hitler and Stalin, stop this messy war, and perfect the fellowship of mankind. You know I do not lie."

Not in the words themselves, but in the totality of their meaning, did Asmodel twist the truth. I tore my gaze away from the demon's nakedness, his deep, warm, amber eyes, and I turned again to look at Raziel.

Raziel had cast his lot with me, with Gisele, with all the rest of us cursed by fate to fight and die in the terrible year of 1939. He would stay with me, even if I chose wrong—especially if I chose wrong. And he would not rob from me the choice only I could make.

"What do you think, Raziel?"

I could not hide from him the desperation in my voice, the strain of the temptation. Raziel leaned in to murmur into my ear. "I was a powerful angel yesterday, Magda. Now I am only a man, and not much of a man, not yet."

He caressed the nape of my neck with his gentle, warm fingers. "It is like this, Magduska. The choice is impossible. You either let Asmodel in and try your best to control him from inside your body, or you keep him locked away, safe but useless.

But beware. Hitler let Asmodel in, and look what has happened. Hitler's evil has only strengthened Asmodel's."

I imagined the cold touch of Asmodel inside my body, possessing my flesh, and I shuddered.

"I don't have the strength to use him," I confessed in a whisper. "And I don't have time to find that gem he speaks of, not before Hitler invades. We will have to find another way, at least for now. Gisele could hold him and not be tempted, but just holding him is not enough."

I looked deep into Asmodel's amber eyes. I could not afford to hesitate any longer. "Go back into the darkness," I said, even as Asmodel's face fell.

To spare us both another struggle I summoned a cone of silence to descend over the tin like a glass dome over a cake. The white tin with the red lettering looked sepia now, like a newsreel, and Asmodel gave me one last, despairing glance as he disappeared through the sifter into the darkness of his prison.

The sudden silence thundered in my ears. I sat at the kitchen table, drenched in sweat, sick with exhaustion, the tin—again scorching hot—clenched in my fingers. Asmodel was trapped inside once more, the stalemate still between us.

The demon was bound, certainly. And unlike most of my countrymen, I knew the time and place that Hitler would strike. I had tried my best to bend Asmodel's will to my purposes, as sages and kings had done in ancient times. But I was no sage. I had failed.

It was Asmodel, even trapped inside his tin prison, who held the upper hand.

✳ 2 ✳

Failure didn't sit well on my shoulders, and after my war of words with Asmodel I wanted to tear out my hair. I was used to outwitting fate in my heretofore dodgy life as a vampire's lieutenant, and I wasn't ready to concede defeat, not yet, not without more of a fight.

Even in the shadow of death, people need to eat. So when daylight failed, that final Wednesday night before the war, I insisted that Gisele and Raziel accompany me to my place of business, the Café Istanbul. My employer, the fearsome vampire Count Gabor Bathory, had doubled my salary before he disappeared only days before, and though the world was collapsing around our ears, his credit was still good.

Raziel agreed to meet me at the Istanbul, but later, once he had found a way to ensure that Asmodel remained well secured inside the paprika tin; a den of vampires was no place to bring an imperfectly secured primeval demon. Given the dangers the Istanbul contained, and the fact I was bringing my little sister within its doors, I was anxious to depart before the sun had fully set. Despite my secret worries, I left Raziel to his labors.

As we paused on the café's threshold, I took Gisele's left hand and tucked it in the crook of my arm, and I pulled her close to me so that we went in as a tightly connected entity. My principal place of business was a café for vampires, and my mortal little sister, untrained in spell-casting, was too delectable a morsel for a vampire to resist. Alas, even my employer, Count Bathory himself, had not been able to keep himself from tasting her in the past.

The maître d' did a double take when he saw us gliding past the huge marble bar on the way to the grand staircase that led to the mezzanine. He ran behind the bar to intercept us, and blocked our passage onto the stairway . . . politely.

By politely, I mean that he kept his fangs tucked away, out of sight, and instead greeted us with a nervous smile. "Bathory is still not here," he said.

I winced at the news that Bathory was still not in Budapest, though I knew all too well where he had gone, and why.

The maître d' shifted his spectral attentions from me to Gisele, and his nostrils flared, not with annoyance but with an epicure's appreciation for the gourmet possibilities of my all-but-defenseless virgin little sister.

"Ma'm'selle, Count Bathory announced with great fanfare, less than two days ago, that he would fly to meet the great Mittel-Europa Vampirrat in full session. He had been summoned. He has not—yet—returned."

He inserted that "yet" out of deference and consideration for me, Bathory's loyal lieutenant, but he and I both knew the truth: Bathory had gone in answer to a summons. And the Vampirrat summoned vampires only to promote or to punish.

My poor count had shown too much independence of spirit to expect promotion within the ranks of vampire nobility, they who of late had sworn fealty to the German Reich. I worried that he had earned a stake in the heart as payment for championing my cause, as well as that of independent Hungary.

My shy little sister, heedless of the danger, bravely and un-characteristically pressed forward. "Sir," she ventured, "my sister here works for the count, Bathory. And she . . . well, she needs her wages. We all need to eat, dear sir."

The maître d' could no longer restrain himself. As his lips parted in a huge smile, he flashed us the disconcerting sight of his long, yellowed fangs. "Indeed we *do* need to eat, ma'm'selle. Indeed, we do."

"Gaston," I said, "she is here with me. The lamb walks under Bathory's protection. Beware."

The smile grew wider. "Bathory? My dear, he can no longer protect even himself."

His words lit my rage like a match held to a gas stove. "Beware, Gaston." My voice vibrated with the force of my power, held in check.

Our eyes locked, and Gaston licked his lips again. Ordinarily, any mortal who met a vampire's gaze was vulnerable to his thrall.

But I am no ordinary mortal.

Gaston stifled a shriek as he stumbled backward and against the balustrade.

"I am not your breakfast, Gaston," I murmured, as bloody

tears welled over the bridge of his nose. "I will summon your dried-up old soul clear out of your body through your nostrils if you do not step aside and let us pass. In Bathory's name!"

I bit my tongue to keep from cursing him, or harming him in a more than transitory way. After all, it was not Gaston's fault that Bathory had gone to Berlin to meet his terrible fate. It was mine.

I eased my grip upon his mind and Gaston slapped his hands over his eyes, breaking our connection. Still half blinded, he bowed deeply and kissed his exposed wrist, the submissive salutation of a lesser vampire acknowledging a greater.

He acknowledged Bathory's power, not mine, but I hardly cared. I patted Gisele's fingers, still tucked into the crook of my arm. "Very well, Gaston," I said, my voice calm and reasonable once more. "Please, we'll be sitting at Bathory's customary table upstairs. Kindly send up Imre when he arrives. It is near dusk, and he should be here soon."

"Yes, certainly, Ma'm'selle Magda." And Gaston wiped his eyes and slunk away.

We climbed the stairs slowly and with a grand show of outward confidence. But Gisele's hand trembled like a tiny creature hidden in the crook of my arm. "Steady," I stage-whispered when we arrived at the mezzanine landing.

The sight of Bathory's table, perfectly set and devoid of its proper denizen, made me pause. With a sigh I pulled Gisele along and installed her in the corner against the wall, where she would be easier to defend. With a flourish I settled into Bathory's seat; I used my witch's sight to scan the entire café for danger.

I surveyed my old domain, the gilded, Levantine Café Istanbul, and a sweet melancholy settled like a taste on my tongue.

Oh, my old haunt was dangerous, all right. The place was filled with hungry vampires who were waiting for nightfall so they could feed. But theirs was the usual dangerous, the known dangerous. I wrapped myself within that familiar peril as if it were a goose-down quilt in February. As much as anywhere, this den of iniquity, with its strange denizens and lugubrious atmosphere, was home.

Settling into my seat with a satisfied little sigh, I unfolded a linen napkin and smoothed it over my lap. "My dear, we are going to have a proper meal at last. Bathory's credit is still good."

Her hand reached across the table to grasp mine, and Gisele half crushed my fingers as she spoke. "Magduska, you are too brave."

"I cannot give up. It would be too easy. Even if Bathory is gone, I can't." My voice caught on the count's name. Even as the world collapsed around our ears, the thought of his destruction was a little too much for me to take.

"But Bathory is still . . . alive, Magduska! I can, you know—I can feel it." Gisi bit her lip and blushed, and my throat tightened with both rage and guilt. Gisele, sweet Gisi, had bared her neck to Bathory in order to survive when I had left her behind in Budapest. He had not turned her vampire, and for that I was forever grateful. But the bond between Bathory and Gisele remained, and it was my fault she had bared her neck in the first place.

I patted her hand with my free one—my other hand she still clutched in a death grip. Café Istanbul had this effect on mortal people; actually, my girl was handling herself pretty well.

The bell attached to the front door gently sounded, and I

glanced over the balcony to the café entrance and looked to see if Imre had arrived.

My heart leaped when I saw it was Raziel, not Imre, who crossed the threshold and entered the Istanbul. His shoulders, backlit by the streetlights, filled the doorway, and I watched him adjust the fedora on his head as he stepped to the bar and looked around for me.

So far away and below he was, out of reach and strangely vulnerable and alone-looking. My mind flooded with a welter of conflicting emotions: fear for him, now mortal and a temptation to the vampiric denizens of the café; pride in his beauty and the goodness that streamed like light from him; and sadness, that he began his life as a man in the encroaching darkness of total war.

Gaston stood behind him, and I half expected him to waylay Raziel, now a mere mortal, before he ever knew where to find me. But he half turned, and as if I had worked some spell upon him, Raziel looked up to where I sat on the mezzanine, and he pierced me with his gaze.

Even from this distance, I saw the desolation in his eyes. I wiggled my fingers in a regal little wave, and a smile broke over his face.

He took the curving staircase two stairs at a time, and arrived at our table not the slightest bit out of breath. "Magduska," he said, voice low. He doffed his fedora and made an absurdly formal little bow.

Gisi laughed and applauded him. "You are charming, Raziel, sir," she said, and patted the seat next to her for him to sit.

His smile grew lopsided, and he instead chose the seat next to me, moving so close to me I could feel the heat of him all along my side.

"Cigarette?" I asked, trying hard to sound elegant, but not well enough to banish the tremor from my voice.

He took my offering with a nod of thanks and placed his hat upon the table. A bit rude, but I couldn't bear to correct him. What did angels know of earthly decorum, and what did fancy manners matter in Budapest on August 30, 1939?

"Where is Asmodel?" I asked in an ordinary voice. I could not prevent eavesdropping vampires from overhearing our conversation; their hearing was so sharp I could not keep them from hearing my racing, galloping heart, let alone our spoken-aloud words. I did not censor my speech; I didn't want the café's staff and nocturnal patrons to think I was afraid, of them or of the ancient demon, either.

The shadows returned to Raziel's face. "He will not stir from his prison, I swear it to you, Magduska. The tin is in the kitchen, right where Gisele left it."

Gisele's eyes widened at the news. "Surely it isn't safe to leave him all alone?"

Raziel shrugged in reply. I lit his cigarette for him, and he took a slow drag, not too deep; he had only begun smoking a few days before. Raziel was still learning how to be a man. "Sometimes you must balance your risks. He is safer locked in your kitchen than almost anywhere else in the world."

I looked at him, watched the smoke curl from his lips. "But it is not safe, is it, my angel?"

His look was sharp. "You may trust my words, Magduska."

I swallowed hard, lit a cigarette for myself. "You, I'd follow to the gates of Hell. I just don't trust that creature in the tin."

I didn't have the money to smoke as much as my heart desired, so I savored the cigarette I had, drawing deeply and watching the tip glow red. And I considered the problem of Asmodel. I could not use him, at least not now. So what next?

The waiter arrived bearing enormous leather-bound menus. I ordered for the three of us, a luxurious, final meal before the war came. And I smoked my cigarette down to a smoldering stub.

"A last supper," Gisi said. She didn't look at me, and though her voice still held music, I could see the weight of her visions on her shoulders.

The poor girl was a frazzled wreck—I couldn't stand seeing her hollowed eyes, her trembling lips, the burden of her knowledge.

"This is ridiculous," I muttered, and I crushed out the last bit of my cigarette. "We cannot sit here, like convicts waiting to be hanged! I cannot master Asmodel, we cannot stop the war, so what is left except to run!"

The two of them leaned toward me, and Gisi held her fingers to her lips.

"No, I won't shut up, Gisele! I don't care who hears me, either. You would have to be a fool or willfully blind not to see the storm on the horizon. I will not just sit here until it is upon us."

"You do not understand," Raziel said. He grabbed his hat off the table, began tugging at the silk edging with his fingertips. "You have already unleashed a storm, Magduska. Asmodel will not stay in that tin for much longer."

The thought of Asmodel loose in Budapest killed my appetite altogether. "Then how are you so sure he is safe in my kitchen?"

"Because he promised. I asked him to stay."

I blinked hard with surprise. "You asked him!" I could not

grasp what he was saying. "You think that anything he says can be trusted, is any more than a lie?"

His smile this time was genuine and dangerous. "I know him better than you do, Magduska."

I shook my head, my nerves still humming from the cigarette smoke. I looked at Raziel again, looked with my witch's sight, and I gasped. His soul's aspect had transformed utterly. Raziel's soul now shone clear and steady, a candle flame instead of a raging storm of celestial godlight.

Raziel was a man. I had known it with my mind before this. But now, in the moment of my need, I absorbed the limitation of his mortality like a punch in the gut.

"But, can you still . . ."

"Can I still talk to him as I did in my angelic form? Better now than before. We are both fallen, we both walk the Earth. I understand him better now, and he thinks he understands me better as well. But that is to our advantage, is it not?"

"It is to Asmodel's advantage, too, I expect."

Raziel shook his head and laughed. He leaned back in his chair and looked at me as if he had never really seen me before, either. "You don't understand what is going on here, do you?"

His words made goose pimples rise all along the length of my arms. "No, I am a fool, I readily admit it. Please, explain."

"Asmodel and I are brothers, Magduska. He was an angel before he fell—I saw him fall. We have been engaged in battle since the world was young, long before your ancestress, the Witch of Ein Dor herself, became the caretaker of *The Book of Raziel*. And now, for the first time, we fight on a different plane of existence, for different stakes."

His words stunned me so that I could barely breathe. "I still don't understand, my dear."

His smile softened. "Perhaps it is better that you don't. Let us instead focus on our present troubles. Stay, or go? We need to solve that puzzle first."

Now I was on more familiar terrain, and I clung gladly to what I knew, terrible as it was. "I don't know what to do. The war will soon engulf Poland, and she will be lost to the Reich. Hungary is safe for now, aligned with Germany. But for how long?"

Despite the loss of the Book, we had fought hard, and with some success. I thought of the imps I had managed to summon only a few days before, without the power of *The Book of Raziel* to augment my own abilities. The option of running seemed the most rational choice, the most likely to preserve our lives.

But my own magic called to me—the magic I already possessed, the spells I had learned to weave in the last few months, and the potential magic I could yet wield, if only I could claim *The Book of Raziel*.

Gisele interrupted my rather desperate train of thought. She leaned forward and kept her voice scarcely above a whisper. "Eva is fighting regardless. She's gone to a dangerous place, a world of deception, in order to serve a larger good. We've got to fight, too."

The mention of Eva made my heart sink. My brave, beautiful friend, with no magic in her at all; she who knew of my sister's prophecy, and who intended to make the most of the advance knowledge.

Now Eva had joined the Jewish fighters. She was a foot soldier of the Hashomer Zionists, gathering weapons and other war-riors for battles soon to come. Now that she was gone, I didn't know what battles she fought in the shadow of the impending war.

"She is a heroine, Gisi. And you know how most heroines end up."

"Well, yes. But we're all supposed to die anyway. You heard what the demon said."

"'We're deader than dead ducks' is what Eva would say if she were here with us," I said, my voice husky.

"Our Eva." Gisele's voice broke over her name. "I know what she would say. It's too late to run, so we might as well do what we can to take our enemies down with us."

Time was running out, slipping through our fingers as we lingered at the Istanbul. Before I could think more on the dismal prospect, the waiter arrived with a sumptuous meal, covered by Bathory's still-good account.

All conversation stopped as we ate, but I had trouble tasting the food, let alone swallowing it.

Still, the meal reminded me of our missing benefactor. "I'll tell you one thing," I said, my voice growing steadier. "No matter what happens, I am going to get Bathory out of his trouble in Berlin. I owe him no less than that. You say he is alive, Gisi. Since that's the case, then I must do what I can to fetch him out."

Gisele stopped chewing in mid-bite, her eyes widening in real horror. "You are not going to Berlin? Please say no. Please."

I smiled at her; making the decision to act nourished me like our meal. "No, I would come to a quick end and be wasted in Berlin. Instead, I will rouse the vampires to save their own."

I knew that every vampire in the place could hear what I said. "I am going to make Bathory's case to the Budapest Vampirrat and make common cause with them. Once Bathory is safe, I can consider leaving Hungary. Not before then."

Raziel shook his head. "Bathory would not want you to risk your life in such a way. You might be safer in Berlin after all, you know. The vampires here have sworn fealty to the Reich on the orders of the MittelEuropa Vampirrat."

"I know that," I said, trying to keep the anguish out of my voice, and the determination in. "But they know Bathory better than I, too. And they know if Bathory can meet such a dreadful fate in Berlin, any of them may well be next. That should give them some real incentive to help him. I have to at least try."

It would also give me something more positive to focus on as the clock ran out and the invasion of Poland became a reality. And perhaps if I survived my encounter with the reigning vampires of Budapest, I would have more of an idea what I must do next, once August became September.

I took Gisele home, and Raziel and I went to try to at least save Bathory, if we could.

The Vampirrat of Budapest resided within a grand old mansion, not far from my beloved, departed Bathory's residence on Rose Hill, in old Buda. I had served Count Gabor Bathory four years before he disappeared into the maw of Hitler's Berlin, and he had never once risked my safety by bringing me through this enormous wrought-iron front gate. But this night, I entered without out Bathory's physical protection, without invitation or warning. Bathory's life balanced on the edge of a wooden stake; I had no time to hesitate.

Raziel stood beside me as I rang the front doorbell. Silent, with the fedora perched at a rakish angle on his head, his face remained blank: he came not as an avenging angel now, but as the lieutenant of a vampire's lieutenant. And he didn't yet know how to play the part to his own satisfaction.

Imre answered the door, and I almost wept with relief. Huge, misshapen, with a heart of gold, Imre was Bathory's enforcer and now I guess he had found a new job. I could count my friends among the vampires on the fingers of one hand—my employment with Bathory had earned me as many enemies as allies among the fanged nobility of Budapest.

But Imre was a friend.

"Hello, you big bruiser," I whispered, knowing my voice echoed in the sensitive ears of the occupants inside.

Imre's puffy little eyes widened and he tried to slam the door in my face, but I was too quick for him and wedged my body halfway over the threshold. Bless him, Imre was strong enough to crush me with the door but his sense of decency made him hesitate.

"Let me in," I said, too quickly for him to get a word in edgewise. "I know you are trying to protect me, but my blood is not on your head, I swear it. Bathory is absolved from seeking my revenge. You can tell him, and he will believe it."

Imre's scarred prizefighter's face settled into a hard, craggy granite boulder. "Get out of here, kid," he snarled low in his throat. "Scram. You'll get sliced into ribbons, and I *should* let them at you for coming over here uninvited."

Imre glanced over my shoulder, and saw Raziel. "Hey, what happened to your wings, eh? Some bodyguard you are, mister."

A sneer had crept into Imre's voice. "It should be you in the door. I bet you don't even have a piece."

I tried to shove my way in but Imre wouldn't let me. "A gun? Here? Are you mad, Imre? I come here with the utmost respect, only to make a humble request. An offer of mutual assistance, if you like."

Imre growled again, and his voice was filled with misery. "Go away. The council will rip my head off if you butt in here. Go away!"

"But think of Bathory. He'll die if we don't save him from the Berlin council. It might already be too late." I looked back over my shoulder at Raziel. His eyes burned like banked coals, and an expression I'd never seen before darkened his features like a thunderhead.

Magic wouldn't get me over the vampires' threshold. I tried one last time to move Imre with words alone. "If you don't let us in, sweet, wonderful, terrible Imre, the public staking of Bathory will be on your head."

Raziel pressed forward, and I could feel his body touching mine. "If you let her in, sir, and if she comes to harm, Bathory may take his revenge upon me when he returns. But I am here to keep her safe, I swear my life on it."

Raziel's words sliced into me. An angel does not swear lightly, fallen or no. And I had never heard of an archangel swearing an oath to a vampire; never!

The air crackled with the tension of all the things the three of us didn't dare to say. After a few moments Imre broke the standoff, silently swinging the enormous door open on its huge, well-oiled hinges.

"Enter," Imre intoned, "but beware." He stood back and Raziel and I were plunged into darkness.

We walked through a grand marble foyer, illuminated, I could see after my eyes adjusted to the dimness, by delicate blue lights. My heart was pounding so hard it hurt. I kept telling myself to keep walking, keep calm; remember, you speak for many who can no longer speak, many who can no longer appeal for alliances.

A low rustling rushed past us, a strange rumbling wind infused with a fetid, ugly magic; I whispered the Ninety-first Psalm under my breath and the wind passed over my skin and away.

I stopped walking, chilled to the marrow. Raziel and I exchanged a silent glance. I saw he understood as well as I why that wind blew evil omens through the hallway to where we stood: vampires cannot work magic; they feared and distrusted it, and yet coveted magic as a weapon against other vampires, and against other magical creatures.

Unlike the vampires, I was a Lazarus, a witch of the blood; even before the great witch of Amsterdam, Lucretia de Merode, had taught me how to work spells, I had been able to summon souls. I was Bathory's favorite protégée in part because of the latent magic in me, and his hope that my magic would be made manifest. Now that I had learned spellcraft from Lucretia, it was my magic I had hoped to trade with the vampires in exchange for their alliance; but unfortunately the vampires had already acquired a magic, however perverted, from another ally.

Foul magic, this. Magic in the wrong place, out of bounds, if you will: unholy magic. And I did not know its origin.

I paused partway down the long, darkened hallway, studied the patchwork of muddy footprints crisscrossing over a parquet floor, and took a long slow breath. "The court meets in the great room at the end of this hallway. I can sense it."

I turned to face Raziel, and he squeezed my fingers reassuringly with his left hand. "Ready to go in, Magduska?"

Tension coursed through my body. "Yes." The calm in Raziel's voice steadied my nerves. Even vulnerable as he now was, yet I was grateful he still walked beside me.

We reached the closed door at the end of the dimly lit hallway. Raziel reached forward and opened the door for me so that we could enter together.

The light inside the grand ballroom was similarly dim: vampires enjoy silence and cool darkness. A faint scent of the grave clung to the gilded walls and dusty parquet floors; for a moment, visions of skeletons clothed in brightly colored skirts, dancing at a ball, swirled through my mind.

"Who disturbs us without summons?" called a voice from the back of the enormous room.

"It's me, Magda Lazarus, lieutenant to Count Bathory," I said, keeping my own voice low. "I come upon an urgent errand."

"Step forward. And bring your companion with you."

Raziel again reached for my hand and we walked across the huge, dusty ballroom, toward a collection of wing chairs and love seats scattered randomly near the back wall. The council was not in session, and the presiding members lolled around, resting between their hunting forays into the night. From what Bathory had told me, I knew they could receive my request and make a decision without a formal session. The council only formally convened for other vampires: the way the Berlin Vampirrat had assembled to judge and probably exact judgment upon my boss, Bathory.

I was close enough to them now that I could smell them, the peculiar, loamy smell of creatures who curl up to sleep in the dirt like earthworms.

Bathory had taught me to avoid the vampire gaze, lest I be captured by their glamour. I seem to be rather immune to the lure of their burning stare—perhaps because I make for unsatisfying prey. Maybe it is my blood, I don't know. Even mosquitoes don't bother biting me.

I scanned the figures, looking for familiar vampire lords. Unfortunately, I recognized them all—and I could not have picked a more hostile panel: hostile to me, to Bathory, and to the urgent mission I pursued.

The highest ranked, as usual, was a female. She lay sprawled over a pile of big, musty-looking pillows, dressed indifferently in a scarlet Japanese kimono, garish against her grayish skin. Erszebet Fekete, princess of the Carpathian exiles. She was Bathory's cousin, and they hated each other with all the virulence of family.

To her right, seated stiffly on a chair, was Attila, vibrating with rage and bloodlust. He was the distant relative of a leading Hungarian Fascist leader, turned by Erszebet only a year ago.

I was surprised to see Attila still alive, actually, let alone an attending member of the council—it was a bad sign. As a bloodlust vampire, he could never attain the rank of the vampire-born nobility, ancient creatures like Erszebet, or Bathory himself. But we lived in perverted, unnatural times. And such a well-connected Fascist had his own sick sources of power.

The final member of this deadly, murderous trio was the ancient, cunning Uncle Jansci, the fattest vampire I had ever seen. Bathory had taught me well the ways of the magical creatures in Budapest before he was summoned away. But he had never had the chance to introduce me formally to Jansci, so the massive creature was under no host obligation to accord me privileges as a guest now.

"Greetings, creatures of darkness," I began. I kept my gaze low and deferential, not because I feared their glamour but because I wanted them to believe that I did.

"Attila, darling, our prey comes into our lair tonight!" Erszebet's scratchy husk of a voice cackled with glee. "Look at that man!"

"The girl smells of death and magic," Attila whined, his body shifting noisily in the creaky leather armchair. Bloodlust vampires suffer from an often fatal lack of control, and I wondered at his current degree of madness.

Uncle Jansci said nothing, but sat as still as an enormous Carpathian mountain peak. His silence frightened me the most, for while the other two creatures were readable, his placidity hid his beliefs and motives. I could not sense Jansci's soul at all.

Despite my nerves I kept my focus, and drew my fear deep inside of me, a hard little pellet hidden in my heart. "I come with the prospect of money and good luck, eternal ones."

Erszebet trailed a bony hand over one meager, exposed breast; I dared a peek, saw her licking her lips, and realized that already she had half surrendered to her own bloodlust. Raziel and I were both in deep trouble, and I had not yet even explained my presence.

I breathed a whisper of protection around Raziel and me, just enough to inflict magical hurt if Erszebet lunged for Raziel's throat. I moved a little closer to him, could sense the slow, steady beating of his heart through the pulse in his fingers.

"Hitler will take Poland within days," I said. "He has his own bloodlust. It is war."

To my surprise, it was Jansci who answered me. "Poland will succumb immediately, like a lamb. Hitler will drink, be satisfied. There will be no war."

"I wish it were so, but it is not to be, ancient one. The Poles have vowed to fight—I went to their embassy not twenty-four hours ago, and they were already on alert. They believe the British and the French will honor their treaties and counterattack."

"The French." Jansci's words dripped with contempt. "Mortal child, you were not born to witness the carnage of the Great War, what murderous idiocy you people are capable of. The French will not attack Hitler's army. Nor will the British. They will speak fine words, and condole the Polish people. And they will hold back while Hitler and his dogs rip out the throat of Poland."

"The great Eastern Werewolf Pack has indeed sworn fealty to Hitler as their pack leader supreme. Surely you don't mean to take orders from them?"

Jansci growled, an impotent, curdled roar of fury. I threw more energy into my circle of protection and it began to hum.

"You're Bathory's girl," Erszebet said, her imperious voice at odds with the shifting red silk and her restless, probing hands that slid over her bony body. "You expect a condemned vampire's name to give you safe passage here? And your companion travels under nobody's protection at all."

"I travel under my own protection," Raziel said. His voice was as smooth as Imperial Tokaji Aszú wine, and I could feel the corded muscles in his arms under the light suit that he wore.

I feared for him.

I returned my attention to Erszebet and her companions, on my guard for Raziel as well as for myself. "We have no need of protection. We come only to say this: the vampire race is too ancient and illustrious to bow to slavering dogs. I offer you magic, my own magic and my sister's, to fight the menace of Hitler. We could stop him even now. Terrible as he is, Hitler is only a man."

"A man with brutal magics at his disposal," Jansci said. Did I detect a glimmer of regret in his voice?

Attila hissed, "Do not speak ill of the glorious German Reich. Our nation stands with our Aryan brothers. Scum such as you will be swept away and Hungary, like Germany, will once more be pure."

He could contain his bloodlust no more, and with a snarl of rage Attila hurled himself at Raziel's neck. Raziel slipped and ducked, and my wards held. Attila bounced backward as if thrown.

"I have brutal magics as well." I held my hands outward to strengthen the spell of protection I had woven. "I am a Lazarus, the eldest daughter of an eldest daughter. I was born with the ability to summon, and I will call the wretched soul right out of your body, Attila, if you insist."

Attila sent up a huge wail of hungry frustration. His fangs flashed yellow in the dim light, long and thin like a cobra's fangs, different from the fangs of a mature vampire. Distracted by them, I was not so prepared for Erszebet's attack.

She surprised me by gliding to the edge of my protection and with her long bony fingers parting the wards like a bamboo curtain. "The Reich bought our fealty with magic, little lamb chop," she said, and laughed as she slid between Raziel and me.

Her sharp-looking fingernails scraped up the side of Raziel's arm and along the base of his neck up to his jaw. She played with his collar and tie as Raziel stood silent, poised to strike, waiting only for my word.

I ignored my rush of fear, and instead I whispered the first verse of the Testament of Solomon. A blue flame licked over the entire surface of Erszebet's body, as if I had lit a gas stove and thrown her onto the burners.

She shrieked and drew back, but I would not let her flee. I spoke softly over her whimpers of pain. "The magic is Hitler's, not yours," I said, so quietly that the other vampires could hardly hear me. I leaned forward; I could smell the coppery blood on her breath. "Erszebet, come to me."

Her soul was old and ropy, coiled tight and hard to unwind. But I whispered her name again and again without mercy, and she scrambled backward as I tugged hard at her soul, to show her how I could yank it clear out of her body. "I come in Bathory's name, to offer you freedom from the dogs."

I could kill Erszebet now, but that would solve nothing. The fetid magic the vampires held in reserve abruptly strengthened, and now stank of vomit and rotting cheese. I had come to parley, but the magic in the Vampirrat could not be disarmed without a brutal, magical fight.

I threw Erszebet's soul back to her, and she staggered out of my wards. She collapsed against the cushions, her upper body now completely exposed, blue-white like snow.

"You reject my parley," I said, "and so it must be that I will save my old master myself, alone, and when he returns he will supplant you all."

Her expression, surprised and embarrassed, drew a short,

hard laugh out of me, and I went on. "Your magic is weak, for it must travel far, all the way from Berlin, and it cannot withstand mine."

Jansci's laugh mocked my pride. "You might withstand the magic the Reich has given us, but you are still a mortal! Only a mortal. You presume too much—your magic is not infinite. You will be crushed by Hitler and his mortal army."

I resented Jansci for his being right, but his tut-tutting gave me time to get Raziel out of their lair alive without having to kill them all and incite a war with the Budapest vampires.

I bowed and inclined my head, showing a respect to them that they did not deserve, but I was willing to give it in order to keep them away from Raziel. "You may be right, Uncle. But can you afford to be wrong?" I dared to catch his eye and smile, a gesture of bravado so futile that Jansci smiled back.

I began to walk backward, and after glancing at me in surprise, Raziel backed away too, still in a fighting stance.

Halfway across the huge, barren ballroom, I paused. "I bid you peace, vampires of Budapest. But I will claim Bathory for myself. In the end, you will swear fealty to him when he returns, or there will be war."

"You declare war as recklessly as Hitler himself." And Jansci's smile widened under the boar-bristle of his mustache, the ends of his fat fangs peeking out from underneath.

A low hiss rose from the divan where Erszebet still sprawled. "Jansci, she must not leave. It is war with her kind, or with the Germans."

"No, lovely one," I said, my voice containing a note of genuine surprise. "I have no particular quarrel with you. I am dismayed you refuse to save Bathory; it is always disillusioning to see strong ones play so small. But my true enemy is in Berlin. Do what you must. But I am not yours to claim, nor is my companion."

Out of nowhere, Attila again hurled himself at Raziel, and this time he was too fast for Raziel to duck. My wards ripped with the force of his assault and hung in spiderweb tatters as the two of them rolled over and over on the floor, the vampire's mouth opened huge with piranha-fangs aimed at Raziel's bare neck.

"Attila!" I called his soul with all of my power. It was as if he was a ravening cur and I had yanked him by a choke collar: his head jerked backward and he bit his own tongue with the violence of my counterstrike.

He reached up to pull at his neck but my invisible grip was powerful at such a short distance. I took a deep, centering breath, and formed my energy around my word of power:

No. No. No.

"You will not have him, Attila, you will not have me, Attila, back, Attila, back, back." With every repetition of the vampire's true name I tightened my hold over him.

Raziel wrenched himself free and caught the vampire with a sharp left hook as he swung away from the monster's long, grasping fingers. Attila lay on his side on the parquet, mouthful of fangs gaping, bleeding from his nose and tongue.

"Let's go," Raziel said as he massaged his bleeding knuckles with his other hand.

I stared at the freely dripping blood as hard as did the vampires. My Raziel now could bleed.

"I've said everything I came here to say." I looked up, caught

Erszebet's gaze and held it, hard and without mercy. An unwilling smile flickered over her lips, and I savored her admiration like a sip of a fine red vintage.

I released her and bowed to Uncle Jansci, the only vampire who had treated me with the respect due to a loyal lieutenant of one of their own. "I salute your chivalry, Uncle, and I offer you my protection should you need it against my enemies, the Fascists."

I darted a glance at Attila, still writhing in agony on the floor. The vile stench of the alien magic still hung in the air, and I rubbed at my nose with the back of my hand.

"I'm done, Raziel. Let's get out of here. You know, your jaw is all bruised."

Raziel met my gaze. For the first time I saw uncertainty in those warm, brown eyes, an amazed frustration at his mortal limitations reflected in them.

I turned away from his disconcerting gaze. I nodded at Jansci; he regally inclined his head in farewell. I made a big show of turning my back and exposing my neck to them as we went. I demanded my due of respect, and would have it from them through my own strength, if not from their own code of honor.

Imre met us at the entrance. He said nothing, only muttered under his breath and opened the heavy wooden door. But before I stepped through the door and into the sticky-hot Budapest night, Imre grabbed my hand and kissed it twice, first formally on the knuckles, then long and passionately on the pulse point of the wrist.

Our eyes met. "The Vampirrat won't lift a finger to save him,

Lazarus. But you have crazy courage, you walk into the fire. Do it, save Bathory, if you can," he whispered.

But I could not deny my doubts. War was close upon us now. I could no longer even pretend to stop it. The only way I could survive was to win.

✳ 3 ✳

"So much for Bathory, my poor count," I murmured. We had made our way far enough down the street for me to be sure we had survived the Vampirrat of Budapest.

A long line of streetlamps shone all the way down the Buda hills. "Come on home—you must be starving," I said. "At least it is not too late for me to save you."

Raziel startled me with a short burst of hard laughter. "My dear," he finally said, after he had gotten his voice back under control, "you were too late the day you were born. Some things you cannot change, no matter what you do or wish."

"I swore to Gisele I would try." My grief came out sounding peevish. "And how can I not?"

I could not bear to look at him, to see in his face the knowledge that I had failed again. Instead I walked, slowly and aimlessly, down from Rose Hill in old Buda, toward the Danube River. It was a very long walk to Dohány Street, but I was determined to take every step, even if it took the rest of the night.

"Magda," Raziel began.

"Don't say it. Don't tell me."

"Sometimes the thing must be said aloud."

"But I already know." I kept walking, walking, the endless night stretching into nothingness around us in every direction.

"The worst will happen, Magda."

I shook my head. "You have fallen, you are a man. The worst has already happened." I took in the sight of him strolling next to me, shorn of his essence and his wings, fedora tipped rakishly to the side as if he had not a care in the world.

"I'm not so sure about that." He straightened the fedora, and I saw how tightly he clenched his bruised jaw. "I chose to choose, if you follow my meaning. Now the Almighty is hidden from me; now I speak Hungarian and Hebrew, and not the angelic speech all living creatures understand. I've lost my language and my wings, yes. But it's worth it to me, Magduska. I am no more a messenger, I am a man. Now I am free to act, to take a side, to do what I know to do."

I considered his words. "You see falling from Heaven as an improvement?" I could not keep the skepticism out of my voice.

His eyes darkened and he shrugged. "I could not bear it any longer," he said. "Safe but bound to do nothing, a mere messenger. Doomed to watch only, as you, your sister, and the world descend into Hell. Perhaps I am a traitor to Heaven, well, so be it. I chose love over fear—I will stand by what I have done."

"You were made for more than minding me!" I blurted out. I couldn't help myself.

He smiled, then winced and rubbed his sore jaw. "That is true. That is why I came."

I wanted to say so much more, about love and gratitude and the waste that was evil. But instead I put Raziel's angelic patience to the test. "Asmodel is the only advantage I've still got. And as you have so kindly pointed out in so many words, I have failed over and over trying everything else."

Raziel took off his fedora and ran his fingers through his thick, dark hair. "Asmodel? But—"

"No, stop. Hear me out. He knows, Raziel. He knows what Hitler plans to do, and he knows the Germans' weaknesses."

"But he will not give you anything, not unless you pay too high a price."

"I tempted him to overreach before, I can do it again. Somehow. Maybe if I invite him into my body to possess me like he wanted. I'm sure you will be strong enough to make sure he does not ruin me."

Raziel hesitated, stopped. We stood together in the street, the mists of the Budapest night rising all around us.

"I know that demon well, know him as a brother," he finally said, so low that at first I thought I only imagined I had heard him speak. "I could not beat him, Magda, not even with the celestial power of my wings. We have battled over the reach of time, and never have I fought him to any more than a draw."

"But I don't intend to fight him. I want to enlist him to our cause."

Raziel took a half step backward and laughed. His thick hair shone in the light of the streetlamps. "That is madness. He has descended far in evil since the beginning, Magduska. He wishes only harm upon mankind, and his essence is cunning."

He replaced the fedora on his head, regarded me with his wise, sad eyes, and he shook his head. "I have seen many things in my time, Magduska, things terrible and wonderful. And Asmodel has seen more. Knows more."

I knew nothing in comparison, but I wanted to believe that my ignorance could be strength. I reached for his hand and threaded my fingers through his own. "The Lord Himself watches over fools, my love."

"You are too ambitious a fool, Magduska. Don't do it."

Bathory was beyond my reach. Raziel was right—even talking with the ancient demon was dangerous. But I had to deal with Asmodel, one way or another. I was running out of time and choices.

We stumbled our way home, across the Chain Bridge from Buda into Pest. The unbelievable reality of Hitler's imminent invasion would manifest in a day or two. If I wanted to get Gisele out of Hungary, I had to do it fast.

When I turned the key in the lock and finally made it alive through my front door, Gisele was awake and sitting at the kitchen table. The poor girl looked ghastly. She had been tasked with the job of guarding the paprika tin, and the job was almost too much for her.

I tried to ignore the circles under her eyes and her slumped shoulders. "Gisele, the time of death is not today, even by the demon's reckoning. Come, time for breakfast, I'm taking you out again."

"Oh, it's you, Magduska darling. You must be exhausted."

Gisele sounded desolate, already beaten. And peevish and resentful too: a mood that did not match my sister's soul in any way.

What had Asmodel done to her in the dark night she had endured alone, guarding him?

I tried to disregard her haunted eyes, her tangled hair. I could not. "Are you all right? Has that creature tormented you?"

She waved my question away with a little flick of her hand. "He cannot torment me more than what I see in my second sight."

After a long moment, I said, "You need a bit of fresh air. I will take you to the Mephisto Café this morning instead of the Istanbul." I could not bear to acknowledge out loud the reality of her continued visions.

I also did not confirm what I knew she was worrying about: that my encounter with the Budapest council had gone so badly that I preferred to take my chances at the demons' café, rather than at my customary café of the vampires.

She gasped, and two livid spots shone on her cheeks as if I had slapped her twice. "The war is indeed come, then, if you must trust me with the local demons."

And with the father of them all, the terrible, barely restrained Asmodel. She didn't have to say a word about him—I could see the awful strain of keeping up my wards etched in every shadow on her face.

I also ached all over from weariness. Raziel and I exchanged a long, silent glance; he looked fresh and rested, and except for the bruise Attila had raised on his jaw, none the worse for wear despite our endless night. He was a man for certain, but was that all that Raziel was?

I shrugged as if the burdens Gisele and I bore were of no account, but I still worried about her. "I trust nobody but you and Raziel. And besides, demons, like vampires, tend to sleep in, of a morning. We won't be in any danger at all at the Mephisto Café."

I could not have been more wrong.

So it was that the three of us ushered in the last day of August from the dubious safety of the Café Mephisto, favorite Budapest haunt of the resident demons and other air spirits. Their coffee was terrible, the pastry often stale, but I trusted the regulars there more than I did the human members of the Fascist Arrow Cross Party, and the vampires now were too dangerous for me to challenge again.

I scanned the headlines of the *Pesti Hirlap*, hungry to read stories of an ordinary day. Raziel sat next to me, his body all but thrumming with tension, while Gisele plowed through a soggy napoleon and a veritable bucket of watery coffee. Most demons do not have a sophisticated palate, and will eat almost anything so long as it is sweet enough.

The paper dispensed with, I carefully folded it back together and rested it on its wooden dowel against the wall.

Far across the expanse of the grand café, the front door swung in with a faint tinkling of bells, and the battered hulk that was Imre shuffled in, well bundled against the morning sun.

He scanned the café as if looking for someone in particular, and our eyes met. He shook his head in disbelief, and his craggy face opened up in a sudden enormous smile.

He trundled around the mostly empty tables, shedding layers of wraps as he drew away from the lead-paneled windows near the entrance. "You still live," he said, all out of breath.

"Not for long, not if I stay in Budapest, eh?" I said softly. "I'd like you to meet my sister, Gisele. You've already encountered Raziel."

Gisele and Imre exchanged a lingering look, and it discomfited me to know they had also met before, while I was off adventuring in Amsterdam. In her desperation, Gisele had come to Bathory to sell her blood and innocence in exchange for survival. I had a hard time forgiving Bathory for that, even though considering the circumstances he had behaved with chivalrous restraint.

"Bathory owes me three months' pay, at double salary," I said, hesitating to disturb Imre's dreamy, Gisele-fueled reverie.

"I know," he said, even as he never took his eyes off my cherubic little sister. "I meant to leave the money with the maître d' at the Istanbul so you could claim it there as customary. But after last night . . ."

"Thank you for finding us," Gisele whispered. "And bless you for all of your help."

Imre's meaty, scarred face softened, and for a moment his prizefighter's features became beautiful. He knelt to kiss her hand, opened up her palm, and put an enormous wad of pengö notes inside.

"Watch out for your crazy sister," he said, and straightened. "Magda'll end up getting the three of you killed." And with a curt nod at Raziel and a tip of the hat to me, Imre wrapped himself up again and slipped away, presumably to go to his customary spot across town at the Istanbul, where his morning libation consisted of something much stronger than a cup of crummy coffee.

"There goes an honest man," I said under my breath as I watched him go. "If only the Imres of the world weren't so terribly rare."

My mind involuntarily strayed to the immediate future, the future that awaited all of us. Once Poland fell, what next? I knew Hitler wouldn't stop there. Aside from the prophecy that specifically doomed Gisele and me, I had a hard time imagining a Europe as dreadful as Gisele's visions. Her descriptions of a world in flames made it hard to think of what to do, how to escape the conflagration somehow.

"I see that you have made up your mind, Magduska, and I for one am glad," Gisele said, her voice very faint. "Shall we head into Poland before or after the war begins?"

I choked on my coffee. "Poland?" I could not keep my shock out of my voice. "I admit it. I was a fool to think I had a chance of preventing the war. But now it is too late. Why ever would we go to Poland, my darling mouse?"

"But the people in Poland . . ." Gisele's voice trailed off, and she carefully, too carefully, licked her sticky fork clean and laid it to rest next to the bone china cup holding the dregs of her awful coffee. "Think of the children trapped there, the mothers. I can hardly bear it; please don't make me go in there alone."

Understanding began to dawn. "Did that Asmodel put the notion into your head?"

She shrugged, and I could see that my guess was right. I could only imagine the terrible things he had told her, in her long watch at the kitchen table. My poor Gisele. Traitorous tears began pooling in my eyes, but my fury at the demon helpfully held them back.

I tried to reason with her. It sounds funny to me now in ret-
rospect that I did, but I tried. "But my darling, going into Poland now is madness. Immolating yourself in the fire isn't going
to save anybody else. How will it help those poor Polish children
if we go in and get ourselves killed too?"

The tears started leaking from her enormous brown eyes, and
I could have torn out my hair with frustration. "But we cannot
do nothing. The fate of those children plays out in my mind's
eye, every waking moment, and in my dreams, too. Their deaths
are driving me mad. How can we just run away, save our skins?
And leave those helpless people to be murdered?" She paused,
then said again, "Knowing what we know?"

I could hardly stand her words. How did my poor little sister
keep from losing her sanity, seeing the pictures in her mind,
never able to close her eyes against those terrible visions of the
mass murder of millions of people? And Asmodel taunting her
with them?

"I don't know what to do," I said again, and suddenly my
voice was hoarse from the lump in my throat. "I don't speak
Polish, I can't kill every German in Poland, I already told the
Poles at the embassy what is happening. There is nothing more
I know to do."

I turned to Raziel, to appeal to his superior wisdom and
strength. There was indeed something more I could do—allow
Asmodel to enter me, imbue my power with demonic resurgence.
Our collective power was almost certainly enough to murder
Hitler himself, ensorcelled or not.

He shook his head no, knowing what I contemplated in my
desperation. And in my heart of hearts I knew he was right. I
didn't have the strength to command such an ancient, malevolent

creature, not without the power of *The Book of Raziel* itself behind me. No, if I tried that I would merely become Asmodel's pawn in a battle with Hitler, and perhaps Stalin as well.

So that left one last choice, to run away. It would break Gisele's heart to run west, and probably destroy her belief in me, but I would rather have her alive and hating me rather than grateful and dead because of my grandiose overreaching. I had already caused enough trouble trying to alter the ways of the world.

But how far could we run, with three months of a vampire lieutenant's pay?

Raziel's sudden burst of amazed laughter interrupted my desperate thoughts. "Look behind you, Magduska. Quick!"

I twisted around in my wicker-backed chair, ready to invoke every dark witchery I knew to protect the two people I loved, who sat next to me at the table in the demons' café.

But no witchery could protect me from the person I beheld.

"Ulysses Knox," I muttered under my breath in shocked disbelief. Though he stood not ten meters away from me, my mind could not accept the reality of his presence, here in Budapest.

"Who is that?" Gisele asked. I shot her a glance, and I could see that she had turned white as death.

"I told you about him. He is the bookseller in Amsterdam, the one who had the remnant of *The Book of Raziel* hidden away in his warehouse. Bathory recommended me to him, but he could not help me in the end."

"Help you . . ." Her voice, stretched tight with fear, shocked me even more than the fact of Knox's presence.

"Whatever is the matter, Gisi? He turned out to be a friend, he helped Eva, and he knows Bathory quite well."

"But he has come to take you away from me."

I looked to Raziel in consternation. The circumstances of my life spun out of my grasp faster and faster as we left August behind.

Before I could reply to Gisele or ask Raziel for help, Knox had made his way to our table, slightly out of breath. His walrus mustache drooped in the August heat.

"You seem to have an affinity for demons, Mr. Knox," I said in French.

He bowed and laughed, shaking his head even as he reached for my hand. Bathory had trusted this American with his life, and my employer's opinion meant a great deal to me. But his appearance at such a time was nothing short of extraordinary.

"I am not here for the demons, Miss Lazarus. And thanks to you, demons are no longer all that fond of me either." I swallowed and my smile faltered at his words, for his spy network of demonesses in Nazi Germany had been violently disrupted as a result of my blunderings in Amsterdam.

But that fact only made Knox's next words all the more shocking. "I came here looking for you—the folks at Café Istanbul had no idea where you had gone. Imre pointed me in the right direction, but it took some doing to find this place."

I covered my confusion by pausing to take a sip of the terrible, now tepid coffee in the bone china cup at my elbow. "Looking for me, are you? How fascinating. But I forget my manners, Mr. Knox. Would you care to take a seat? This is my sister, Gisele, and my . . . friend, Raziel."

If Knox registered my stumbling over Raziel's name he gave no sign of it. "A pleasure to meet you," he murmured in French as he maneuvered his well-fed body into a chair that looked too frail to bear his weight.

"Neither of my companions speaks French, dear sir," I replied, and for at least the thousandth time since she had gone to join the Zionists in their battle against the Nazis, I wished for my friend Eva Farkas. Eva not only spoke impeccable French, she could charm Satan himself into doing her bidding. Whereas I am prickly, and preoccupied, and too serious to charm the denizens of polite, nonmagical society. Especially an upstanding, steady American Mason who had just happened to endure unspeakable havoc as the result of my activities in Amsterdam.

I glanced at Gisele and almost spilled the dregs of my coffee. The girl stared at Knox with huge, saucer-shaped eyes, as if he were the Angel of Death come to finish off her napoleon pastry and then take her away.

There was nothing for it. Premonition or simple case of nerves, Gisele was going to have to tolerate his presence. "Smile and say hello to Mr. Knox," I murmured under my breath in Hungarian.

Her eyes blinked once, twice, and her lashes fluttered as if she were going to faint. "Hello, sir."

My heart tightened with worry even as I slid my chair closer to hers, but I kept my voice playful, light, as if we were talking about a play or the price of sardines. "No fear, nothing is going to hurt you here, my darling," I murmured.

"I did not think to say farewell again to you so soon, Magduska!"

I restrained a sigh of impatience. I had nothing to fear from the bookseller. He had a soft spot for murderous demonesses, vampires like my old boss Bathory, and even for fierce and somewhat confused witches like me.

"Let me talk to him," I said in Hungarian to Gisele. "See why he is here. Maybe he can help us now. We could use all the help we can get."

My little sister hiccupped and said nothing more, only looked so miserable I almost gave up on the job of reassuring her and instead let her run away. But another glance, this time directed at Raziel, made up my mind. I had to find out what Knox's sudden appearance portended.

Raziel nodded at me to go on. "Magduska, you know there are no such things as coincidences."

The fact my angel was right did not render our surprise coffee klatch any less awkward. When I returned my attention to Knox, he inclined his head ever so slightly in my direction, as if he could sense both Gisele's consternation and Raziel's encouragement. "I will translate from the French for my companions, if you do not mind, Mr. Knox," I said.

"Certainly. What I say is not for your ears alone." He leaned back in his chair and sighed, taking in the whole of the Mephisto Café with a single, weary glance. "I have come all this way to find you."

I hesitated, then decided to speak the truth to him. "If you come seeking Count Bathory, sir, you will not find him. Bathory is no longer here in Budapest."

Knox leaned forward, his face flushing. "I know. He is in Berlin, facing the MittelEuropa Vampirrat."

It was my turn to blink in surprise. Few nonmagical mortals, and even fewer Americans, had any inkling of how the vampires of the world organized and governed themselves. But Knox was no ordinary man, and for an American he was astonishing.

"It is because of his plight that I have come for you. I still have friends in Berlin, and they warned me of Bathory's fate. I need your help, and believe that you need mine too."

I translated his words in a nearly inaudible rush of Hungarian, and Raziel nodded for me to go on. Perhaps Gisele was right and I was soon to leave Budapest alone. Knox looked so rotund and harmless, so innocuous and bland, but apparently he had come on a perilous mission. It would be dangerous to underestimate such a man.

"I am soon to become a refugee myself, as I believe you know. Tell me how I may help you, though I am not sure I can help even myself at the moment."

"Well, Miss Magda, let's be frank. You have nothing left to lose. Do you realize what kind of power that gives you?"

Knox's vehemence caught me off guard, and for an awful moment the hopelessness of my situation threatened to overwhelm me and shut me down altogether. I reached for my purse and rummaged around for a cigarette in an effort to stave off a sudden terrible despair.

"I don't know about the power of nothing, monsieur. All I can say is that my situation is dreadfully precarious. But I am happy to entertain your notions."

"I am here to get you out of Budapest," he said, his voice low and urgent. He reached across the table and grabbed one of my hands, squeezed my fingers until I stopped fidgeting. "You are almost out of chances, girl. I have a plane waiting on the runway for you, filled with Polish dignitaries headed west."

I could not suppress a gasp at this information. "Why would there be any room on that plane for me? And do you mean me, alone? I couldn't possibly leave the country without Raziel and Gisele, not now."

Even as I pushed him away, I searched his face for the truth hidden in his words. If Knox meant it, he was an angel of salvation, not death, and he would extricate us from the east before war trapped us here to die.

"I need your help," Knox said again, and his fingers tightened around mine. "You . . . know things. You are in a position to find out more. There are people who need the information you possess."

"People? What kind of people?" I said. I could not keep the roughness out of my voice. "People have killed me before for what I know, for what I wish I knew. They didn't get what they wanted out of me. Why should I willingly give up to a stranger what I have left?"

I pulled my hand away, and began translating for Raziel and Gisele. "He cannot pay me enough," I muttered to them.

"Don't be so stubborn," Gisele said, surprising me anew. "Bathory adores this man, yes? The least you can do is hear him out. Even if . . . he means to take you away from me."

Lord, I needed a cigarette. My sister did not mean to torment me, but her mysterious little pronouncements drove me crazy sometimes. "He's let me down before," I said in Hungarian, playing devil's advocate against myself. I desperately wanted to trust Knox, wanted to go west for any reason, or none. Anything to flee from the horror of Friday, September the first.

I appealed to Raziel with a glance, but he half smiled and wearily shrugged, looking like he had been born and raised in Budapest. "What do you have to lose, Magduska? The bookseller is correct, of course. But do not go with him simply to run away. You will have to go into the storm, and I think that is what he is going to ask of you in the end."

My two beloveds had given me little in the way of comfort. I sighed and resigned myself to hearing him out. "Let me see if I understand, monsieur. You propose to put me on the plane with the Polish diplomats, yes? To go west? But why? And what must I pay for the chance to run away from my death here?"

Knox looked up at the ceiling of the Mephisto, as if he were appealing to his own army of angels to overpower my nonsense. He squinted hard as he studied the crystal chandeliers above our heads. "No less a personage than Winston Churchill wishes to consult with you regarding the impending war," he said, his voice flat and noncommittal. I searched his face, but now he avoided me and studied the ceiling of the Mephisto instead.

Before I could force a word past my strangled throat, Raziel murmured in Hungarian, "Who is this Winston Churchill?" Clever man . . . he understood no French, but had caught the name in the torrent of Knox's foreign words. And while a clever man, he had not been one long enough to know who Winston Churchill was, and what he would become.

"A great Englishman," I replied. "One who has warned the world against Hitler for longer than Gisele has, and who has been ignored pretty much as thoroughly as she."

I spoke to Knox's meaty chin. "Is Churchill still out of power in the British government?"

"Yes. But that is bound to change should England enter the war."

My mind could not think past the words "Winston Churchill." I shook my head hard, as if I could dislodge the man's name from my mind. "What would such a powerful Englishman, one with no magic, want from me? He knows better than I do what kind of enemy he has in Hitler."

"I cannot speak for Churchill. I bring you as a favor to him." He tore his gaze away from the dusty crystal chandeliers that hovered like swords over our heads.

His eyes were bloodshot. "You do not have the Book," he whispered. "But should we get it away from the Germans, you alone can use it. The British are the only ones strong enough to stand against the Nazis now. Winnie has an extensive network of his own throughout all of Europe. You may know something, a fact meaningless to you, which is of profound import to him."

I shook my head in stark amazement. A headache had started between my eyebrows, as if a tiny imp were bashing me between the eyes with a ball-peen hammer. "You have no problem telling me this in a café full of demons?"

It was Knox's turn to shrug. "Demons care little for human affairs. They want chaos, misery, and their own freedom. You know this. You met my demonesses and set them free yourself. In some ways they are the natural enemies of the German Reich, if you consider the matter. So what do you say, Magda? The plane is waiting on the runway and it's leaving Hungary within the hour, whether you are on board or not. What's it going to be?"

I translated the gist of Knox's offer to Gisele and Raziel, and before they could ask any questions and cause me to hesitate, I said in French, "I will go and speak with the honorable Mr. Churchill. But only if there is room on the plane for Gisele and Raziel."

My thoughts turned to the paprika tin and the elemental

demon trapped inside. Now that was a worthy gift for a man of Churchill's stature, but I did not believe there was a wizard left in Britain with the wherewithal to keep him bound.

Knox's voice pierced my ruminations. "Absolutely not. There is only room for one, and the plane leaves immediately. I have a cab waiting outside. I need an answer, and I need it right now."

My headache abruptly got worse. I closed my eyes and rubbed at my eyebrows, but even as I considered the dilemma before me, Gisele sliced through it:

"You must get on that plane, Magduska. And I mustn't. You go, my darling, and I will stay."

With a groan, I forced my eyes open. "You are insane, my little mouse! What will you do here all alone as Hitler smashes Poland?"

Gisele trembled under the storm of my words, but she did not back down. "Don't you see? We can't stop anything, we're too late. But maybe we can tip the balance for the winning side. This Churchill fellow, he could use your magic, my darling. And someone needs to babysit Asmodel, no?"

"Then Raziel must stay with you!" I could barely get the words out one by one past the lump in my throat.

"I can manage the tin," she said. Her face was mild and calm as always, but her voice was choked with tears. "All I have to do is keep up the wards you built. You did the hard work, Magduska darling. And the Germans are invading Poland, not here. Maybe . . ." Her face became dreamy for a long moment. "No, it is too much to hope. But Friday is not yet. September is not yet. Go, Magda. And you must take Raziel with you."

She did not say why; Gisele was innocent of the world's dark and bloody ways, and that very ignorance would protect her. I was much less able to resist the siren call of the world to commit evil, to act with malice even while pretending to myself that I did good. Gisele would guard Asmodel, while Raziel would guard me. But at that moment I did not yet understand the price that Gisele would have to pay. In my own strange way, I was still an innocent too.

I saw the two people I loved most in the world exchange a long look and nod in conspiratorial assent, and saw that I was doomed to do as they wished.

"Knox, I will go to England," I said, my voice full of a confidence I did not feel in the least. As I spoke I looked to Raziel, and it was his hand I clasped. "But I must have a bodyguard or I will not leave Hungary."

The cab lunged across the city, to bring Gisele home and me to the airfield before it was too late. I held her close to me, and I could not help it—I cried into the crown of her head. It was too sudden, this separation, it was too sharp, and promised a finality I could not stand.

I breathed in the clean smell of her hair as I spoke. "Swear to me you do not talk to Asmodel, you do not lift the top of that sifter for even a moment, Gisi!" I muttered fiercely into her curls.

How could I leave her alone with that monster in the house, with war just over the border? It hurt to breathe, just thinking of the look on her face when I had found her in the kitchen.

She opened my hand and planted a kiss on my palm, the way our mother used to when we were tiny girls leaving for school in our northern town of Tokaj: a kiss to hold in reserve.

That was pure Gisele, able to demolish me with a single little gesture. "Magduska, he's already done his worst. I swear I will not talk to him, Magda. I will not say a word, and I will not listen to anything he might try to tell me. Please, please, now I know why you are always begging me not to cry!"

I tried to focus on practicalities instead of my heart breaking. "Knox says I will be back in a couple of days. I will leave a message with Gaston at the Istanbul if not." We had no telephone at home, no other way to communicate other than the mail, and I did not believe a letter would reach her in anything like enough time to save her if disaster befell our plans.

The cab screeched to a halt in front of our apartment building. A pair of boys leapt backward. They were Hasidic, their black coats reaching all the way down to their scruffy leather shoes. The older one twirled his earlocks as they resumed their progress toward the Great Synagogue a few blocks away, on the same side of the street.

"Farewell, my darling," Gisele said, and she gave me a final hug, so tight that for a moment I could scarcely breathe. "Be brave; do what you must."

That courageous admonition sounded strange coming from my little mouse's lips, but I engraved every word of Gisele's valediction on my heart. "Send a messenger to Eva if you need help. She would defy even the Zionists to help you, my love. Farewell, little mouse. I will see you again, I swear it!"

Gisele's face stilled. "Don't swear to such things," she said. "Such things we cannot foretell." And something hidden in her words chilled me to the very marrow.

I had no time to pry her worries out of her and fix them. Instead, I kissed her on both cheeks, whispered a few final en-

dearments in her ears, and she untangled herself from my arms
and tumbled out of the back of the cab. She leaned in the front
window, where Raziel sat in the front passenger seat, and whispered something in his ear, too low for me to hear. He nodded,
evidently too overcome by emotion even to speak, he embraced
her through the open window, and then she was gone.

The cabbie shifted into reverse and stomped on the gas pedal,
careening the wrong way down Dohány Street back toward the
Danube River and the Chain Bridge.

"Will I ever see her again, Raziel?" I said. My tears had gone
now; I spoke in an ordinary, casual tone of voice.

"Don't ask such questions, Magduska," he admonished me
in reply. The cab rattled so loudly on the cobblestones that further conversation became impossible.

The cab lurched to a stop outside the dusty airfield. I gaped at the
sight of the Polish bomber perched like an enormous bird of prey
at the end of the runway. With a roar, the twin propellers burst
into life, and the gigantic plane began to taxi along the runway.

The taxi driver, an emaciated-looking Pole, cursed in an im-
pressive polyglot of languages and drove the cab to the edge of
the wire fence enclosing the airfield. He screamed in Polish at
the befuddled-looking guard, and the man unlocked the fence
and swung it open.

The cabbie shot the cab through the fence and directly into
the path of the bomber. "Are you crazy!" I yelled over the unholy din of aeroplane engine, squealing taxi brakes, and unceasing cacophany of Polish curses. "You'll crash right into the plane!"

His chauffeur's cap blew off and out the open window, just past his elbow hanging out of the driver's side. He waved frantically at the pilot, perched high above us, and the plane slowed, then stopped. The propellers lost their power, turned more and more slowly.

The door swung open way above our heads, and Knox himself stuck his head out to see what the commotion was about. "Get in!" he bellowed, waving his homburg wildly at us, then at the ground crew to bring boarding equipment back onto the runway. "We've got to go!"

I stammered my thanks to the cabbie, got an incoherent growl in reply, followed Raziel up to the top, and for the first time in my life stepped inside an aeroplane.

A luxury airliner the PZL.37 Łoś was not. The pilot and passengers sat in a single area, the hard, unpadded seats were bolted in, and the floor beneath us was roughly girded metal. It seemed to me that if I stamped my foot hard enough, it would go right through the floor and punch through the skin of the plane.

The other passengers stared at us blankly. One of them, an older, sinewy gentleman, shook his head and spat between his feet in what looked like a show of angry despair.

"What's wrong?" I asked Knox.

"What's wrong is that man's assistant could not ride on the plane because your bodyguard would take us over the maximum weight. We removed the bombs, but we have . . . other cargo, very heavy cargo, and the pilot is extremely unhappy with all of us at the moment."

The entry door slammed shut, and the pilot yelled for us to

take our seats—at least that is what I think he yelled, as I do not speak Polish.

"How much can this gigantic plane carry?" I shouted over the roar of the engines as the plane again began to taxi to the head of the runway for takeoff.

"About nine thousand kilos including the plane. Believe me, with the passengers, the extra fuel tanks, and the . . . well, the cargo, we are straining the limit of this bird."

I had never flown before, and I already hated it. But before I could say anything more, the bomber began bouncing along the runway, and directly after that, the plane fell upward, into the sky.

It is about a thousand-kilometer ride from Budapest to England's Gatwick Airport, freezing cold, and by the time we all but crashed onto the airstrip outside London I had been nearly shaken to pieces. It took us almost nine hours to get there, with no stops for refueling, food, or anything else, and my legs had turned to rubber by the time I emerged from the back of the plane and stumbled down the stairway to the sweet stillness of Mother Earth.

England. The air was cool and leafy; we had left at noon or so in Budapest, and it was only about 6 P.M. on the island of Albion. I had never seen such green, lush grass in my entire life, certainly not at the end of August.

Knox gave me no rest, hardly a minute to take in the fact that I had alighted in the land of Beefeaters and kippers. "Let's go, m'dear. Winnie's waiting. He's expecting us for a late supper, and miracle of miracles, the flight went faster and easier than I expected."

I shook my head; my teeth felt loose in my gums, and the roar of the engine still shouted, a ghost in my ears. "Easy? Fast?"

Knox laughed then, a big belly laugh that I could not have imagined from him in Budapest. London, a free city with only limited magic to be had, suited this man well. "No one shot at us or tried to stop us. And we flew over German airspace! Try that after next week and see what happens, Miss Lazarus!"

Poor Raziel looked rather shaken to pieces himself, but he said nothing, only adjusted the knot of his tie and ran his fingers through his hair. Knox folded the three of us into another cab, this one an enormous humpbacked creature, and we smoothly disappeared into the dusk, on the left side of the road.

"What will happen to those Polish gentlemen?" I asked.

"The diplomats? They will be meeting members of Chamberlain's government tonight, without a doubt, begging for help from the English. Too late for that now. The British have promised to stand with them in case of war, but they will not antagonize the Russians before war officially breaks out."

I thought of those stiff, starved-looking men sitting hunched over in their cramped metal chairs bolted to the floor of the Polish bomber, looking like they had left their souls behind in Poland. They knew as well as I did that we all danced on the edge of the abyss.

My plan was to dance and sing for my supper, as well as I could. I would give Mr. Churchill what he wanted, and in exchange I would get what I wanted—a safe haven for Gisele in

England, and a place for me to hide from the Nazis while I figured out what we must do next.

Surely that was not too much to ask? Surely England could spare a useful friend such a small compensation for services rendered? It was time for me to find out.

✳ 4 ✳

Mr. Churchill's estate, Chartwell, was some distance outside of London proper. Its verdant opulence almost wiped my mind of language.

That such a refuge could exist in the same world where I scrabbled for scraps in Budapest boggled what was left of my faculties. It began to dawn on me how august a personage was this Mr. Winston Churchill, and how dangerous in fact my pilgrimage could prove.

Such powerful men as he did not have to repay favors made; they did not have to acknowledge the bare existence of one such as myself. I had magic of my own to be reckoned with, but it did not intersect with the money, nobility, and worldly power that Mr. Churchill possessed.

The car pulled into the circular drive at the front of the grand old estate house. Huge leaded windows rose high above our heads, reflecting the light of the setting sun.

"We're early," Knox said. "All the better."

A butler met us at the front door, his eyebrows beetling at the sight of us. Knox nodded at him, and the old man bowed and motioned for us to follow. We passed through an enormous pair of heavy wooden doors, then through a veritable warren of hallways to a back door.

To my surprise, the butler motioned for us to follow him outside again. I all but had to run to keep pace with the old butler as he shuffled along at surprising speed.

I was at the point of asking Knox where the devil he was taking us, when the servant led us down a gently sloping hill to where an old man worked with his hands on a muddy-looking brick wall. Knox tugged at the butler's sleeve and they spoke quietly together as I pressed forward.

The old man, dressed in canvas pants and a white workman's shirt, straightened when he saw us and swiped at his face with a filthy handkerchief.

When he saw Knox he smiled, and motioned to the butler for a cigar, which he lit with a flourish. As the smoke wreathed his face like a garland of victory I suddenly recognized him.

The bricklayer, hands caked with clay, was none other than the English lion, Winston Churchill.

I resisted the sudden urge to curtsey; instinctively I knew the great man wouldn't like it. "It is a profound honor to meet you, Mr. Churchill," I said in my best, most formal French.

His eyebrows shot up, and he took a few puffs on his cigar before replying. "It is a flaming purple witchery I see," he said, in very bad French, and he bowed deeply from the waist.

I offered him my hand—I could not care less about the clay—
and he kissed my hand most chivalrously. Knox appeared by
my elbow in a flash, and cleared his throat.

He whispered in my ear, in the worst Hungarian I had ever
heard, "No. No. French. Bad. French. No."

Even if I could decipher Knox's concerns, I was not so quick
to accommodate them. My first imperative was to win over and
even to befriend the great Churchill if I could.

I continued in French. "I have come, Monsieur Churchill,
from the east, to share with you what I know."

Churchill's eyes widened, and he straightened up again to
smoke his cigar awhile. The smoke rose, dancing between us.
Knox said something to him, quickly and low in English, and
Churchill's laughter rumbled out of his chest and over the hill.

"He says he wants more than that," Knox said quickly, before
Churchill could attempt a direct reply in French.

Churchill patted my hand, and we began strolling back toward
the great house as if we had known each other for years. Churchill
and I led the procession, with Knox hurrying directly behind.
Raziel and the butler brought up the rear.

As we walked, I racked my brain for a way to bridge the language barrier, and sighed in frustration. As an angel, Raziel
could have spoken with any creature, mortal or magical, without turning a hair. Now, he spoke only Hungarian and Hebrew, and I felt his loss of angelic speech more sharply than he
seemed to.

I turned around to look for him, and instantly Raziel was at
my side. I whispered in Hungarian under my breath, "This is
impossible. I trust Knox, but he cannot translate well enough to
satisfy me."

Raziel smiled back at me, unruffled and undisturbed by our epic rattling journey to the west. I clenched my jaw to keep myself from saying something unladylike.

Raziel laughed and shook his head. "After all that we've been through, a little thing like this is what finally sends you over the edge? Peace, Magduska. Remember who you are, and what you can do."

The breath caught in my throat. His calm words were as good as a rebuke for shaking the nonsense out of my head. I was simply unused to gentleness as a goad, or to possessing any power myself.

I had survived the last few dangerous years in Budapest, first as a penniless sixteen-year-old orphan, then as the loyal assistant of a courtly but murderous vampire. But now I was something more, a witch with magic manifest, and the possibility of gaining tremendous power, should I possess the power of the wayward *Book of Raziel.* So much had changed in a few short months; so much had altered inside of me. I needed to act more in keeping with what I had become.

The procession had come to a halt, and we stood on a great patio overlooking the grounds. I looked at Knox and held up a hand. "I must speak with the honorable Churchill myself. I mean you no offense, kind sir. But our minds must meet, and it is difficult to accomplish such a feat through an intermediary."

His eyes widened, and Knox whipped a handkerchief out of his pants pocket and began to wipe his spectacles. "You cannot," he finally said in a low, headlong stutter as he leaned to me, looking unsteady on his feet. "You speak no English, he speaks no Hungarian—and even worse, speaks a little French. You mustn't! This is too important a mission!"

I waved him away, studied the tips of my fingers, and concentrated on the problem. Englishman, words, letters, languages . . .

My magic is rooted in words, in the language of Hebrew and the angelic tongue. I wielded spells most effectively in Hebrew and the old languages, but all words retain a native power.

But I needed no incantation to summon. This gift, to call forth souls of any kind, was my birthright. Spellcraft or not, I was born with the ability to call.

I made up my mind and raised my arms to Heaven. Churchill took another puff on his cigar and blinked up into the fading August light.

"Angel of England, come to your son in need," I called. I did not know the angel's name. "Angel of Mons, the angel over the British Isles, Churchill himself needs you."

"Her name is Albion," Raziel said, low and quick.

"Albion, your brother Raziel awaits you here." I did not, strictly speaking, compel her to appear—such a compulsion runs counter to the Lazarus creed, the first tenet of which is to summon no unwilling soul—but I imagined the combination of her name and Raziel's would prove hard to resist. Though angels are celestial messengers, and not granted the free will of mortal souls, they are still as curious as the rest of us.

The air between Churchill and me began to waver, and two ivory-delicious wings began to shimmer into being. Knox stumbled backward and gasped something frantic-sounding in English, but Churchill only waved him away and laughed.

Good fellow, this Churchill. He was no magical, only an Englishman born to rule his people, but he did not allow fear or even prudence to rule him. He simply watched, his eyes twinkling, as the air rearranged to admit the reality of an angel, a breathtakingly beautiful female angel, into our midst.

Her first words were not for me and not even for Churchill, but for Raziel. "Brother, bless you, have no fear," she said in a musical concordance of sounds that scrambled my senses. By now I was used to the visitations of angels, and still I could hardly retain my bearings in her celestial presence.

"Albion, you are a blessing. Thank you for joining us here," Raziel replied, the roughness in his voice belied by the transfixed expression on his face.

My heart constricted at the sight of her, of her wings. How could a world that contained creatures of such beauty also admit of child murder, Nazi sorcery, and my sister's terrible visions?

"I need to convey a message to Mr. Churchill," I said. "You are the only one, the perfect one, to carry the message from me to him and back again. Please endow us all with the ability to understand one another."

She nodded her head and smiled. "It is a miracle, but a small one, and you need not endanger your soul with sorcery for such a minor gift as this. It is done, my dear girl."

And to think I had, not so long ago, hesitated to call upon the angels for help, believing it was too close to a soul-summons and therefore a grave impropriety, for messengers of the Almighty should only be compelled by Divine command. Her celestial perfection reminded me of the first time I had encountered Raziel, and my nerves were stretched almost to the snapping point by the calendar and the urgent nature of our mission in England.

I bowed my head to hide the trembling of my lips. "Thank

you for heeding my call, and for giving Raziel comfort here on Earth."

She shrugged and laughed. "Answering prayers is what I am supposed to do. How many prayers are directed to me by name, in Hungarian no less? More than none, but not very many for all of that. Churchill is my favorite charge, not that he needs much help from me. You do what you need to do without angels or the devils to interfere, Winnie!"

Churchill threw his head back and roared with laughter, waving the lit cigar dangerously close to the angel's outstretched, delicately feathered wings. "Very good!" he finally managed to force out. "My angel has a sense of humor. It is meet, it is fitting, it is delightful! And they say there is no proof of an Almighty! My marvelous Albion, it is a distinct pleasure to make your acquaintance due to the intercession of this lovely Hungarian witch-girl. Whatever else she may have to say, making such celestial introductions will forever endear her to me."

He winked at me, the marvelous old rogue, even as he bent to kiss the angel's hand as he had kissed mine. The sun setting behind us limned him in a brilliant golden glow.

The angel curtseyed in reply, then straightened. Her wings, tinged with gold, stretched even farther before she folded them against her back. "Lazarus, the time is short. Tell Churchill what you will."

Churchill sat down on a wicker chaise with a rumbling sigh. "Forgive me," he said to Albion, "but I must never stand when I can be sitting." She inclined her head in assent, and Churchill returned his attention to me.

I sighed and brought us back to the terrible reality all of us faced. "Hitler will invade Poland in the early hours of September the first, Mr. Churchill."

His expression grew grave, and he nodded once. "Of course. Our country has been mobilizing against the Nazi threat, and well I know that war has come for us. I fear it will be some years before I will again paint in peace in the South of France."

"My sister has the gift of prophecy, sir, and she tells me . . ." I suddenly could not bear to go on, spill such ugliness into the cool, soft air and reveal such ugliness to this refined, delightfully mad, charming gentleman.

"Please proceed, Miss Lazarus. This is why my friend Knox, here, thought it important to bring you here to Chartwell before it is too late."

"My sister foresees mass murder," I managed to croak out. "We are Jewish, Mr. Churchill, and the Jews of the Reich . . ."

His round face grew serious. "Times are most precarious for your people. Much as I have admired the fighting mettle of the German race, I cannot abide this stain of hatred that mars their thinking, their ambitions, and their mad leader."

I forced myself to go on. "Millions murdered, sir, men, women, and even children. Systematically; an industry of death. The blood will cover over all of Europe."

"But there is hope, my dear Miss Lazarus. There is always hope until the final breath is drawn. In some cases," he said, his eyes narrowing as he puffed on his cigar then flicked the ashes away, "hope may be sustained even after the last breath dies. Or so I have been informed."

I turned to look at Knox. He shrugged and motioned for me to continue. "I have come to offer my skills to you, sir," I said.

"My sister's prophecy holds that after September the first, if I do not have *The Book of Raziel* in my possession, my life and my sister's life will be forfeit, along with the lives of the rest of our people."

"You may not be as doomed to defeat as your prophecy may have led you to believe. Prophecies often only make sense after the fact, you know. We all must do as we must. And success consists of persisting, failing over and over again until your opponent finally wearies of you and you win. Indeed in my service during the Boer War . . ."

And Churchill launched into a fascinating but only marginally relevant tale of his escape and flight across Africa in his youth. Knox wrung his already destroyed handkerchief around in his fingers, and Albion shook her head—apparently she had heard this story more than once before. Only Raziel listened enthusiastically, his expression rapt.

"Winnie," the angel interrupted him, "this girl has the ability to stop Hitler himself, but only if she retrieves the true *Book of Raziel.*"

"What is this? A book—what? Could stop that madman, Hitler? Who has this Book at the moment?"

I could not restrain a sigh. "The original has been lost to time, Mr. Churchill. But Hitler himself is in possession of a fair copy. I had thought it was destroyed, but Hitler's demon, Asmodel, has informed me the original still exists in this world. Contained within a lost gem, a sapphire. I will be too late, but I will search for the true Book until my time runs out."

Churchill stubbed out his cigar in a great urn filled with sand, and motioned to the butler for a fresh one. "I suppose Knox has told you about me."

The change in subject caught me a bit off guard. A breeze began to blow over the now-darkening hills, and the first star began to shine overhead. "A bit, sir. And I know your name from the newspapers, of course. You are England's best hope."

"Well, Chamberlain learned late about the Nazi evil, but at least he learned. I will serve king and country as best as I may. We all must fight on, in the battles we are ordained to fight. And even if we fall, our struggles may prove a final victory in the grand tapestry of the world."

I tried to keep the Budapest sarcasm out of my voice. "I suppose, but I prefer to think of survival as the ultimate victory. And I offer you my services in exchange for survival, mine and my sister's, and Raziel's, too."

"Now you listen to me, Lady Lazarus," he thundered, low in his chest like a growling English bulldog. "You are not mankind's only hope." He lit his new cigar and puffed away avidly, the fat tip glowing red in the dusk. "That last hope would be me. And not yet, Miss Lazarus, but all too soon.

"Still, you have a part to play in the coming madness. Whether pawn or queen, all of us must play the game. You are no different. From what Knox tells me, you have been gifted with the infernal powers of a Jewish witch. I cannot be a party to you hiding your dark magic away for a rainy day. For the day has come for you to wield that dark magic, my girl."

A slow burn caused color to rise into my cheeks. "Jewish martyrs' lives are cheap," I replied. "I will give you my all, become Churchill's witch, but fat lot that will do to change the world. Yes, Mr. Churchill? Correct me if I am wrong."

Churchill wouldn't budge. "Mere survival isn't enough though, my dear Miss Lazarus, and I suspect you know it. Martyrdom is not my preferred state of being, I assure you, but I will not run from any fight. You must fight, my dear, you must not run. You must not."

His words hit me harder and affected me more than had the appearance of England's angel. He knew, he could read me, he could sense my fear, my desire to flee from the conflagration despite my noble promises, the vows I had made to my sister to save her from despair. It was not even the first of September and already I was tired. Part of me wanted to negotiate a peace with my enemies. *Fine, you take Europe, let me run away to Zanzibar.*

As if he could sense my thoughts, Churchill leaned forward and looked into my eyes, the smoke curling up from the stub of his cigar. "You cannot run, Miss Lazarus. Not if you possess such a powerful magic. The Nazis will not let you go—and neither shall England, nor France. Not now that it is time for war."

The lights began to twinkle in the windows of the house, over Churchill's rounded shoulder. Easy for a great man, swaddled in his wealth and fame, to speak courageous words.

But, damn his fine words, Churchill was right. I stole another glance at my beloved's face, and Raziel smiled. "Magduska, join the man's service. Give your magic to something greater, and I will stand with you, no matter what happens."

Raziel's words, so brave and yet, in a strange way, so innocent of life in mortal skin, pierced me clean through. I tried one last time to resist. "Fine, but I cannot bear to see Gisele immolated on the altar of my supposed heroism. I never could."

Raziel reached for my hand and kissed the back of my knuckles. And that small, tender gesture gave me the last particle of courage I needed, to weigh the scales on the side of the right but doomed thing.

I held on to Raziel's hand as I faced Churchill in the dying light. "What can I do, Mr. Churchill? Sometimes life demands more of you than you think you have inside of you. Very well, then, I am your witch. But keep my little sister safe. She is a seer, but she is not quite of this world, Mr. Churchill. She is too innocent to survive this war, prophecy or no."

"I will do what I can. Why has she not come with you now?"

I sighed again. How could I explain Gisele to a pugnacious, worldly strategist like Churchill? I shot Knox a sharp glance, and he looked away uncomfortably. He knew why she wasn't here, but I would not embarrass him by explaining that to Churchill.

"My sister . . . isn't like other people, sir. She is not quite of this world. She saw Knox, knew he meant to take me away from her, and yet she refused to come to England. She waits for me in Budapest, and there I must return to protect her, war or no war, prophecy or no. Once I've made sure she's safe, I will come back here to serve you until Hitler is no more."

"That's lovely, Miss Lazarus, but you are not a British subject. With all due respect, you do not belong here. And no matter where Hungary ends up—though with old Horthy in charge, I am sure your nation will fall obediently in line behind the Reich—you will be no refugee. You are fighting alongside England, now."

"I don't understand."

"It is quite simple. I have maintained a far-flung network throughout all of Europe, on my own private initiative, for nearly five years, ever since it became clear to me that Hitler's annexation of the Rhineland was only the beginning, and not the end, of his territorial ambitions. I have independent, volunteer operatives in Paris, in Amsterdam . . ." He turned to Knox and smiled, and Knox made a short bow in response. "And I have them in Warsaw. Go home, make your arrangements, and I will have a contact now in Budapest as well. No matter what you must do, you will be your own witch, not mine. Knox will see to the practicalities."

Churchill gave me a long, level look, and I felt distinctly that he could look into me as deeply as my vampire employer Bathory ever could. "You have already fought a number of skirmishes. But you haven't seen anything yet, Miss Lazarus. Stay with me here overnight, have some excellent beef Wellington, some lovely French champagne, and a good night's sleep."

He looked from Albion to Raziel and, I swear it, Churchill winked.

The night before the world ended, I retired early, needing my rest, but wondering how I could possibly sleep knowing August was almost gone.

Raziel shut the door behind us; I had called him my fiancé and that was enough to satisfy Churchill's sensibilities. We stood, staring at each other, alone at last.

"What do we do now?" he asked.

His question sounded portentious, given the circumstances, but I could tell by his uncertain smile that Raziel meant something much more prosaic.

"We get ready for bed," I replied, my voice light. "We need to sleep, my dear, or we will be worn to a frazzle. Churchill's staff has been kind enough to supply us with pajamas...." I waved vaguely at the neat stack of nightclothes on the chair by the window. "We get changed, we wash up for bed, and we ... go to sleep."

Raziel shrugged his jacket off, piled it on the chair, on top of the pajamas. He pulled at his tie, but the knot would not loosen. "How do I get out of this?" he said.

He still hadn't gotten the trick of knotting and undoing his tie. I drew close to him, and, fingers trembling, I worked the knot of his tie loose, slipped it off.

He looked down at the buttons on his shirt. Before his fingers could pull the buttons off by accident, I reached for him, undid the buttons one by one, and slid the shirt off his shoulders.

"You'll learn," I whispered, holding his shirt in my hands. Raziel stood in the moonlight, muscles rippling beneath his undershirt.

I swallowed hard and slipped away to hang up his shirt and jacket on a heavy wooden hanger. Such a contrast, between the mysteries of the world Raziel kept as secrets, and the little routines any schoolboy would know how to do.

I gathered up the pajamas and held them out to him. "Try to put these on," I said. "It's good practice. I'll go freshen up in the washroom. . . ."

And I fled the sight of him, wrestling half naked with the nightclothes, and got ready in the enormous marble washroom instead, splashing my face with cold water until the burn in my cheeks subsided. When I returned, dressed in a white silk peignoir, he had managed to get his pants off and pajamas on, and we were at least both decently covered up.

By agreement, Raziel took the floor near the enormous leaded bedroom window, while I took the high, narrow bed. I got over the fact that I slept alone with Raziel at Chartwell, and, exhausted, I sank into sleep like a stone into dark, cold, murky water. I escaped into the past through sleep, and joined my mother and father in a time before war, when we had enough to eat and could love each other without dangerous complications.

I was eating an apple at the circus when someone shaking me roughly summoned me unwillingly back to life.

It was Raziel.

I held my breath, as if I could stop time that way, and Raziel and I could hide from the world together if only I kept still. He did not smile, and I understood why. It is much more difficult to watch your beloved suffer than to fly into the storm yourself. But I wasn't going to stay out of the fight just because Raziel suffered for it. He didn't want me to run, either.

Weariness broke over my head like an enormous wave, but I refused to go under. "These big marches of armies, deep thoughts about the fate of nations . . . it's all too much to contemplate. And yet we must."

The silence became huge between us as he slipped into my bed, and I curled against Raziel's chest as he sheltered my body in his arms. I refused to cry the tears that clouded my vision, instead pressed closer against him. There was nothing I wanted more than this stolen moment, this touch, this human gentleness.

In the morning, war would rip this tenderness away. I refused to lose Raziel by giving up, running toward a false safety. I stood by my words to Churchill: I had resolved to fly into the storm. But neither could I give up my passion for this man. I didn't want to stop touching him, stop kissing him. I wanted to show Raziel how much I loved him, as a man and not as an angel.

We came to rest in each other's arms on the high, soft bed, twined together like flowers. He tucked my head under his chin with his hand, and I listened to the steady beat of his heart.

The next I knew, the light of dawn woke me and I lay in the

perfect pink silence for a long time, my head still resting on Raziel's chest. I listened to the sound of his even, soft breathing, and to the gentle beat of his now human heart. And Raziel awoke to my desire.

We kissed and kissed, as if we were saying farewell forever and for all of time. His fingers traced my lips, my neck, my jaw, and I let my hands wander over his arms, his chest. But we did not do more than this.

Both of us were virgins, though we had already seen and survived much. And unspoken between us ran a solemn agreement: we would not let tragedy dictate our burgeoning love's expression.

I was young then, and innocent. If I could only now return to that final night before the war, I would have made love with my fallen angel until daybreak, given him every last thing I had to give. But I held back. May God forgive me, I held back.

Now it was too late. It was September. And war.

✳ 5 ✳

The next morning, Raziel and I returned to Budapest on the first available plane. The war had officially begun and I could do no more to stop it; I now had my marching orders and a larger cause with which I could align.

As the plane roared at three thousand kilometers, too loudly for Raziel and me to speak as mortals do, I considered his fate as well as Gisele's. He had chosen mortality for the chance to fight on the side of the innocent. Did he yet regret his choice? I was afraid to learn the answer.

After a long and wearing journey, the plane dropped back to earth in Hungary, half shaking the brains out of my head. The astral travel of my dreams, and even the wanderings of my soul when I had twice died, did not cause as much distress as these desperate wartime journeys in the air.

Night settled as black as ink over Budapest. I was wild to see Gisele again, but we had no taxi waiting for us, let alone Janos, Bathory's driver, in his big black Mercedes. Instead, Raziel and I walked to the tram line that would take us back inside the Ring Road, to the heart of the city I still, unwillingly, loved.

By now Budapest knew of the war; by now the innocence of everyone around me had already been taken. And yet, I gaped in disbelief when I saw the people promenading in the night on Andrássy Street and Váci Street in their summer suits and silk skirts, as if nothing had happened, as if the world was still the same as it had been the day before.

The signs outside the Pushkin Theater blared: "Newsreels of Polish Provocation!" But none of the fashionable strollers seemed to take the slightest notice. I couldn't believe it.

"They don't want to know," Raziel said, his voice husky. He cleared his throat and we stood together at the corner of Andrássy and Dohány streets, only a few blocks from home. "They want to believe in their dream of a life, not the death that hunts them. It has been ever thus, Magduska. Do not blame them for clinging to their illusions."

I tried to achieve Raziel's long view, but couldn't do it yet. The best I could do was to ignore them and focus on our reunion with Gisele.

We reached our apartment building just after midnight. I scanned the street and the building itself for demonic or vampiric intruders, and found none. Only the darkness of Asmodel in my kitchen, blotting out the light on the third floor.

I knocked on our front door, waited for the sound of Gisi's scratchy little voice; that front door was thin as parchment paper. But she never answered.

I knocked again.

Nothing.

We stood together, Raziel and I, in front of the closed door. I turned to face him, slowly, as if in a nightmare. The single lightbulb down the hall flickered and sputtered out, leaving us in darkness.

With a curse under my breath, I called up a dim witchlight in a circle around us, and again searched for evidence of demonic tampering or vampiric hunting. Nothing.

"What do you see?" Raziel said. He crossed his arms across his chest and frowned, the most he would reveal of his own worry.

"Nothing, my dear. No vampires. No demons. No threshold trap. But no Gisele, either."

"Is Asmodel—"

"Yes. He is still on my kitchen table, still safely contained in the paprika tin. But Gisele . . ."

Of course I feared the worst. I could all but see her round little body sprawled out across the rag rug in the parlor, her throat ripped out, her lifeblood pooled all around her; her soul stolen by sorcerers. . . .

What we found in reality was almost worse.

I turned on the electric lights, and they worked inside the apartment. No Gisi dead in the front room, no Gisi at all. A quick search revealed that her good dress was gone from her wardrobe, as was her valise.

The cylindrical paprika tin stood silent on the kitchen table, the bald lightbulb hanging above it all but imperceptibly swaying as if in a faint breeze. The lace tablecloth beneath it was scorched in a widening circle around the tin, much as I had imagined the circle of blood around Gisele's missing body.

The paper tucked under the tin's corner was smudged with char, and had half burned where it touched the nearly red-hot metal. I plucked it away and flicked the folded note open with a single movement.

Gisele's careful, childish handwriting told a horrible tale:

My Beloved Magduska:

Please forgive me for what I must do. You have your fate, and I have mine. I tried not to listen to the old soul inside the tin. I tried, but he conjured my own terrors into life.

He told me everything. What will happen to you and Raziel, what will happen to me, even what will happen to himself. I know, he is the master of lies, but it was the truth that convinced me. The truth! I could not defend against the truth. They say that truth is beautiful, Magda, but I could not see the beauty in his visions. Terror and death have no beauty for me.

I am walking dead, my love. I must sell my life as dearly as I can, save as many innocents as a foolish girl like me can do. I have no choice. You know, my love, where I have gone and what I do. Poland.

The vampire's kiss burns in me. The ancient one, the demon, tried to tell me he had to come with me to Poland. I could resist him in this. The safest place for the ancient one is here, and I sense you will return in time.

So I go, and leave the old prince of lies behind. I waited for you as long as I could, but once the radio

*was full of the news I could wait no more. If I don't
leave today, I will never get inside Poland in time.*

*I kiss your hands, my beloved sister. May we meet
in the next world, before you return to this one once
again to fight on the side of the angels, as you are fated
to do.*

Bless you and farewell,
Gisele

Her terrible visions had gotten the better of her at last. Gisele
had snapped.

I dropped the paper, and it fluttered to the floor. "My God," I
whispered, "she's gone into Poland. Alone. To warn the Jews of
their fate and get them out somehow, on her own, in the middle
of a shooting war."

"Why did she do it? What did you tell her?" Raziel's voice
remained calm, but something in it made me look up sharply.
His hands clenched and unclenched at his sides, and he stared
at the tin with something closer to hatred than I had ever seen
on his face.

I realized Raziel spoke to Asmodel, not to me. "Peace, my
love," I said quickly. But not quick enough: a low, horrible curdle
of laughter bubbled up from inside the locked-up tin.

"You meant for her to go," I said to Asmodel. My heart was
now stone cold: I could feel nothing: no rage, no grief, no fear,
just a numbness throughout my body; I felt as if I had died once
more, and could now fight disembodied, unconnected to anything except my determination to claim my revenge.

"Of course I did!" the demon chortled. A low, slow column of
paprika rose in a shimmering cloud. "I knew how to get her

away from you, and I did. I just magnified her visions, played upon her despair. And you will go after her, won't you? Into Poland. You will take me with you."

I started shivering, I was so cold, despite the fact it was still summer in our stuffy, sealed-up apartment on the third floor; despite the heat radiating from the paprika tin that held the demon. Before I knew what I was doing I took three steps forward and grabbed the tin in both my hands. I dimly registered the fact that it was hot enough to burn my fingertips, but I couldn't stop myself.

I shook the tin hard, and Asmodel's laughter cut off abruptly, as if he finally realized he had pushed me too far. "Asmodel," I began, my voice shaking with fury. "Go to the next world, I unravel your soul for you thus. Asmodel, -Smodel—"

"Stop!" Raziel cried, and he shook me by the shoulders even as I shook the tin. "You cannot dispatch a spirit of the air that way, Magduska! You will only set him free!"

The pain from my fingertips and palms brought me back to my senses. I dropped the tin onto the table, where it lay on its side and rolled to and fro, gently rocking the infernal soul within.

"Peace, Magduska," Raziel said, in imitation of my bossiness, and he laughed bitterly. He wrapped one of his powerful arms around my shoulders.

"What now?" Raziel said. He shifted from one foot to the other, nervous energy rolling off his body in waves.

The fact that he asked *me*, that the mighty Raziel didn't know, filled me with confusion, and for a moment I lost my bearings altogether. He had no injured pride to salve, and as a result his honesty jarred me even more. It galled him, I was sure, not to know his way, but Raziel was strong enough not to pretend.

I spoke as if in trance. "We must go in after her, my love. Get her out again before it is too late."

It was a long trip over the mountains of northern Hungary and across the Slovak plains to the Polish border. How could we get into Poland before it was too late?

I racked my brains for an answer, and came up empty. What did I know? Who? I had little money, but I was rich in contacts thanks to my dangerous work with my missing Count Bathory. I needed a Pole with good connections and an edge of desperation as sharp as my own. The Polish embassy was worse than useless; in any case, the diplomat I had seen there most likely had already fled to England by now.

My mind groped for a name, a friend of a friend, any vague hint of a connection I could grab on to. I was so convinced we had reached a dead end that when a name and face appeared in my mind, the knowledge shocked me into hard laughter that jolted me like a racking cough.

"Antonio," I said. "Oh, by the Witch of Ein Dor, we may call upon Antonio."

I opened my eyes and took in the sight of Raziel, who stood alone with me in the whirlwind.

"Who is this Antonio?" he asked, slowly, as if he had to drag each word out of his mouth.

"Bathory turned him vampire, not even six months ago. If he is still . . . alive . . . he will be wild to go back to Poland. His mother still lives in Warsaw."

Raziel's face blanked. "Bathory? But you told me how much he prides himself on his control."

"That is true. I have never seen him surrender to his blood-lust. But Antonio begged and begged, and as a gesture of thanks for many favors, Bathory turned him vampire at last. The blood-lust has driven Antonio crazier than before; Bathory watched over him as best as he could. But now Bathory is gone. And Antonio's mother lives in Poland."

"But why do you think he can help us?"

"He is a pilot, and he has access to a plane. An old junk heap that he's tried to convince me to fly in before. He's crazy enough to do it, Raziel."

If I only had time I would have bought a bottle of Eger bull's blood wine, the vampire's vintage with real bull's blood in it, as a gift to my mad vampire, Antonio.

I knew in my bones this insane plan could work, and that I would not see Budapest again for a very long time, if ever. I had nothing left to lose in my native city. Everyone else I loved was already gone.

✳ 6 ✳

Bathory's driver was no vampire; I am not sure what Janos was. But he was loyal, and he knew how to drive fast. After exchanging my pengös for Polish zlotys, we found Janos loitering at the Istanbul, and we were lucky to find him; the big, lethal-looking Mercedes shot across town to the Thirteenth District, Angel Fields, like a panther on the hunt.

By now, it was the early morning of September 2. I had high hopes Antonio was still lurking in his lair: if the vampire had not made it back to the safety of his retreat by morning's light, then he was finished, staked or simply ripped apart by another magical creature.

Janos kept the car idling outside the abandoned warehouse that Antonio called home, while Raziel and I slipped inside the broken, unwarded front door.

The heat inside leapt like a wall of fire that sucked all the air out of my lungs, an all but physical presence pushing us back. I took a hot, dusty gulp of air and forced my way into the boiling darkness.

"Isn't it dangerous to disturb a vampire in his lair?" Raziel asked.

I was so frantic to get out of Hungary to find Gisele that I had to force myself to slow down long enough to reply. "It's so dangerous it's stupid. But we don't have time to come up with something sane." The dark air was so thick, dust-filled, and hot I could barely see my own fingers.

I murmured under my breath the words of sending. I reached with my life force to summon the life inside the warehouse, so that I could sense at least the shape of my quarry and if he lived.

Antonio was here. He was perched way up near the ceiling, on top of a narrow metal catwalk that ran all the way along the walls, some ten meters off the ground.

"Up there," I whispered, and pointed with my chin at the spot. "How do we get up there? Wish I could fly."

Raziel's hand reached for mine, and I realized with a start how stupid I sounded. As soon as I said it I wished I could take it back.

I bit my lip in consternation; Raziel squeezed my hand but said nothing in reply. It was dangerous for him to speak aloud now, and he knew it.

"There must be stairs," I whispered, and I pulled him toward the wall, yelping quietly after bumping my shins on something in the murky dark.

I was right: looking around, I saw a rickety, broken staircase, the railings encrusted with a thick scab of rust. By now, my eyes had adjusted to the dimness, and I let go of Raziel's hand so that I could grab the railing and test the stairs.

They bore my weight, however creaky they were, and we started climbing the stairs to the balcony. Rust fell from them, landing like clots of red snow on the cement floor far below. Halfway up, Raziel's foot went through a slat completely corroded by rust, and I had to wrench him free to keep him from crashing down.

But the danger of the stairs was nothing compared to the risk of surprising a bloodlust vampire asleep in his lair. Turned vampires are all half crazy, at least when they are first claimed by a vampire born. And Antonio was crazy even before Bathory granted his fervent wish.

I whispered a spell of binding under my breath, the one that the ancient witch Lucretia de Merode had taught me a few months before in Amsterdam. A restraining mantle slid softly over Antonio's skinny shoulders and as he slept it held him fast, a magical straitjacket.

I had done all I could. I crept forward, muttering little gypsy wards around us. I poked Antonio in the shoulder, hard, the way Gisele did to me when she wanted me to wake up.

He didn't stir, so I poked him harder. "Wake up and face the sunshine, sleepyhead," I said loudly.

My voice woke him where my prodding hadn't. With a huge snarl, he was upon us in a furious blur, and glad I was that I had tethered him before he woke. He managed to get his hands on me but he was too well restrained to get his slashing fangs within reach of my neck.

Raziel pulled me away from the vampire's grasp and together we tumbled backward and sprawled in a tangle on the catwalk.

The rusty bolts holding the whole contraption together groaned in protest. Would the entire thing collapse?

"Good morning, my Antonio," I said, my voice calm, even as my hands shook.

My salutations were met by an incoherent snarl and violent scrabbling against the bonds I had fashioned. I could not stop to make him more comfortable: no time. "Your beloved Poland is being attacked."

His struggles abruptly ceased, and I suddenly understood: his father had been a drunkard baron from some decrepit estate in Ruthenia; but his mother was an ersatz princess of Poland, and when his father died she had repaired, in relief, to Warsaw.

Antonio already knew.

"The German bastards," he said, his voice choked by rage into an all but incomprehensible growl.

"Yes, we come to seek your help in coming to Poland's defense. We need to get to Warsaw immediately: so do you. Do you see? It is fate that makes you vampire now: feast upon the German soldiers and set your mother country free."

It was a patriotic nonsense I wove like a spell with my words. But Antonio was a romantic fool; he pretended to titles of nobility and magical powers he did not possess. He lived in a fantasy world of his own making, one that kept unpleasant realities at bay. He was a poor dreamer, who denied himself life. But here was a final chance for Antonio to redeem himself.

He huddled against the metal latticework at his back, squinted with a blurry, unfocused stare, and I realized he was not just vampire-tranced but also half drunk.

My blood ran cold in that dark and dusty furnace. "So how did you get the news?"

"My mother left a message for me at the hotel." Antonio used to meet his pets at a seedy hotel that served the factory workers of Angel Fields. The place, a scene of many messy accidents, did not much care what happened during Antonio's deadly assignations.

"Is your mother still—"

"In Warsaw. Yes." His voice slurred over the words, and his eyes looked deeply into mine. He did not look insane, staring into me like that. He looked terrified.

Every moment we dithered here in Budapest, the Germans thrust deeper into the Polish countryside on the way to Warsaw. And Gisele following behind the German army, alone and undefended.

I could no longer restrain my impatience. "The Nazis are—"

"You told me. And I already knew it." With a groan, Antonio strained against the bonds I had looped around him like a spider's gossamer threads. "The plane is in the back. Let's go."

His reply stunned me. I had expected to have to resort to official maneuverings, fake stamps, that sort of thing, to get permission to leave. The kind of subterfuge that can take days to orchestrate. But Antonio didn't need any of that to fly.

So, to Poland.

✳ 7 ✳

The field behind the warehouse was impossibly small, choked with weeds, and it was encircled by a crumbling but still quite substantial looking wall. I supposed if I died in a wreck I could return, as long as the plane did not burst into a fiery inferno upon impact.

But Raziel . . .

I held my breath as Antonio spun the propeller and I punched the ignition button. Antonio's plane was an ancient Fokker Spider, held together by a tangle of wire, insubstantial and flimsy looking, but the tiny four-cylinder engine obediently coughed into life.

Antonio leapt onto the pilot's seat; Raziel and I shared the passenger seat in the back. The Spider shuddered nose to stern, and with a puff of acrid, oily smoke, we began bumping over the grass and rubble. The brick wall came closer and closer with greater and greater speed.

The engine began to whine, and the plane shook so hard I thought a wheel was going to bounce right off. The roar of the engine became deafening and I could see every crack and crumb of brick breaking off the face of the wall in front of us.

In my mind, I imagined Gisele's voice like a breezy caress, encouraging the plane to rise. And flooding through my senses, cool and exhilarating, came the clean scent of mountain Tokaj pine, and the cool breeze that tickled the far-off branches swaying against the sky.

My fear fled from that beautiful vision as the plane gave a terrific lurch and hauled itself from the earth. The brick wall fell away directly below my feet, and with a groaning snarl from the engine we were airborne and on our way out of Hungary.

Compared to the lumbering Polish bomber, this was like flying without a plane at all; the sensation intoxicated me. Budapest shrank below my feet, became compact and singular, a dusty jewel set in the mosaic of the earth. This, I thought, is how the world once looked to Raziel.

I watched the city bank and turn below us as Antonio pointed the airplane's nose to the north. Far below, now, I saw the Chain Bridge, the huge and ornate Parliament building, the brilliant Danube flashing sun diamonds over its murky surface, now crowded with boats of all kinds. Somewhere far below us was Dohány Street, the Great Synagogue, and my home, but I could no longer make out the different streets and apartment buildings.

We had abandoned the flat on Dohány Street to its fate. I had entrusted our few homely treasures to the neighbors upstairs, the charming, shy, and delightful Ady family. As long as they were safe, our few mementos would be, too.

But how long were the Adys to be safe? Were they safe, even now, from the storm we now flew into?

I yanked my thoughts away from the buildings below me, and redirected my gaze to the northern horizon. We had a long way to go, and I didn't know how far the plane could fly without more fuel. Perhaps more important, I had no idea how long Antonio could drive himself, in full daylight no less, before his bloodlust once more overtook him.

Contrary to human lore, vampires did not instantly die from exposure to sunlight. Perhaps the legend arose from the extreme sensitivity to the sun that vampires do endure. But though the sun cruelly burned a vampire's skin, he was much more likely to die at the hands of irate villagers finding him abroad and vulnerable by daylight. Antonio would burn, but the sun alone would not be enough to kill him.

We stopped to refuel in Tokaj, of all places, and then our journey north took us across the rolling, lush Slovak countryside and over the Tatra Mountains. Antonio flew erratically now. Before, I hadn't realized the difference between merely hazardous flying and about-to-die flying. But the difference, once one is presented with it, is unmistakable.

The engine began to sputter as first one wing and then the other tilted into the air like a seagull's wing.

Once again, I could hear Gisele's voice in my mind, blessing the airplane, the engine, and the pilot. As we lurched along I imagined Gisele's sun-kissed chestnut curls whipping like a flag in the wind.

Like me, Gisele was a born witch but untrained; and also like me, the misfortune of war brought her gifts to the surface out of desperation. I had always known my sister was uncommonly sweet-tempered, humble, and patient with her harum-scarum older sister; I never had imagined how those traits could manifest in the world through her witch's powers. And that power had taken her from me and driven her into Poland.

The engine coughed and for a terrifying moment the propeller stopped spinning. "Go! Turn!" I could hear Gisele in my head, now; I wove my magic through the memory of her pure spirit.

The acrid smell of burning hay rose to where we buzzed along like a half-dead fly. I craned my neck to see far, far below: a battle was raging.

It was tanks and artillery versus Polish cavalry. The horses were tiny, courageous specks, running into the path of Panzers. Through a scrim of smoke, I saw that the field was covered with fallen horses and men, and I could not tell whether the fire had been set intentionally or if an errant shell blast had lit the dry grass in the field by unhappy accident.

I had seen my share of death before this, but never actual battle, not even at a distance. Antonio bellowed curses in Polish and shook a blistered fist at the battle. He shoved the nose of the plane down and we plunged toward the battle, losing altitude.

I again craned my head far over the side to make out the details. But before I could learn any more I heard a roar rising from behind us.

A black Luftwaffe plane with a swastika bloodred along the side screamed out of the smoke and directly for us. In the airstream directly behind the Stuka I could faintly discern with my witch's sight the figure of a woman, leaning forward like the prow of a ship, bearing a spear and a sword.

I summoned her name: Freda; and her creed: she was a valkyr, a German war spirit. In the same way that seafarers linked their fortunes to sea spirits who rode the prow of their ship, the pilots of the Luftwaffe often flew under the protection of the valkyrie. The Teutonic war spirits protected their planes and attacked other air creatures; without the valkyr, the Stuka would have been just another warplane, more vulnerable to both conventional and magic attack.

"No," I murmured, and felt my magic grow dark and hot around me, coming to a rapid boil. The sight of the carnage below only fueled the intensity of the magical charge building up inside of me.

With a hard jerk, I summoned Freda out of her perch, and she was so surprised by my presence that I tore her completely free and threw the Luftwaffe plane into a tailspin. I folded her wings together hard; with a terrible scream she plunged downward to annihilation onto the field far below.

The Luftwaffe plane recovered itself before the spin became fatal: the pilot was excellent. And the plane was suddenly bearing down upon us once more, bullets tracing and exploding in an arc above our heads.

I threw a cone of protection over us, but it was terribly difficult to keep it steady in the face of Antonio's erratic flying. However, our jerky, unpredictable flight made us a difficult moving target, too, and by keeping the plane's attention on us we spared the Polish soldiers below: for the plane had been strafing them when we came upon it in the sky.

I gathered a dark ball of energy, a malignant grenade of a spell, and I hurled it with all my might at the Luftwaffe pilot's head.

Direct hit. I could not hear him screaming, but I saw the plane shudder with the impact. It all but glowed with heat, and though the gunner kept shooting the shots now went wild.

The plane went into another tailspin, but this time I knew the pilot would not revive to pull them out of it. The plane spun faster and faster, like a child's whirligig, until it smashed into a column of German infantry and exploded in a flaming fireball.

Exhausted almost to fainting, I released my wards with a gasp, and wildly scanned the sky for another plane, but I could see none. My head drooped forward onto my forearm and I watched the wrecked plane burning far below us. Neither the pilot nor the gunner had jumped free of the plane in time.

We had gotten a little bit ahead of the battle, deeper into Polish territory, when the plane's engine, despite all my encouragement, finally gave up and died.

For a moment we hovered in the air in complete silence, the clean-scented orchard air as sweet as wine. Then the nose of the plane hitched up a little, dipped gracefully, and we went into a spin like the one that had killed the Luftwaffe pilot and his gunner.

I could not summon a soulless plane back into the sky. But Antonio was a better pilot than I had given him credit for: he pulled us out of the tailspin and we crashed into a big field of corn, badly rattled but at least not burnt to death.

We sat together, stunned, in the sudden silence, and then I heard Antonio. "Get out. Quickly. This plane could still burn."

The vampire's presence of mind saved us. We scrambled free and into a grove of linden trees at the edge of the field, right before the engine belatedly caught fire and exploded.

Antonio had a broken arm, and I had a long scratch all up my leg that fatally laddered my silk stocking and spotted my best skirt with blood. Our valise, still inside the plane, must have been burned up.

But the zlotys were safe, tucked into my brassiere. I checked my breasts, and basked in the knowledge that with this money we could get anything else we needed. I sighed, and just like that I blacked out, as if the lights of the world had been shut off by a giant hausfrau in the sky.

When I came to, Raziel was sheltering me in his arms. I kept my eyes closed and pretended to be still gone. It wasn't hard to pretend: my head was exploding with a headache, and waves of nausea rolled through me as I lay there.

"Is she dead?" Antonio said, voice hoarse. It took all my concentration to keep my lips from twitching with a smile: he sounded terribly excited by the prospect.

"No, just stunned a bit," Raziel said, his voice soft.

"Excuse me, sir," Antonio said. "Is she your girl? Your fiancée, if you know what I mean?"

A long pause, and I held my breath, the better to hear Raziel's answer.

"Why do you ask?" he finally said as he cradled my body closer against his legs.

"I must . . . feed. Or by full night I will be crazed, I will rip apart the first person I meet, man, woman, or child."

Tension hummed through Raziel's body like a coiled wire pulled tight. "No. You cannot touch her."

I melted against him and sighed: a mistake, because Raziel could now tell that I had come back. "Look, she's stirring."

My eyes fluttered open and I could not help a little groan. "So dizzy," I muttered.

"Try me, Antonio," Raziel said, his voice quiet.

My head hurt worse; I knew exactly what he meant.

"Feed from me," Raziel said. "I can trust you."

I tried to sit up and failed. "Are you mad? He'll kill you!"

My head spun, and then abruptly the world steadied itself.

"We do what we must," he said. "Our ideals become golden calves at the moment of truth, Magda."

"But—"

"No buts, not anymore."

"I don't think you understand."

My face flushed when I saw the expression on Raziel's face; I hadn't meant to speak to him as to a child. I hoped he knew I meant no offense. I still remembered who he was.

Raziel smiled back, not defensive at all, but he gave no sign of changing his mind. "Antonio is our brother in this war."

It hurt me to imagine it, even worse than the thought of Bathory feeding on Gisele. Gisele had the remnants of her innocence to protect her; Raziel had seen too much in his long existence to entertain any illusions about the state of our Polish friend's tormented soul.

At least I didn't have to worry Antonio would turn him: bloodlust vampires can only kill; they can't make more vampires. But I wasn't so sure Antonio could control himself once he got started.

The heat of the still-flaming airplane pushed at our bodies like a giant, invisible hand. I could not speak; only nodded my reluctant assent. Raziel kissed me, hard, and he got up. "I am ready, Antonio."

Without a word or hesitation Antonio bent to his wrist and slashed. Raziel grunted with pain, then sighed, a strange groan that mingled pain and an animal pleasure. Their connection was too intimate to watch; I turned to look instead at the burning plane, and abruptly was dizzy again.

I returned my attention to Raziel—I could not look away any longer. Expressions passed over Raziel's face like fast-moving clouds: fear, shock, pain, an atavistic longing to complete the connection. Ecstatic union is the vampire's attraction, the lure they use to attract their prey. I had taught myself immunity to the vampires' charms, but the temptation to surrender was always there, lurking like any forbidden desire, just under the surface.

The air smelled of burning engine fuel; of apples and wheat. The countryside of southern Poland unrolled from beneath our feet.

My throat tightened as I again remembered Raziel's sacrifice the night we had battled Asmodel at Heroes' Square in Budapest.

And then suddenly my entire body jolted with a terrible realization, one that meant our immediate and certain death.

"Raziel," I called, in a sudden panic.

My voice pulled him out of his trance, and Raziel pushed Antonio away from him. He turned to me, blood dripping drop by drop from his wrist.

Raziel saw the horror overtaking me and he closed the distance between us in an instant. "Something is wrong. Tell me."

"My powers and creed, the tin. The *tin*."

"What? You're not saying . . ."

We both turned, not toward the vampire still licking Raziel's blood from his lips, but to the melting wreckage of the burning plane.

I had leapt to safety, leaving everything behind. Including the paprika tin containing the bound demonic spirit of air, Asmodel.

"Fire is his native home," Raziel muttered.

A low cackle rose from the flames. The sound made my skin crawl.

I wrapped my arms around Raziel's waist to keep myself from fainting. "I've got to catch him again . . . and please, somehow, you've got to help me."

✳ 8 ✳

Asmodel answered me. The cackle rose to an unholy scream, and the flames rose high above us, taking on Asmodel's demonic form.

I recognized well the curving horns, the huge fangs, the protruding tongue, all of it now encased in fire.

Asmodel gave a roar of triumph, and I staggered backward in the blast of heat. But I held my ground. I had to.

"No," I began. I said it three times, louder and louder, even as the demon grew before my eyes into an evil inferno. Raziel stayed close to me, and I half turned. My body shook with exertion, and I had not even begun to do battle with my escaped adversary.

"Magda, you must contain him."

"Help me, Raziel!" I tamped down the panic as well as I could: terror was Asmodel's friend, not mine.

"I am here." But frustration roughened Raziel's voice: not so long ago, he could have helped in obvious ways, using a celestial sword and angelic powers bestowed upon him by virtue of his station. Now all he could give me was all of himself.

That gift was precious, and it would have to be enough to stop Asmodel from getting away. Or I would unwittingly become a key element of Hitler's victory over Poland. And I could not live with that knowledge.

"Sing psalms, Raziel," I said urgently under my breath. "Sing!"

He immediately launched into the most heart-rending rendition of the Twenty-second Psalm I had ever heard: "My God, why have you forsaken me?" It was not what I had expected: I half hoped he would sing a warlike psalm about smiting evil or something similar.

But Raziel knew our adversary better than I did. Asmodel hesitated, and a strange expression came over the demon's crackling, flickering face: shockingly wistful. Orphaned. I knew that pain all too well.

As Raziel sang, the psalm changed me. I rose against my enemy with more compassion than before, and though compassion is dangerous because it often leads to softheartedness, it keeps you human.

I raised my arms and began to sing the Testament of Solomon, in harsh counterpart to Raziel's psalm. Asmodel flinched away from the sound and bellowed, trying to drown out the sound of our voices. But my song was spell and could not be silenced with a scream. His voice only augmented the power of the spell I wove, tied us closer together.

"Asmodel," I said. "Come forth, out of the fire!"

He squirmed and shrank, flickered in and out of the flame. Then, before I could restrain him, he shot out of the fire and over my shoulder.

I whirled to face him, but the demon was intent on flight, not battle. I turned fast enough to see where he was headed: to where Antonio had crumpled to the ground.

I could not help crying out: Antonio's face was ashen gray, the color of death. Raziel had not given him nearly enough to revive him; a fine foam of spittle and blood pooled on his lips and chin.

The force of the demon's blow knocked Antonio sideways. And before I could stop him, Asmodel entered Antonio's body and asserted full possession.

I could see it in the way the eyes glowed red, in the self-assurance and the vampire's swagger, an arrogance poor Antonio had never displayed in life. His broken arm had hung limply before; now Asmodel waved it wildly, disregarding the terrible pain he must be causing his unwilling host.

"Leave him," I warned, but my voice trembled. I had never even heard of a possessed vampire, let alone seen the horrible spectacle for myself.

"Die, bitch," he snarled in reply. He launched into a biting diatribe in Polish, ending by vomiting violently through Antonio's bloody mouth. It was all Asmodel at the forefront; Antonio's spirit, if it was still there at all, was crushed to the back of his own skull.

Without warning, he lunged for my throat, fangs fully extended. Raziel put himself between us, and blocked the now-possessed vampire from reaching me. Man and demon fought together on the ground, fists against fangs.

I threw my magical muscle into the fray. "No!" I screamed, and the vampire's body flew backward into the trunk of an aspen tree, hard. The trunk snapped like a matchstick and the tree toppled, the crown slowly falling away.

The impact had broken Antonio's back. The demon tried to make him walk, but the effort was pointless; he looked like a marionette tangled in his own strings. With a roar of frustration, Asmodel exited through Antonio's lolling, open mouth, stretching it too wide and breaking Antonio's jaw as he left.

I caught him inside the energy I held between my hands, a fly caught in honey, and held him fast, my arms aching with the effort. "Asmodel, be still," I ordered, tears of exertion streaming from my eyes. "Stop."

He squirmed furiously between my hands, and broke free. With a despairing cry I once again ordered him back, but he was too fast. Asmodel tore through the tree branches, across the field, and was gone.

With a stifled sob, I ran to Antonio. He was dead, his skin still smoking in the afternoon sunlight. The life of a bloodlust vampire is precarious in the best of circumstances, and Antonio had lived for longer than anyone could have expected.

But the fact remained. I had killed him. I sank to my knees and covered my face in my hands. Raziel's voice called to me from a great distance.

His fingers caressed my arms, and Raziel held me close. "You are shaking like a leaf," he said.

He let me fall to pieces and for two precious minutes, three, I cried. Then he stroked my hair and kissed me on the top of my head.

I looked up at him, my eyes puffy with tears, and he kissed me full on the lips, hard. The touch of his lips on mine shook me harder than if he had slapped me.

His voice was full of steel. "We must go now. Asmodel is very fast, and he may well have already invaded another host. We have to stop him."

He stated the obvious, but his steadiness brought me back to my senses. "I can cast and see where he has gone. We will hunt him, right, Raziel?"

"Yes, and you have power enough to bind him again."

I turned to contemplate the awful sight of Antonio, crumpled and mangled on the grass. I sent out my witch's sight, a scout in hostile territory. Great waves of rage and death and fire knocked me off balance, but I closed my eyes and reached.

War raged not thirty kilometers behind us. Battalions of souls marched off to Heaven in formation, soldiers unwilling even in death to abandon their comrades. I dug my fingers into the dirt and watched them go. The forest spirits and earth spirits of this place had fled their ancient domains and now hid deep in a great forest about ten kilometers ahead of us.

And aside from the battle lines, the land itself cried out to me, an old lament, a song of pain it had cried many, many times before. "Not again, no, not again. . . ."

I turned my focus deeper in, straining to hear where Asmodel had gone. North, toward Warsaw . . .

I opened my eyes to see more clearly. Souls, some doomed, others saved, flew through the thick clouds above the battlefield, an immense plain of destruction that bled over the western boundary of Poland. The Germans' drive was for Warsaw.

A darting spark caught my attention in the midst of this slaughter. Asmodel triumphant. He was not far, less than five kilometers away, a straight arrow shot to the north.

"He's almost to Kraków," I said under my breath, not knowing the words until I spoke them aloud. It was the sight that spoke, not me. "He grows weary. He wants . . ."

I shuddered, took a deep breath to steady myself. "He wants to kill. Take his revenge. Punish. He seeks a host."

I pulled my sight back, looked up to where Raziel stood. I was nearly in despair. "How can we stop him?"

"Let us track him. You search for magical signs; I will look for physical evidence."

I nodded and unsteadily rose to my feet. We started walking, Raziel easily keeping pace with me. At the edge of the field I hesitated, looked back over my shoulder at Antonio's body.

"We don't have time to bury him, Magduska," Raziel said. "The farmers will find him. And his bones will rest in his mother's country. He could have met a worse fate, poor soul."

And so we left Antonio's broken and abused body tangled up in the long grass at the edge of the field. The airplane was a torched, blackened shell, and the fire still burned.

✴ 9 ✴

We walked for two hours through the softly undulating hills, hiding from the few farmers we saw and finding telltale signs of Asmodel's progress: a hideously flayed cow; a dead flock of crows; a blackened, reeking patch of corn.

Our pace was slow but steady; Asmodel's was speedy but erratic. After his initial burst of speed, Asmodel meandered, first west toward the continuing, bloody battle, then back south, as if to go on the attack against us.

As the light began to fade into a golden, molten sunset over the fields, Asmodel's path became straight again. And it led due east.

"He's heading into a forest for the night," I guessed. "It doesn't make sense. Shouldn't his power grow stronger by night?"

"Travel may not be his intent. Destruction tempts him always,

Magduska. Destruction and pain fuel his power. So he may be drawn to something innocent in the forest to destroy. Wood sprites, perhaps, or a remote farm with children."

Guilt over my failure to hold him drove me forward; the thought of those defenseless souls seared me. "We'd better hurry, then."

Though Antonio had barely begun to feed before Asmodel's escape, Raziel showed clear signs of exhaustion. Even his prodigious strength was now only human, and we had not eaten a bite or had even a sip of water since we had bid Budapest farewell. But he nodded in agreement. "We'll catch him, Magda, even if we have to track him through the night."

My fear and consternation goaded me onward with more than enough energy, but I considered Raziel by fading light. "He must be hunting Gisele." My fear tasted like ashes.

Raziel sighed. I could all but feel his weariness weighing down my own bones. "We must catch him first then, Magduska."

"What if I can't find him?"

Raziel looked into my eyes, willing me to stay strong. "Forward now. It is not time yet to entertain such questions."

I wiped at my sweaty forehead and cast yet again for a sign of the escaped demon. My feet were a welter of bloody blisters, and my stomach yowled for food. Rage kept me moving, one foot in front of the other, trudging over the endless fields of Poland.

And a crazy hope kept me going, too. Asmodel was my satanic bloodhound, leading me unerringly to the goodness in Gisele. Even as Asmodel pursued his purpose, he also, unwittingly, served mine.

So, the glimmer of pure light I discovered in the forest meant all the more to me when I found it. I would not have traded that sight for a crown encrusted with diamonds.

"Asmodel seeks a haven," I said. I spoke unwillingly, as if the beautiful emanation I had found would be harmed by my discovery of it.

"There is a soul that shines like a sapphire in that forest," I continued. "And the demon is zeroing in on it."

Raziel turned in the direction where I pointed, and started walking again, faster. His shirt was soaked with sweat and stuck to his broad, muscular back.

I hurried to catch up with him. "But what if we don't get there in time?"

I hoped that Asmodel had found Gisi, but shuddered at the thought of him reaching her before I did. The thought of that innocent light becoming prey to Asmodel acted as a spur and I broke into a half run. Our first day in the war in Poland was almost done.

We walked another hour, into a forest that grew thick and dark all around us. I tried to cast as I walked, though I could not draw power from the earth that way; it tired me terribly, but I did not want to pause for even a moment. The beautiful golden light shone steady and kindly like a candle in the darkness lighting the way to a lost and wretched soul. And I could sense Asmodel's hunger to consume that bright flame and snuff it out.

My thoughts and worries became darker and more jumbled with every step that carried me deeper into the woods. The night rustled with life all around us: creatures still oblivious to the human destruction bearing down upon them; night spirits that came to hide from the moonlight in the shade of the sweeping branches over our heads.

A great owl hooted as it flew across the face of the moon. "We are almost there," Raziel said, his eyes narrowed nearly to slits.

We stumbled upon the source of the light almost without realizing we had arrived. Only the specter of Asmodel, a blot against the sky, gave me confirmation that we had found him. But where . . . ?

I looked around. We stood in a clearing, by a small river. At the edge of the clearing, all but indistinguishable from the night, stood a small, decrepit cabin, a hut, really, with a sloping roof thatched with grass and a heavy wooden door that stood ajar.

The light emanated from inside that doorway: it was invisible to my ordinary sight, but when I trained my witch's sight upon it I was dazzled by its brilliance.

I glanced again and gasped. Gisele stood before me, basking in that light like a bird at sunrise. But the brightness in the dark did not emanate from her.

With great presence of mind, I made myself useful by stepping forward and, quite gently, capturing Asmodel in my hands like a firefly in a glass jar.

The light had so mesmerized the demon that he hardly struggled in my grasp. He sighed and fell into a deep sleep, condensed into a ball of dark energy between my palms.

I could not believe my success. Before I could call to him, Raziel was by my side, and though he looked exhausted, his face seemed to shine again with a celestial light. "A great holy man is here," he said.

⁜ 10 ⁜

I don't know what I expected to see after a statement like that. A tall magus in striped robes and an exotic jeweled headdress, perhaps? A swami in a cotton loincloth?

After a moment, the holy man appeared. He looked exactly like what he was: an elderly watchmaker from the city of Kraków, short and potbellied and utterly ordinary. A small man, in every material respect.

He was a mortal man, only a mortal man, with no magical gifts I could discern. But when I looked on him with my second sight, I was again dazzled, all but blinded by the radiance of this man's soul.

He looked at me and smiled, then spread his hands open in greeting. "Good evening, my dears, you have arrived in time for supper," he said in thick Galician Yiddish. "I am Yankel Horo-witz, at your service."

I scanned around the place for signs of deception or spiritual rot and found nothing. And I stared at Gisele, half disbelieving that I had actually found her at last.

Mr. Horowitz caught me at my surreptitious scanning of the place, and he straightened his spectacles on his nose. "Oh, you'll find no funny business here, miss. Just a place where strangers are welcome."

I wanted to believe him, but the fact that he did not look twice at the demon I held trapped between my palms gave me pause. Without a word about Asmodel, he bowed and smiled, and re-turned to the hut, presumably to see about supper. As soon as he had gone I turned, careful not to disturb my hold on the demon, and faced Gisele, who still stood by the hut's doorway.

"Little mouse," I whispered, my relief choking the words in my throat. "Thank the Maker I found you in time."

Her smile was so sweet and sad that it nearly broke my heart. "Did you really find me, or did . . . he?" She tilted her chin to in-dicate Asmodel, who was trying to wriggle out of my bonds.

I whispered a spell of binding, and the demon stilled again in my hands. "It doesn't matter. We're together again." But be-fore I could say any more, Raziel impatiently interrupted me.

"This is one of the righteous ones of the world, Magduska, what the sages call a *zaddiq*. I expected him to speak in the holy tongue, like the angels."

"Well, he doesn't speak Hungarian either," I said, my voice gentle. "He may be a righteous one, but he speaks only Polish and Yiddish, and Biblical Hebrew, I'm sure."

Raziel shook his head and sighed. "It is difficult, this Babel of languages. I am used to speaking the angelic tongue, which all creatures understand."

That was all he said; but his sadness hung in the air like the smoke from the smashed-up plane.

"Try the Hebrew, Raziel. It will work, I am sure."

"How do you know Yiddish so well?"

He surprised me. "Do you not know? My father was a wine merchant in Tokaj, and did a lot of trade with partners of ours in Galicia. They spoke no Hungarian, we spoke no Polish. I learned Yiddish at my father's knee, as they negotiated things like inventory and dates of delivery."

The man returned, carrying steaming pierogies on a silver tray; I found out later he had a small camp stove. I had not realized how ravenous I was until the scent of those salty potato dumplings rose to meet me.

Mr. Horowitz put the tray down on the tablecloth laid out on the grass. He then tilted his head to peer at me from over the tops of his spectacles to where I sat awkwardly, the demon now squirming again in my hands.

"He's a lively one, isn't he," Mr. Horowitz said, nodding at Asmodel while stroking his long cascading beard, the color of bridal linen.

"You are the wonderworker of Kraków," Gisele said, her voice dreamy. "You will help us, I know. We have come all the way from Budapest to find you."

That wasn't exactly true, but I did not disabuse either of them of the notion. Gisele spoke in Hungarian, too—her Yiddish was not as good as mine, her head not suited to business or to acquiring languages—but to my amazement, the man seemed to understand. Gisele and the wonderworker of Kraków were children of the same tribe, and spoke the same language of another world.

It was his lack of fear that awed me the most, and it made me love him. Mortal or magical, all of us had lived in fear for years. Raziel had not known fear before now, but the burden of it, I could see, was beginning to settle on his shoulders. Yet this little old man lived free of fear and its constraints.

"First things first," he said. "This restless fellow you're sitting on needs a home, *nu*?"

"He's tricky, all right," Gisele said. Raziel sat beside me, watchful and silent, listening to the cadences of Mr. Horowitz's mild Yiddish, as if he understood the essential goodness of the man and didn't need to know anything else.

It was full night now, and Asmodel's power waxed stronger . . . and in my exhaustion my own power ebbed. "I will help you," Mr. Horowitz said. "Let him go, my girl."

I gaped at him in amazement. "But you—don't you know what he is?"

He nodded sadly and sighed. "Poor soul. We must hold this wild creature fast."

Asmodel decided the question for me; with a savage slash at my arm he wrenched free of my grip. He whirled on me, all claw and fang.

I raised a cone of protection around us, and Mr. Horowitz clambered awkwardly to his feet, shaking his head. "All right already," he admonished me.

In surprise, I let my defenses drop. And we all waited for something, the demon and mortals arrayed against each other in the darkened clearing.

Asmodel broke the tableau first; he swept along the semicir-
cle we mortals made, and his low laughter crawled up into the
small of my back. "Your strength fails you, Magda Lazarus."

I could not speak. The specter of seeing Asmodel loose again
struck me mute. Only the pure light of Mr. Horowitz's soul had
lured the demon to a place where I could recapture him. But
now I was too exhausted to hold him.

The hateful sound of Asmodel's laughter echoed through the
trees and night. "Evil is stronger than good. If you were worth
possessing I would do it, witchling. But you are not powerful
enough to suit me. Now, as for Raziel . . ."

The demon circled around to face Raziel directly. Raziel refused to lower his eyes in deference to the demon's contempt,
and the two faced off as Asmodel snarled. "You would be worth
living in. You have seen enough of this world to imagine the
taste of power. But you would die rather than have me, wouldn't
you, my brother?"

Raziel said not a word. But the intensity of his gaze would
have discomfited any mortal man.

Asmodel snapped with his fangs at Raziel's face. I could not
help crying out, but Raziel leaped backward in time to escape
getting ripped by Asmodel's terrible jaws.

The demon manifest was a hideous thing. The sound of
laughter again rang out in the darkened forest clearing. But this
time it was not the demon who laughed.

To my astonishment, it was Yankel Horowitz who laughed.
And he did not laugh in terror, or in bitter derision; the old
man sincerely enjoyed the spectacle of Asmodel made manifest
in the flesh.

"Oy, wonderful. Wonderful! Great is Hashem's creation!" He started clapping, and then Yankel began dancing from one foot to the other, hands upraised in the air.

"Glory, glory, glory!" he sang. "All of the Lord's hosts, holy!"

Asmodel roared and clapped his huge clawed hands over his large, veined ears. "Stop it, curse you!"

"No. Bless you, Asmodel, holy one of God!" Yankel exclaimed, his face shining like the sun. "Bless you, ancient one come to stand upon the earth like a son of Adam! Bless you! Come, eat, eat!"

Yankel spoke in a mix of Yiddish and Hebrew; his words assailed Asmodel like a swarm of hornets. "Stop it!" The demon's screams shook the very trees.

"Hush, Asmodel." Yankel clapped his hands, and Asmodel collapsed. He spoke no more, but held his head in his hands and groaned, curled up on the grass like a naked madman.

I dared to look away from the spectacle to make sure Raziel was unharmed. Tears sparkled in his eyes like stars. "Now this is a righteous man, Magda, as heroes were in the days of old."

Yankel's performance had left me stupefied. After stumbling about to find my Yiddish again, I finally sputtered, "So, righteous one, are you going to dump him in the river?"

The smile faded from Yankel's lips, but only slightly. "For shame, Lazarus, to talk such a *shanda*. This ancient one is safest in a hidden place. Hm."

He glanced at Gisele. "Quiet one, do you have a pretty thing that you love? An earring, a bracelet? A watch would be perfect, my love."

He spoke in Yiddish, but again my little sister understood.

She reached around to the back of her neck and unclasped a tiny gold chain that always hung around her neck. "My grandmother's locket," she said in Hungarian. "My mother left it to me when she died."

I knew that little locket well, had secretly grieved when I found my mother had bequeathed it to Gisele and not to me. It was a little red gold cameo locket my grandmother used to wear, dented from where Gisele had cut her teeth on it as a baby. Now, Gisele held out the locket to this stranger, eager to share her most precious treasure.

Yankel took the locket with a smile and a grateful nod. He began to pray over the locket, rocking slowly at first then faster and faster, a furious gabble of Hebrew rising like an army of spirits into the sky.

Periodically Raziel punctuated Yankel's prayers with an ecstatic "Amen!" And Asmodel twitched and snarled at them from the dirt, as if trapped inside a hellish dream from which he could not waken.

Yankel finished his prayer with a triumphant *"Kadosh! kadosh! kadosh!"* And a ring of fire surrounded all of us in a sudden shower of blue sparks. I managed to stay silent, but only barely: Yankel's prayer was so infectious that I wanted to leap to my feet and cry Holy! Holy! Holy! myself.

"Amen!" Raziel cried out, and a bolt of light blinded me. When I blinked the dazzle out of my eyes, I took in the scene with a gasp.

Asmodel was gone.

"Won't it be too heavy to wear?" Gisele asked, her voice sounding completely ordinary in the fading whirlwind.

I rubbed my eyes and saw that Gisele now stood next to Yankel,

the locket nestled in her outstretched palm. Raziel stood behind her, and the three of them leaned in to see the locket.

The scene would have seemed quaint and ordinary to the
unknowing eye. But the entire clearing crackled with magical
power, and the demon's essence imbued the locket with a terrible,
electric darkness. The locket dragged the very air down into it
like a hole in the world.

"How did you do that?" I demanded, my voice shaky. This
scrawny little man was no wizard or warlock; in fact, from what
I could tell, he was possessed of less innate magic than my old
friend the Zionist Eva Farkas. But Yankel Horowitz had just
performed the most powerful act of magic I had ever seen.

"I did nothing." For the first time a shadow passed over his
ebullient old face. "The Almighty accomplishes all through
me."

He gave me a significant look. "Magic is not something you
do, my Hungarian stranger. It is the means by which God
transcends death."

The words thundered in my head. I swallowed hard, stood
completely still. It was as if the Almighty Himself, who had
hidden from me even in the second Heaven, now spoke to me
through this man's words.

"An angel is a messenger of God," Yankel continued, his voice
now gentle, as he leaned forward and returned the gold chain
and locket to my sister's neck. "But God Himself is the message,
nu?"

"I don't understand," I said, my mouth dry.

He worked the clasp on the locket, then straightened. "I know,
my poor child, I know." He smiled, held his hands open, defense-

less, in front of him. "Maybe the message is not that you should understand, but that you should trust.

"He is more securely restrained by gold," Yankel continued. "The locket is further strengthened by the bonds you have to your sister and grandmother. It need not stay closed, even." And to my horror, with an expert flick of his thumb, he opened the locket.

I was prepared to fight, but Yankel was right. The only sign of the demon's presence was his face, flat and serene, a portrait superimposed over the photograph of my father tucked inside.

Trapped and still, the fangs hidden from view, Asmodel's fine features revealed his celestial origins. Not for the first time, I pitied the demon's journey farther and farther from Heaven.

Yankel must have seen the expression on my face, for he closed up the locket again and stroked the black-and-white cameo on the front. "It is sad to see an Angel of the Lord so debased. But he chose it! And he could go back if he chose, too. Instead, he wants to drag you down with him."

With a final check of the clasp, he let the locket come to rest over Gisele's heart, and he gave me a long, significant look. "This girl Gisele must carry Asmodel. But it is you I worry about, *mamele.*"

✳ *II* ✳

Dinner with Yankel, Gisele, and Raziel was as surreal as a fever dream. My joy at our reunion was tempered with the knowledge that we were in the middle of a shooting war in Poland. Gisele was sure her fate remained here. But if she stayed in Poland, should I stay, too, to protect her?

The war had already smashed what remained of my old, comprehensible life. But despite the dangers, Raziel's presence made even the burden of Asmodel bearable.

Raziel protected me. Some men in this world find shelter in their academic degrees, their social status, or their money. They thrive in fine society and never learn what they are really made of. My man, Raziel, had no money, no social connections, and no academic laurels upon which to rest, a self-made, self-reliant man. And in this savage new world, he was well suited to fighting the grim battles we faced.

After our meal, Gisele and Yankel went to sleep inside the hut, while Raziel and I stood guard outside in the clearing. I thought of my man's attributes as I remembered our discussion with Yankel during dinner.

I let my fingers stray to Raziel's arm, and I stroked the cabled muscles as I spoke my thoughts aloud. "Did you hear what Yankel said about the salt mines where the Polish resistance is already gathering?"

I bit my lip as I reached his hand and interlaced my fingers with his. Raziel looked deeply into my eyes, and a smile played over his lips. "I know what you are thinking. Don't go chasing after Polish partisans, Magduska. Not yet."

"I love it when you say my name."

Raziel leaned forward and stole a tiny, perfect kiss. "Don't try to change the subject. The people in the salt mines will not welcome us. We are not Polish."

"But what should we do instead? Gisele is as safe with Yankel as she would be alone in Budapest. Maybe safer," I said. "But I don't know what to do. For now, we will find a connection in Kraków with Yankel's help. I owe Mr. Churchill no less, yes?"

Raziel considered my words. "Do you speak any Polish?" he asked. He now understood the importance of fluency in a world divided by language.

I suppressed a sigh. "No, but I speak French. Hopefully the assimilated Jews in the city will know some; the people of Poland have long had a love affair with France."

"Will that be enough to convince frightened people that they can resist the Nazis?"

The wind picked up around us, and I shivered . . . but I wasn't sure whether it was from the cold, or because I couldn't stop thinking about my worries.

After an uneasy night, my concerns only multiplied in the morning. I asked Yankel to make introductions for me in Kraków.

But he refused. "You are dangerous," he said, his voice kind but his expression grim. "An untrained Lazarus witch! For shame. You have too much dark blood in you, too many fallen angels in your bloodline, for you not to understand what you are. You think you use Jewish magic, but I cannot let you leave without helping you learn to master yourself."

I looked over Yankel's shoulder and Gisele nodded at me. She wanted me to learn Yankel's ways.

"Time is short, sir."

"Bah, time is always short. I know a very nice boy in Kraków who can help you. But first you must learn about your lineage. Who you are, *mamele*. Poland is not Budapest."

Before my mother had died four years earlier, she had failed to give me my magical inheritance, knowledge of the Lazarus creed and the limitations of our magic. It wasn't her fault; at sixteen I was too wild to learn what she had had to teach.

Now Yankel wanted to give me an introduction to what I should have learned. He crossed his arms across his narrow, sunken chest, and we sat down by the banks of the little stream.

"You are the eldest daughter of an eldest daughter, the last of the Lazarus line," he began. "You can summon souls, including your own, from the dead. Your little sister, the second daughter, has the gift of the second sight, the ability to foretell. These gifts are all governed by the Lazarus creed . . . but you never learned it! I cannot teach you your creed. Instead, I will teach you what I know. And somehow that will have to be enough."

He was no Lazarus witch. But once he taught me his own rules, Yankel Horowitz would be content to unleash me upon Kraków, and keep my sister safe with him.

I had recently been schooled in magic's rudiments by the enigmatic Lucretia de Merode, courtesan extraordinaire and matriarch of the clandestine Daughters of Arachne coven. But now Yankel taught me the greater lore that governed us all.

But he would never call what he taught me "magic." In his parlance, he taught me Kabbalah, Jewish mysticism, the wonder-working of the great rabbis and sages of renown. The fact that I was a godless, bacon-eating female from Budapest seemed not to matter to him in the slightest. Though I was a terrible Jew by any conventional reckoning, in Yankel's eyes I had a ferocity of spirit and an indestructible Jewish soul, and therefore I was a worthy instrument of the glory of the Almighty and His wondrous works.

"The world is made of holy sparks," Yankel began that cool, clear morning in September. "Our job is to collect them together to hasten the end of days."

That made me hesitate. I couldn't care less about the end of days, unless it meant the end of the Nazis and their enormous army first.

But I held my peace and strained to understand. I felt sure that had the war not upended everything, I never would have

met such a man, and if we had somehow encountered one another, he never would have considered teaching me the secrets
he now revealed.

But in his way, Yankel was even more desperate than I, and
more willing to compromise his ideals. For he understood, in a
way I had not yet done, how short our time together would be.
He had no other young disciple to teach; Yankel had resolved to
do his best with me.

We started that day with golems. "Have you heard of the
golem of Prague?" Yankel asked.

I had to admit that I had not. Yankel stroked his beard and
tsked. "That you could do so much, untaught, and still not
know such things!" he marveled. "You have been very lucky."

I told him about the remarkable Lucretia de Merode and all
that she had taught me in her Amsterdam bordello: how to cast
spells, how to throw witchfire. But Yankel dismissed her les-
sons with an impatient wave of an old, gnarled hand. "Parlor
tricks," he said, shaking his head.

I privately, and vehemently, disagreed, but it did not matter.
I nodded for him to go on.

"Now, you will soon need an army, *nu*? We could do worse
than an army of golems. They are made of mud and holy sparks
from holy words. They are hard to kill because they aren't really
alive."

"But how much harm can they do, really?" I asked, skeptical.

"Well, less than guns. But I am not speaking of harm, but
protection."

Again I remembered the great battle Raziel, Gisele, and I had
fought at Heroes' Square in Budapest, how an army of imps had
followed my brainchild, an imp called Leopold, into battle

against Asmodel and his brother demons. And I thought of Asmodel, trapped inside Gisele's locket.

I hesitated to say what I was really thinking—and then I decided that I didn't have time to play coy. "Why do we only consider protection? An army should do more than hide. Could we not call upon an army of demons?"

Yankel didn't find the prospect as scandalous as I thought he would. "It is an interesting idea," he said, after a moment in which he was lost in thought. "But I see some problems with it."

"Like the damning of my soul," I said, a statement, not a question.

"No, not at all," he said. "We are not Christians, and certainly not Catholics. I love and admire the Christians. They are, after all, Jews of a sort."

I found that assertion rather amazing. "But the Christians imagine Satan as an enemy general, in a fight against God. And demons aren't?"

"Some are, yes. They are air creatures, like the angels and the seraphim. Some are fallen angels, degraded by their hatred of human beings, their jealousy of mortals. But others were made that way, the way mosquitoes and asps were made. All serve the glory of the Almighty. Even the Adversary serves a greater plan—that fact drives the demons crazy because they know it, too."

My own personal imp, Leo, had gloried in serving the greater good, even if only to better his own station in the world. I tried to open my mind to the world as seen through Yankel's eyes, a view that expected miracles to ripen like fresh fruit, part of the natural unfolding of life and its seasons. "Can demons ascend?"

"Certainly. They are made of holy sparks as well. All will be gathered up, into the great One. It is that gathering up that the demons can't stand."

"Because it is like death." I was with the demons on that particular point.

Yankel sighed again. "It is *not* like death." He paused, seeming to search for the right words. "Death is not celebrated in the Jewish tradition. We accept it, we support our brethren when they lose their loved ones. We move on from it as the *mitzvot* decree we do. But each soul is a world. The death of that soul is the death of the world.

"The gathering up is different. It is a return to the world as it was before creation. One singular creation . . ."

His voice trailed off, and Yankel glowed with that pure light I had loved from the first moment when, lost in the forest, I had found it.

But we lived in a world where the sparks were still scattered. "I cannot bring the demons into the light of creation, but I can summon them, whether they want to come or not. And if I were only strong enough, I could, like King Solomon or my ancient great-grandmama the Witch of Ein Dor, compel an army of demons to my will."

Yankel turned from his contemplation of the heavenly dance of angels and shot me a dirty look. "You can force them to show up, Magda. But how well do you think they would fight?"

"I can call up the spirits, too. Don't you think that Jewish ghosts would fight to save their living descendants?"

Yankel muttered something unintelligible under his breath; my obstinacy seemed to be wearing him down. "Those souls have important places to be, Magda. You may cause more harm by calling them here."

"But am I forbidden by the Lazarus creed to call them?" I held up a hand so that I could finish my thought. "If they knew they could save their children, their grandchildren, I think they would come. If I am able to call them."

"My dear, the Lazarus creed is not the point. But let's talk about the creed anyway. I do not know all of it, but I do know it says you can't return after you have been dead for three days. Am I right?"

I thought of my mother, who had refused to return after she had died four years before, and I sighed. "I don't know the exact wording, but yes. My mother told me that."

"The creed is saying not that it isn't possible to do it, but that you shouldn't do it, it's not kosher to do it. Listen, like eating pork kielbasa, you can do it, *mamele*. Come back, anytime. But you just might find that the maggots that now live in your corpse won't go away so easy, they ruined your body too much to make it nice to come back. A practical rule, the three days."

I tried to keep the impatience out of my voice. "But what does kielbasa have to do with calling up an army of the dead?"

"We were talking of the creed. Just because it is possible for you to do something, doesn't mean you should do it, *mamele*.

"You have the strongest gifts I have ever seen in one who is unguided," Yankel continued, his voice rumbling deep in his chest. "But I have to warn you against two things: calling up dead spirits, and seeking to harness the power of primordial demons, the ancient ones that fell in the early days of the world."

Demons like Asmodel, I was sure he meant. I looked down and listened as contritely as I could.

"Such demons have been wielded by kings and sages," Yankel continued. "But these are debased times in which we live, and you do not have the power to force such creatures to serve the Lord—not without doing great harm to yourself."

Binding Asmodel is a good enough deed. And my mother wants to come fight, I know she does, if I could but reach her again. I will not throw away the few advantages we have.

But I did not voice my protests aloud.

Yankel looked at me for a long time, then seemed to make a decision about me. It wasn't until he smiled and I relaxed that I realized I had been holding my breath.

"I will teach you how to raise golems," Yankel said. "And how to call down the wrath of Heaven. But let go of this idea that you have, that you can fight Hitler himself, army against army. Let it go, *mamele*. To hell with Hitler. He is the Lord's problem, not yours."

To Hell with Hitler, indeed. That is where I intended to send that man, as soon as I could. Surely it would alter the terrible visions my sister had endured: millions murdered, factories of death.

But first, golems.

Yankel and I worked by day, ate pierogies with Raziel and Gisele by night. And then, after only a few short days of instruction, Yankel Horowitz sent me on my way, to Kraków.

✳ 12 ✳

Yankel sent Raziel and me with a woman, Chana, the blessed maker of his pierogi, who also brought Yankel bread and firewood. Before we left, he promised to look after Gisele and Asmodel while we were gone, which I found a comfort.

Kraków reminded me of a little Budapest. Its city squares, with their beautiful, oddly Mediterranean-looking stucco and archways gracing curved, cobblestone streets, seemed more the architecture of an Italian city.

Our guide took Raziel and me to Kazimierz, the Jewish district, and we were soon installed in Chana's brother's place on Miodowa Street, in the heart of the quarter.

I could not believe the calm in Kazimierz under German occupation. The first week of September was done. Warsaw still resisted, but here where the battle against the German invader had already been lost, Poles strolled along the street, lingered in cafés, and read their newspapers as if the war itself had never happened.

When I mentioned these observations to Chana, she shrugged. "Warsaw is fighting like a lion, at least," she said, her eyes puffy and red despite her defiant words. "England and France have declared war. They will soon squash Hitler like a bug. The war will be over by Chanukkah."

I stood in her brother Asher's stuffy little parlor, and I said nothing. They had not yet heard Gisele's prophecy. The Poles, in their crazy determination to fight and resist until the Western powers intervened, filled me with a profound admiration. But I feared it doomed them.

I tried, as gently as I could, to tell Chana what I already knew. I explained Gisele's foreknowledge of the murder of the Jewish people, explained that we had come to try to stop the invasion by magical means, get them all out in time if we could.

She simply would not believe me. "Palestine?" she said, incredulous. "Why would I go to Palestine? Everything I know is here, my family is here. My beloved husband is dead, how will I survive in some strange desert full of Arabs? No, the Lord put me here, so here I will stay."

Raziel interrupted me, and I translated for him, my voice shaking with my frustration. Chana was much safer with the Arabs than with her Polish countrymen.

"Never mind," he said, his voice as gentle as a feather. "All we need is to talk to the local Hashomer."

The boy Yankel knew was with the Hashomer in Kraków. And Chana's brother Asher, a more worldly character with a big watch on a chain which he kept taking out of his vest pocket to check, knew where we could find them. "I will take you to meet Viktor," he said. "But you need to wash up first."

So it was that I got a nice bath, a decent meal, and a new dress the morning I found the Zionists of Kraków. Chana's sister-in-law was zaftig and I was thin, but I didn't care. The borrowed dress was cornflower blue, my favorite color, and I resolved to take that as a good omen.

But my good omen was belied after meeting Viktor Mandelstam, the leader of the Hashomer in Kraków, Poland.

Raziel and I met Viktor after following Asher down and across Miodowa Street to the pharmacist's shop, then up a narrow, high staircase smelling faintly of pinewood and cigars.

The landing at the top of the stairs revealed a single door, the leaded glass unmarked by any sign. Asher knocked, then swung the door open; it was unlocked. He introduced us briefly, bowed, and to my surprise, disappeared down the stairs.

I shut the door behind me and took the measure of the man who sat behind the desk. Viktor Mandelstam sat behind an enormous desk covered with piles of paper, a ratty-looking desk blotter, and a black, squat telephone with a rotary dial.

He surprised me with how young he was, how dapper, and how overwhelmed. He wore a double-breasted suit with a thick chalk stripe in it, as elegant as any I had seen in Paris the previous summer.

But his eyes. Startlingly blue, and sharp. Yet, looking into Viktor's eyes, I thought I already could see defeat.

It wasn't Viktor's fault: his job in Kraków was impossible. The Germans were still going through the motions of politeness to the citizens at large in the city of Kraków: there had been alarming, but isolated, reports of mass arrests of academics, magicals, and mystics in the past few days, when the Germans had first installed themselves in town. But as yet, none of us (except Gisele, really) knew what the Germans had planned, and hardly a building had been destroyed by the invading Wehrmacht.

Only the Jews had been mistreated, and from the very first. Aside from the sneering contempt they encountered from the Germans, nothing official had yet been done. But I remembered my sister's prophecies and I shuddered in Viktor's dusty little office on the second floor, remembering the future as Gisele envisioned it.

"We have no time to lose," I said. My Yiddish was pretty basic, so I had no way to gild the truth to make it less ugly. "Hitler means to murder us all. We must get the children at least to Palestine, now. And the religious—if the Catholics will go, they should. The gypsies, too. All will be in special danger under the Nazis' boot heels."

Viktor lit a cigarette and offered me one, which I gratefully accepted. Raziel waved away the proffered cigarette and matches—he still didn't really know how to light it himself without burning his fingers.

Viktor gave him a long, contemplative look. Raziel spoke no Yiddish so he could not help me convince Viktor. But he didn't need to say a word.

"My God, you two look like the veterans of a big war already," Viktor said with a sigh.

"*Parlez-vous français?*" I asked with a sudden flicker of hope, and to my delight, Viktor responded in French. He and I could have a real conversation now.

I decided to give Viktor everything: he was in the Nazi crosshairs in a way that Mordechai, the Hashomer leader my friend

Eva worked for in Budapest, was not yet. I told him about my summer's misadventures, Gisele's prophecies, everything. Even that Hitler of late had been possessed by a demon: anything to get him to see how serious was the threat to every decent person in Poland.

"It is no secret," I concluded, "that Hitler sees every Pole as subhuman. So far, he has treated you humanely—perhaps he does anticipate an attack by the French or the English."

"The West will certainly honor their treaty with us and stand with Poland in her hour of need." He still thought of himself as a Pole, and of Poland as a nation instead of a possession of Nazi Germany.

"Please," I concluded, already nearly at the end of my patience. "Don't wait for anything more. Just send these people to Palestine."

"But if we enrage the English, it may interfere with their battle with Germany. The Palestine Mandate is under their control, after all, ever since the end of the Ottoman Empire. The English need the Arab oil to fight this war."

"Can't you sneak them in? Not even the children?"

He took a long drag of his cigarette, slowly blew smoke. We stared at each other in the half-lit, dusty silence of his office.

"I believe you," he said, finally. "Why else would you risk your life and run into Poland while the rest of us should be trying to get out?"

"So you will help these people?"

"Help? We are trapped here ourselves."

I refused to accept his fatalism as the end of the matter. "Let me call the Budapest Hashomer. If I establish a pipeline to Budapest will you send people there? You'll at least be getting people out of here—Hungary is still technically neutral. Even if they don't go any farther, the children will be safer there than here!"

He took a long look at Raziel, his hollow cheeks, hungry-looking eyes, and dirty fingernails. Viktor crushed out the end of his cigarette in a gigantic crystal ashtray on his desk that was already overflowing with dead cigarettes.

"All right," he said, and pulled the phone to him. "The telephone service is spotty at best—we are likely to be arrested by the Gestapo in any event before the end of the day."

"In that case, I will hide you in the forest. They don't know about me yet, and I can keep your operations running in Kraków until my cover is blown." I meant it for a grim joke, but Viktor's blue eyes lit up, a bright, fierce fire. He didn't look like someone who had been born to do a bureaucrat's job behind a desk.

Viktor lifted the receiver and began the long search for an operator willing to try to patch through a call to Hashomer headquarters in Budapest.

The operator said she would buzz when she had made the connection, and if not, would try again in ten minutes. Viktor laughed at that and lit another cigarette. His eyes narrowed as he studied me sitting across from him.

"So your sister says none of us are going to survive."

I could not bear to say it again, so I just nodded yes.

"But what about you?"

I sat glued to my seat, thunderstruck.

"You and the other magicals, the vampires, the demons, all of you—to you, dying is a cheap parlor trick. You ask of us to come to fight and die based on your little sister's prophecy. I will fight to the death for my people, but fighting to the death means nothing to you."

I swallowed hard, my cheeks burning with the backhanded slap of his words. "I grieve as much as you do when my people die," I finally ventured to say, my voice hoarse.

"You may grieve," Viktor said, the anger in his voice now palpable. "But you cannot understand. Death has dominion over us."

"Only if you allow it," I said. "Besides, you can kill me, or a demon, or a vampire, just as dead as any ordinary mortal. It just takes more doing, that's all—and it often takes another magical to do the deed."

Viktor tapped his fingers on the surface of the desk, his nerves seeming jangled by the cigarettes, or by the war, or my unsettling presence, or by all of it together. "The Hashomer has a policy not to deal with the magical folk. We are ordinary mortals. In many ways, Magda Lazarus, you are as much of an enemy as the Nazis. For you fight on death's side of the battle."

"No, I don't. I fight for Churchill." There, my last weapon, and I used it to the hilt. "Not two weeks ago, I myself met with Winston Churchill. I am his witch, and I have come to establish a spy network for him here in Poland. He is ready enough to use magic to serve his cause. For God's sake, why will you not?"

I leaned forward, rested my hands on the far side of the desk blotter. "Nazis do not hesitate to use magicals. They seek to enslave demons and to raise a demon army. They so far have failed only because magicals like me are fighting them. They have made alliances with the MittelEuropa Vampirrat and the great Eastern Werewolf Pack . . . but vampires and werewolves are natural enemies, and we all know a pact with those lying Nazi bastards means nothing. Look at Czechoslovakia! The

British and French deserted and betrayed them to make peace. How long did that last—a year?"

I had to make Viktor understand; the Hashomer had to hear me, or we could not fight our common enemies. "Viktor, you cannot fight vampires, demons, werewolves with ordinary weapons."

Viktor took another drag of his cigarette. His fingers trembled. "Precisely. That is why mortals must shun the magical."

"No. Wrong! I am your weapon. My sister is your weapon. Fight magic with magic, Viktor. With magic in your arsenal, you can negotiate with the likes of the vampires, and perhaps get them away from the Nazis altogether."

I thought of Gabor Bathory, my elegant, melancholy vampire boss, now imprisoned in Berlin for daring to love the idea of a free Hungary. Surely Bathory wasn't the only vampire unwilling to enslave himself to the cause of Nazi Germany. "Don't throw away the advantages you can use to survive. To save your people and mine."

"But the Hashomer leadership—"

"To hell with them! Who are they, some eminent old men in Jerusalem or someplace? They are not here, fighting! They left you, the young men, the children, in the slaughterhouse to sacrifice you for the cause. I come here to say 'Live.' Surviving is victory. Let us join forces."

He stubbed out his second cigarette in the ashtray, looked from me to Raziel. "You can't die. Neither can he."

"We can die. And Raziel here can die as easily as you. He is a mortal now. He was magical once, but he sacrificed his magic to fight the Nazis."

The truth was, of course, rather more complicated than that, but I had delivered its gist. He looked again from me to Raziel, this time with a completely different expression on his face. Now, he looked, I thought, as if he was evaluating our value as deadly weapons in his fight.

The telephone on the table buzzed loudly, and he picked up the receiver, eyes still fixed on Raziel as he spoke in Polish, then French, then German. After flirting, cajoling, and screaming into the telephone, Viktor, miraculously, got patched through to Budapest.

He spoke rapid-fire French for a bit, so fast that I had trouble following him. A smile passed over his face and was gone, like a flash of heat lightning.

He held the receiver out to me, gingerly, as if it were a loaded revolver. "Some girl named Eva is on the line. She says she knows you, and she has found a vampire for you, one that is ready to join your cause."

Her name stopped my breath.

Eva, my old friend, not a drop of magic in her, but braver than the rest of us put together. I never thought I'd get to talk to her again. Viktor handed me the receiver, then leaned back and contemplated me and my conversation.

But at that moment, I left Viktor, the Hashomer in Kraków, and all of the war behind. My Eva was on the phone, alive and safe and still ready to fight.

I swallowed hard and composed myself. "Eva!" I said, embracing the Hungarian I spoke like a lover. "It is so good to speak to you. It is a miracle."

"You sound clear as a bell, too," Eva said, her voice as melodious and cheerful as ever, never breaking. "My darling little star, how busy I have been. That vampire is in trouble indeed. A world of trouble. He is in vampire jail and the trial is scheduled for next week!"

There was a crackling, then silence on the phone as I gathered up my wits to speak on the open line. We were certainly being listened to, by a phone operator who might or might not understand Hungarian, or by some Hungarian Fascist. We spoke in Hungarian still, but I spoke the truth in riddles.

"What is the charge against him?"

"Who cares? The punishment is public staking."

"Oh, horrible, Evuska. The whole arrest is garbage. We have to get him free."

"I have been working on it."

I could hear the twinkle in my girl's eyes, and could not restrain a smile. "I am sure you have."

I changed the subject. Who knew how much time we had left before we were cut off. "The cousins are doing well up here in Kraków, the little ones, my, how they have grown."

"I can only imagine."

"It's like there are hundreds of the little darlings. And can you believe, they *all* want to visit their Auntie Eva in Budapest!"

She laughed, but the sound was hollow. I was not surprised; I had just asked her to take in hundreds of Polish Jewish refugees, all children. "Where would we put the little bonbons, in my tiny flat? The little mousies would overrun the place, and there is the hungry cat on the white horse to consider."

She meant, of course, Horthy, the grandiose regent on a white horse, making a great show of Hungarian anti-Semitic jingoism and the glorious Austro-Hungarian past in an effort to keep the Nazis placated and out of Hungary.

Eva said, "I would love nothing more than to take every single one of those little cousins. They are so sweet and adorable—I would never let them go back to their mamas! But my landlord . . . I don't know if he would let me."

The leader of the Hungarian Hashomer, Mordechai, was fierce and unbending in his ideology. He would say no on principle just because it was me, a magical, who proposed to save the children of Kraków.

"Well, I will have my landlord talk to your landlord. My landlord here likes my idea."

"Well, my landlord is out looking for a bigger apartment house as we speak. Once he finds a great, giant one, as many cousins can visit as you like."

I had a flash of inspiration. "My uncle has an enormous, fantastic mansion on Rose Hill. You know the place? It is huge, and he lives alone. When he returns from that trip to Berlin, he would let you rent the place for nothing."

I heard a gasp on the other end of the line. She knew I meant Bathory's place. "But isn't that cat even more fearsome than the cat on the horse?"

"No, no. This other cat is hungry, but he only eats willing mice. It is a point of honor."

"I have never heard of such an honorable cat." Eva's voice was as sour as a corked bottle of Tokaji wine. I had to laugh, I couldn't help it.

"I know that cat well. But you have to save him from the dogs."

"I can do that. But have your landlord call my landlord before you send the little cousins down here unannounced."

I had no idea how Eva would manage to save Bathory from death. But she was resourceful and brave, and she had worked as a human courier for Bathory and survived. If she meant to save him, Eva could make it happen. But at what price? I put grim thoughts out of my mind and forced myself to smile. "I love you, sweetheart. I will have my landlord call today."

"Miracles are still your specialty then, Magduska. I kiss you a thousand times, my darling."

I meant to tell her that Gisele was fine, but the line went dead in my hand. I looked up at Viktor, who was waiting with an expectant expression.

"She says she has to talk to the leader of the Hashomer in Budapest, and that you and he must work out the details. Eva is working on getting safe houses lined up to protect them. But let's get the children out of here as fast as we can. We have no time at all."

✳ 13 ✳

And that was Viktor Mandelstam. A man who dared to dream of victory even in the midst of defeat. I will give Viktor this: despite our many disagreements, he moved fast and with a ruthless efficiency. A couple of phone calls later, and after some messengers sent as couriers, he had collected, within half an hour, two dozen young, likely-looking fighters from the Hashomer, unarmed and untrained, but too clear-eyed to disbelieve Viktor's message of death, and young and brave enough to fight anyway.

I was surprised to see that more than half of the contingent were girls. Some of them were tiny, delicate-looking things, but they, like me, burned to fight. They had given up more than the boys had, I imagined, defied their parents more, to join the Hashomer in the first place. Now they had less than nothing to lose.

I too had defied my mother and the old ways to claim life on my own terms. I had broken with the past, with my mother's restraint, and I well understood these girls' ferocious despair.

We fought the good fight, together. Thus began a brief, but brilliant reign of terror orchestrated by the Hashomer against the Nazi administration in Kraków.

With Asher's and Chana's help, we disappeared into the forest, set up our camp not far from Yankel's clearing. The boys and girls dug hiding places into the ground and brought provisions for the little army.

And then we planned our first attack by night, not three days after we arrived. I translated for both Gisele and Raziel, and back again for the Hashomer.

"The Nazis are flexing their muscles," Viktor began. "We got word that they've arrested dozens of professors from Jagiellonian University, and shut the banks. They are proclaiming Kraków an ur-German city."

Raziel and I looked at each other. "You know what that means," I said. "Anyone not German is going to cease to exist."

"Nonsense," Viktor said. "They will need workers, lots of workers to feed the war machine. They may hate us, but they need us."

I looked at Gisele, who was sitting near the cooking fire with her hands folded. I expected to see her twitching, crying, or otherwise in the throes of prophecy, but she sat quite calmly, a smile playing over her face.

"They need us to die," Gisele said. "They need us to die to feed their killing machine. Demons need tormented souls. Vampires need blood. Nazis need ideology, they need to grind the innocent into the dirt. You seem to think that Hitler's army is Napoleon's, reborn. No. These are the servants of Moloch. They worship death and evil. Either we stop them, or we all die."

I translated her dark words in a monotone. We all sat, struck dumb by Gisele's happy little speech, thinking no doubt of all that we had already lost.

Yankel's voice pierced the silence. "The girl speaks true. I have sensed this evil as well. A great calamity is upon us, and long have I prayed to the Lord to avert the harsh decree. He answered me. He sent you all. We may die fighting these evil men. But at least we die fighting."

"To live is a more effective victory." Viktor's voice was dry; he alone seemed unmoved by Gisele's and Yankel's words. "We must retreat, if what you say is true."

"Yes, but it will not be enough to stop the Germans," I said. "No place is safe, retreat is not possible. Get those who cannot fight away, yes! But those of us who want to fight, must fight."

"I will stay and fight," Yankel said. The words seemed absurd: Yankel was too feeble to lift a gun, let alone fire one. But his declaration of war electrified the very air.

All of us now understood that the battle we fought was fundamentally a magical one, a clash of wills. And in that invisible, cosmic battle, Yankel's power was formidable indeed.

"Every day, troops and supplies come in through the main rail yard. That is the Nazi nerve center of Kraków," Raziel said.

"We've got to blow it up," I said.

"It won't be easy," Viktor said with a sigh. "You really think a dozen, two dozen people can do it?"

"With the right people, yes. And you have a witch of the blood on your side."

A heavy stillness settled over the group. I knew my magic

frightened and disturbed them, but it was better to address their fear directly now, before we got down to the serious fighting.

"With the proper spells, I can blow that rail yard into oblivion better than a kilo of dynamite."

"But—"

"Say it, Viktor. I'm as bad as the Nazis? No. I'm a danger to the mortals around me? Again, no."

He sighed. "The central committee of the Hashomer will have my head for this. We Zionists have pledged to win our battles honestly, without magic."

"Well then, die with integrity." My patience was at its breaking point. It was only with great difficulty that I kept my voice calm. "Or, fight magic with magic, and live to see your precious Palestine."

A low murmur rose among the Hashomer, and Viktor's girlfriend Mina whispered urgently into his ear.

"Mina says you are worse than demons. If that is so, good that you fight on our side."

Viktor's smile was grudging, but it meant we would attack the Nazis together. It gave me deep satisfaction to resolve to fight, and to use everything that I had in me. Now that fate had brought me into Poland, I meant to stop as many Nazis as I could, and I would do it whether or not I had mortals to help me.

I had Raziel, I had Gisele and Yankel. And, as my final, secret weapon, I had Asmodel. I could secure his services for a fatal price, but if I had to, I was willing to pay it.

We would attack the rail yards later that night.

6

It was time to gather, witching hour, four in the morning. Yankel and Gisele joined me, Raziel, and the Hashomer in the forest to say good-bye.

"I promised you," Yankel said softly, his face gray with weariness. *"Refesh, Ruach . . ."*

He muttered the Hebrew prayers under his breath, sounding careless and unmoved; I stole a glance at Raziel. He nodded in time to the watchmaker's words, completely engrossed by Yankel's casual-sounding prayer.

Suddenly, a chill shot down my spine. My body responded to his words before my mind could understand them.

Yankel was raising golems.

The ground itself began to undulate at his feet, as if the mud had turned into ocean waves. Gisele, standing behind him, touched the locket at her neck.

But Yankel had no need of a demon to work his miracles. As he had said the night I'd met him, Yankel's miracles came straight from heaven, no magic required.

His prayer became a little song, nothing special or operatic, a lullaby, a nursery rhyme. And a half-dozen men made of crumbly, wet mud grew up out of the ground.

Yankel raised his hands, and Hebrew letters glowed upon their half-dozen muddy foreheads, blocked in places by dead leaves or little twigs, but clearly legible to anybody who could read them.

The mud men joined hands, shuffled around Yankel in a clumsy hora, then turned to face us, the fighters.

Yankel's song was done. We stared at the golems in the sudden and complete silence. This was the stuff of Jewish legend; the Hashomer accepted the golems into our ranks without a word of protest.

Our band now included Raziel, sixteen Hashomer, and myself, with the six golems raised by Yankel to serve as an unkillable rear guard. The golems made me nervous; they smelled like swamp water, and they left a wake of footprints clearly marking our passage. A signpost could not have pointed the way to the refugee camp more clearly than those muddy tracks.

We were in a fierce and murderous mood. Thoughts of consequences and reprisals did not yet trouble us. Our goal was simple: destroy the rail depot in Kraków and make it that much more difficult for Nazis to ship weapons, soldiers, and supplies into the city. Viktor insisted that we also concentrate on remaining alive: if this action was a success, he wanted to tell the entire underground network in Poland, and accelerate the uprising as quickly as possible.

"Perhaps we can end the war almost before it starts," I murmured to Raziel as we marched along through the darkness, following Viktor and his blond girlfriend back into Kraków. "If we stop the Nazis in Poland, kick them out even, the French and the English—"

"Forget the French and the English," Raziel said. Unlike the rest of us, he sounded war-weary, pessimistic. It reminded me how very old he was compared to the rest of us. Raziel was no stranger to martyrs, noble and pointless sacrifices, to empires crumbling and entire peoples disappearing in conquest. "They won't come to our aid. It's Czechoslovakia all over again."

"But this time the French and English both declared war against the Germans!" I said. A little stone had worked its way into the heel of my shoe, and I paused a moment to get it out before it raised a blister on my heel. The Hashomer stretched ahead, not pausing for us, and the golems mindlessly lurched behind.

I saw that Raziel's shoelaces were untied, and after a moment's hesitation, I reached for his feet and tied them for him. I smiled up at him from where I knelt, and then I rose to stand beside him.

Raziel and I stood together in the moonlight. "What were you saying?" I asked, for the first time wavering in my determination to kill Nazis. "Are you saying that we are doomed to fail?"

For answer, he leaned forward and kissed me, not gently as he had the day he had first come to me as a man in Budapest, but roughly and with bruising passion, the kiss of a man fighting for his life.

I had no choice but to surrender to that kiss: it electrified me, sent shock waves of desire through my body. Finally he released me, and I looked up into his eyes, my lips whisker-scratched and tender, my pulse racing.

"We will blow up the rail yard," Raziel said. "And the Nazi hornets will swarm. Undoubtedly, it will distract the Nazis from their work—but their focus will be upon us."

He raked his fingers through my hair, hugged me close to him, and again he bewitched me with his scent of cinnamon and musk, with his wildly beating human heart.

I pulled him along the muddy track the golems had left behind, and together we raced to rejoin the others. But now my heart was heavy, where before it was innocent and well armored for battle.

At this time of night, the tracks were all but deserted. Two of the Hashomer made a diversionary attack on the guardhouse, and a large group of soldiers responded to their shouts and gunshots by leaping out after them, in the other direction.

"Quickly!" Viktor whispered, his face covered in a film of sweat. "Do it now—or it will be too late."

I have no facility with inanimate objects. Other witches refract magic through gems, and goblins often work iron. My magic is of souls. I can summon them, find them, compel them to my will. I can protect them with my wards, and I can pull a soul right out of its living body.

But a railroad track has no soul.

In the far distance, the mournful whistle of a munitions train sounded. I sensed the frantic agitation of the engineer, his unverified but unshakable conviction that something was terribly wrong.

I forced the engineer's hand to push the throttle forward, to make the train speed up, not slow down.

"Put a barrier on the tracks!" I screamed above the rising din. The engineer tried to put on the brakes, but I sent a burning into his left hand. He tried to let go of the throttle but I wouldn't let him.

The Hashomer tossed a veritable junkyard of wire scraps, junk metal, and cinders over the tracks. Raziel shoved a huge barrel of pitch onto the tracks, and it fell over and split open.

Viktor's girlfriend Mina raced forward and uncoupled the tracks by using the manual switch. If our pile of junk didn't derail the train, it would fly off the track a hundred meters down the line, right before the guardhouse.

"Get back!" I screamed, my cries now drowned out by the shriek of the onrushing train. We leapt into the darkness and hid in the shadows as the train plowed into the pile of garbage at full speed.

The barrel of pitch disintegrated with a splintering crash, and the wheels scraped over the piles of baling wire, pieces of fence, and the cinders with a sickening crunch.

The train crushed over it all and hit the uncoupled tracks, slowed only a little by the debris. The train hurtled off the rails, and like a giant fist the engine smashed into the guardhouse itself.

The engineer emerged, screaming obscenities in German, and Viktor picked him off with a blast from the shotgun—he and I were huddled only about ten meters away.

The rear car contained a small contingent of soldiers, sent, I suppose, to guard the ordnance on the train, and we started shooting at them from the shadows.

Raziel shot into the overturned side of one of the cars, and a ragged explosion blew over the top: the car contained gunpowder or ammunition. A fire began to rage, and bullets began popping like popcorn in the flames.

A siren sounded in the distance; I was nearly deafened by the explosions. "Let's go," Viktor yelled, and Raziel simultaneously waved us away with his arms.

We ran for our lives, the golems staying behind to make a muddy last stand. We wanted the Germans to think that the golems alone could achieve this level of destruction, to focus on golems instead of human partisans.

I heard the silent shuffle of their great, muddy feet, their swampy bodies like walking sandbags taking the force of the bullets aimed at us.

All of us had survived the initial attack, even the two Hashomer who had courageously attacked the guardhouse. Our mission was a success.

But as we ran for the safety of the forest, my heart remained heavy. We had not taken any ammunition or weapons off the train for ourselves. Only the Nazi engineer had died, not even the soldiers for sure. Raziel was right: all we had done was stir up the hornets' nest. Time to see how hard these hornets could sting.

If only I had used Asmodel . . .

Yankel had his own path to miracles, the way of his fathers. My mother had learned and followed the Lazarus creed, before she died. As for me, I didn't know what the Lazarus creed would say about my spellcasting, whether according to my people's law I was doing right or wrong. I was going to have to figure out my path for myself, to survive a world that had come undone.

And my fate was all tangled up in Asmodel's. Without taming him or destroying him somehow, I could do no more than I had done in the Hashomer raid on the rail yard.

The raid was a tremendous success, and it still was not enough. In the end, our triumph endured less than a week. But while it lasted, it was glorious.

✳ 14 ✳

Gisele did nothing to put my worries to rest. Raziel led the war-
riors back to the forest, while Viktor and I, in a last-minute decision, made for Hashomer headquarters in Kraków. We wanted
to spread the word of our exploits, and plan how to make the
most of them.

Imagine our surprise when, opening the door to Viktor's dusty
little office over the pharmacist's shop on Miodowa Street, we
found my sister Gisele, framed by the big window by Viktor's
desk, the new light filtering through the venetian blinds and
striping her face with strange, tribal bars of shadow.

"How did you get in here?" Viktor said warily.

"It's my sister, you know, and she speaks no Polish."

I was angry with her, for instead of greeting us with joy, as conquering victors, Gisi merely stood by the window, her enormous eyes as wide as a baby doll's, her rosebud lips pursed tight.

"Let me speak to her. This won't happen again."

Viktor shrugged and lit a cigarette, and after a long appraising look at the two of us, he slipped back out the still-open front door.

We listened to his footsteps reverberating down the creaky wooden stairs to the street. As soon as the sounds faded away, I turned on her, barely able to restrain my annoyance now. "What are you doing? Viktor, Mina, and the rest are spooked enough by the two of us. Why are you sneaking into his office and scaring him worse?"

"I had to come, Magda," she replied, low, in her soft, scratchy voice. She leaned her head against the dusty windowpane and sighed. "Chana got me here and the door was unlocked. I let myself in."

"But how did you know I would be coming here and not to the forest? Even I didn't know until after we were finished at the rail yard."

But I didn't need to ask that question. Gisele had always just known. Her magic didn't manifest itself in great works, in terrible spells. My little sister just knew. About too much. It was a great gift and a great burden, all at once.

She stared past me, as if I were a ghost. "I'm afraid for you, Magduska." Her voice trembled, and she gave me that big-eyed look again, as if she were looking at a ghost.

I took refuge in my grumpiness. "Don't waste your time worrying about me." I sauntered to Viktor's desk and sat down on his creaky office chair with the cracked leather. It felt so good to get off my aching, blistered feet.

I surveyed the world from behind Viktor's desk. From this vantage point, Gisele looked small and frightened and helpless—a problem, an obstacle to victory.

"I came here to warn you." An edge of my mother's judgmental voice crept into Gisele's from beyond the grave.

"Warn me of what? That fighting Nazis is dangerous? My darling, I could have told you that."

Gisele took a half step toward me, then seemed to think better of it. She shook her head. "You know the attack on the rail yard was madness."

I had to laugh. "Since when has that stopped me? Sanity would have us meekly marching into the ovens you foresee, you know."

"You don't understand." She sighed with frustration and hugged herself. "At first, being with Yankel stopped my visions. I thought it was his goodness but now I understand, after this night—I have entered my visions, we are living them now. I see you in the darkness. It's like a nightmare become real. Eva's gone too, into a place of danger and death. Did you know she has become a spy? She is hiding within a world of illusion, but you are in more danger than she is."

My heart twisted when I realized Gisele's visions now included me—and Eva, too. I cringed at the thought of her lost in a tangle of lies and espionage. "Eva? What's happened to her? What do you foresee?"

Gisele shook her head impatiently. "This isn't about prophecy, it's about you. Eva dances with the devil, but she knows what she is doing, the price that she must pay. And she serves the greater good. But will you? I see you heading into a dark place, with a fearsome adversary. If you don't stop now, part of you will die there."

Poor Gisele, I could never have borne her burdens. But I still had my own battles to fight, no matter how much she suffered. "You must admit, in the short term, this was a brilliant strike, the rail yard." I was still too proud of our success to succumb to her dire words. I was sick of having to believe her; her visions were so vividly awful.

She swallowed hard and stared miserably down at her shoes, as if she was about to puke on them. "Oh, so brilliant. But it was a mistake all the same. Remember why we are here."

"We? I'm here because you came. Why are you here, Gisele? You speak of madness, but you are the one who ran into Poland when everybody here who could was running out on September first."

She wiped at her eyes and looked straight at me. "I just couldn't stand it anymore. I am sorry, Magda," she said, so hoarse I could hardly understand her. "Please, forgive me."

"Forgive you?"

"Me and my prophecies," she said, and laughed again, a hiccupping little half cry. "Some good they do—I tell you the world is ending, and what are you supposed to do about it?"

"Whatever I can. You are making yourself sick, poor thing . . . we will do our best, that's all we can do."

"It's just—" Gisele bit her lip and looked away.

"What now?"

"The trouble's plain enough, Magduska. You don't have the Book. If you had the Book, Raziel wouldn't suffer so, and . . . our story would have a different end."

The thought had occurred to me, quite often in fact since Raziel had come back. Our great-grandmama the Witch of Ein Dor herself had warned us: without *The Book of Raziel*, our lives were forfeit.

The Book had slipped through my fingers and into the hands of Adolf Hitler himself. And though the German Führer had no inherent magic of his own, it was my darkest fear that sooner or later he would find the magical key to unlocking our ancestral Book's terrible power.

With my natural-born gifts I could summon demons to my side. But I could not bind them to do my bidding, to fight and defeat the German Army of mortals and magicals, not without the spells encoded in *The Book of Raziel*.

I ached for that Book, lusted for it. "How do we get it back, Gisele?" I whispered. "It must be in Berlin somewhere. And where is the original sapphire? Asmodel knows, but—"

"I don't know," Gisele said, her voice heavy with misery. "It's not even the same Book anymore. Asmodel said the wizard Staff transformed it entirely before he died."

"Gisele, I hate to say it, but . . ."

"But what?"

I gathered up my strength, then I spoke aloud what I had brooded over since the day I'd captured him. "Asmodel himself must be the key. To using the Book and bringing my full magic out."

"No, Magdalena! I know that gleam you get in your eye. . . ."

"As if we weren't in the most awful trouble already, Gisi. How much more do we have to lose, anymore? If I only had the Book," I continued, "I could kill every Nazi in Poland inside of a long night. You think the attack on the rail yard was good? It would be just the beginning."

Gisele ran to me then, and hugged me so tight I could hardly breathe. "But that is what I'm afraid of, what I came to warn you about. When you talk like this. Without the Book, we die. But with the Book . . . oh, Magduska . . ."

"Sweetheart," I said, half buried under her tumbling chestnut locks. "Why did you come to Poland? Why would you tie my hands to keep me from fighting?"

She whispered low in my ear, as if we were surrounded by enemies—which, I suppose, we were. "I came to save the mothers, the babies. Warn them in time. It was foolish, I know, Asmodel tempted me and I gave in. I didn't think you would come after me. I've probably killed you, too. And I fuss at you, while I still have time, because . . . I am afraid of what you might become."

She released me from her embrace and fingered the locket hanging at her throat, as tears streamed steadily down her face. "This, my most precious possession. Now the home of an evil that could destroy you."

I leaned against Viktor's desk, half exhausted by Gisele's misery. "I'm good as dead anyway. But that doesn't mean I should give up now, right? In fact, if I stop fighting now I die a lot faster and messier, *nu*?"

One corner of her mouth tilted up as I imitated Yankel's lilting Yiddish cadences. "All of this will go into the fire," she said, looking around the office wildly. "All of Kraków. Everything. And so soon."

"So let me kill the damned Nazis first. Give me Asmodel, little mouse. Let me have him, and Book or no Book we will have our victory."

She blinked hard and her tears stopped flowing. "Some victories are not worth winning," she whispered, the locket now clutched in her fist. "I will murder you with this locket if I give it over. I can't do that."

I kept my voice calm and reasonable. "We don't have the Book. Instead, we have a million Nazis and more in Poland, on the march. And Asmodel. All you can do with him is hold him fast. But I . . ."

"All you will get with Asmodel is a dark victory, Magduska. A dark victory, indeed." Gisele's voice sounded muffled, trance-like, as though the words emanated from deep underground.

"A dark victory is better than none, my darling."

"He's the one who tempted me into rushing into Poland in the first place. I'm not as strong as you think I am, Magduska. Not so virtuous."

I didn't reply, only waited.

Instead of unclasping the chain, Gisele suddenly slipped it over her head in one fluid movement, her curls tangling in the golden links. "May God forgive me," she managed to say through new tears. "Here, you have him. I'm not strong enough to hold him, I shouldn't pretend. But don't let him overpower you. That is no victory at all. No matter what happens, Magda, swear on my head that you will remember that."

I hesitated, my fingers mere centimeters from the dangling locket. "You mean . . . don't let him enter me?"

"I mean, do not let him become your master. If you do, you will surely defeat Hitler. But Asmodel will defeat you, and that would be the beginning of the end of everything."

Well, I did what I had to do. I promised her, swore on everything holy and her very life that I would mind her words. I slipped the chain onto my own neck, and immediately felt the force of Asmodel's enchained power, whispering to my own.

"I promise," I whispered. But I knew even as I said it that my vow would be hell to keep.

After the attack on the rail yard, I feared the Nazi subjugation of mostly-conquered Kraków would escalate as the defense of Warsaw grew more desperate.

Sadly, I was right. I remember with painful clarity September fourteenth, the day Hans Frank, the new governor-general of the Protectorate of Poland, arrived with his motorcade into the heart of Kraków.

Warsaw had not yet fallen. There was as yet no true German protectorate: Poland was still fighting for her life, though she was weakening. After our destruction of the rail yard, the Nazis wanted to crush the partisan resistance in Kraków, and were so intent upon their success they sent their man early to set up shop sooner than any of us had expected.

He was a mortal man, the way Hitler was a mortal man. But he was important enough to be surrounded by a retinue of SS werewolves in their lupine form as he emerged from his Mercedes limousine at Wawel Castle, the historic seat of Polish government and a Teutonic pagan worship site to boot.

Using binoculars to search the face of Hans Frank and his men, Raziel, Viktor, and I watched them hoist the swastika over the castle. My blood ran cold at the sight of the werewolves. I knew such creatures well: a pack of them had tried to rip my throat out not long before, on a train station platform in Vienna.

Hitler had handpicked this man to ruthlessly suppress all partisan activity in Kraków and the surrounding districts, and to subject the Jews to a brutal regime of unprecedented severity.

It was our job to stop him.

I handed the binoculars to Raziel, but something about the expression on my face kept him looking at me. "Don't do anything impulsive," he said. Despite his words, his face remained serene.

"No, I won't," I said, but reluctantly. "I'll take my time. I want this man to die so dramatically his end will be a warning in itself. And that will take planning, not impulse."

Raziel was in the middle of raising the binoculars to take another look at Hans Frank and his retinue. He lowered them slowly and stared at me for what seemed like a long time.

"You sound like a killer."

He said the words softly, but they rattled me nonetheless. "This is war," I replied. "You've pointed out the fact to me many times."

Raziel nodded, then handed the binoculars to Viktor, not bothering to look again at the meaningless pomp of the ceremony at the Wawel. "I don't know why," he said softly, "but you have suddenly become a warrior who fights without hesitation. That is a victory for us, I think, and a big problem for Hans Frank."

He reached out with his fingers and touched the dented locket now resting against my heart.

Viktor cleared his throat and raised the binoculars to look at the Wawel again. "So you mean to assassinate the governor-general himself," he said.

Gisele's warning still echoed in my mind, but I willed myself to ignore her words. "Hans Frank must die," I replied.

⊚

The first thing we did after Frank arrived was to increase the exodus of refugees from Poland, as fast as we could. We had a lorry running from Kazimierz, Kraków's Jewish district, to Yankel's woods, and from there to the Polish border. As long as the Hashomer's bribe money lasted, we'd smuggle the children out of the country. The greatest challenge so far was convincing the parents of the terrible danger their little ones faced if they stayed in Poland.

Eva had telephoned to beg us to slow down, but when I was done telling her about Frank's arrival and what it meant, she ended up by pushing us to move faster. "We'll find a place for them," she said. "Somewhere."

I could hardly bear to ask about Bathory, but he was never far from my mind, what with all the Nazis overrunning the city. And I couldn't ask Eva about what Gisele had said, that she was tangled in the deceptions of a spy. Spying on who, and why?

Eva reassured me about Bathory, at least. "Don't give up on him yet," Eva said, her voice sounding weary across the line. "Uncle's still in the hospital, poor old codger. But the doctor says to be patient: there's still plenty of life in the old fellow. And I won't rest until I find a doctor to save him, if this doctor won't."

So: it was too early to give up all hope. Eva was working on some improbable scheme or other that would lead to his release from the Vampirrat. The trail to Berlin had not yet grown cold, and she had no definitive information on his fate.

By now, over a thousand refugees, most of them children, had been spirited across the border and into Budapest. It was a drop in the bucket: over three million Jews lived in Poland, and then there were the Catholic priests and nuns, the Gypsies, the homosexuals, the seers and country witches, and all the others who would not survive a Nazi regime. Of course, given the Nazis' murderous ideology, no ordinary Pole was safe: according to Gisele, Hitler's plans included enslaving the entire nation.

The day after Governor Frank installed himself and his enormous retinue within the fortifications of Wawel Castle, a group of Hashomer and other partisan leaders met in Viktor's office, above the pharmacist's place on Miodowa Street.

It was me and Raziel, a big bear of a man named Levin for the Communists, and Viktor and his girlfriend Mina for the Hashomer. The Polish nationalist partisans had promised a representative, but none showed.

"There must be a thousand partisans holed up with that Catholic priest, in the salt mines," Mina said wistfully. She tucked a lank lock of blond hair behind her ear. "It would be good to join forces with them."

"Forget the miners," Levin the Communist said in a low growl. "What are you going to do to Hans Frank?"

"It won't be easy to get to him inside the Wawel," Raziel said, his face imperturbable as ever.

"We will have to watch him and his retinue, see if he falls into a pattern of behavior," Viktor said. He lit a cigarette and watched the smoke dance lazily toward the ceiling. "Once we know what he is about, then we will know what action to take."

"Don't wait too long," I warned, but the meeting was effectively over. These wary, brave, desperate people were looking to buy time more than anything else. Every day they stayed alive and out of the Gestapo's clutches was a victory of sorts by itself.

Viktor muttered under his breath and took a deep drag on his cigarette, and Levin crossed his huge arms across his barrel chest and glared at me, not bothering to hide his hostility. The Nazis eagerly used Teutonic sorcery to achieve their war aims; in contrast, the Communists sought to gain supremacy over magic and religion by outlawing both.

Lenin had proclaimed religion the opiate of the masses; the Communists also believed that magic was the cyanide, administered by rootless cosmopolitans like myself. Instead of working magic, the Soviets studied it as a science, conducted horrifying, barely secret experiments at the Institute for Brain Research in Leningrad. They studied the subtle energies of magic to control it, subjugate it, root it out of the greater Soviet, for the good of the proletariat.

Viktor was right. These people didn't have the luxury of returning from the dead; I was the only magical in the room. If anyone was going to take supernatural risks, it was going to have to be me, because death was surely part of the plan.

It was beyond dangerous. Gisele had warned me as clearly as she could. But that did not change the fact we had to stop Hans Frank somehow. And I already knew, no further investigation required, that the only way to stop the governor-general was to kill him.

"Let me see what I can do," I said.

I began that very night. Once I had slipped out of Kraków and returned to the forest, I called on my personal creature, Leopold. I had inadvertently created him the first time I had died, but I had never regretted making that particular mistake. Leo had become a trusted ally, and I was in no way above using an imp in the service of the greater good.

I called him, and Leo came instantly, bony as a starved, wet cat, his neat little whiskers bristling in anticipation of action. "Mama, shall we fight?"

"Not yet." We met near the river; by now, the young volunteers from the Hashomer had burrowed a series of all but invisible dugouts in the underbrush behind Yankel's hut. Some two hundred people could live in our camp now, as they waited to be evacuated by Viktor's lorry, but such was the Hashomer's skill in hiding them that except for the smoke from the cooking fires, the place looked more deserted than when we had first arrived.

I thought of the last man I had killed face-to-face, the Nazi sorcerer Staff, who had come to hunt me down and who now reposed deep in the earth, beyond our reach. "I need to send you on a mission, Leo, dear."

He puffed out his chest and stroked the base of his skull with the tips of his long bony fingers. "A mission! I will do it, Mama, do it gladly."

"There is a new man in the town, an evil man. Hans Frank is his name; he is the new governor-general of this part of conquered Poland. He arrived in quite a rush; I think they sent him sooner than they had planned, because we partisans have been giving the Germans lots of trouble."

"Hm. Evil. I like the taste of him already. Yes . . ."

"Yes. He has installed himself in Wawel Castle. It is heavily guarded; no mortal being can get in and out again alive, not even me. I need you to sneak inside, find out what you can about this dreadful man."

He mulled over my words, walking back and forth on the cool mossy bank of the stream in the moonlight. Leo paused, and looked over a scrawny shoulder, back at me. "Information? What kind, Mama?"

"Anything, Leo. But it seems to me you are a specialist of passion, of those things that quicken the blood of mortal men."

He shot me a knowing look, and laughed deep in his chest, a hoarse little growl. We both knew he was born of my primal fury, that he was a stray spark of my own turbulent soul. My rage was our fundamental link, my grief for Gisele's fate the connection that made it so easy for me to call upon him at my need.

Leo would know Hans Frank's pleasures and hatreds when he saw them.

"Seek entrance to his mind through his dreams," I said. "You are an air spirit—it should be easy to meet him in the sphere of dreams."

"I will see if he takes baths," Leo said, his voice soft as he spoke his thoughts aloud. "Many a man, alone and naked, has waking dreams in the tub. . . ."

"Now, that is good thinking," I said. "Do you need a spell to send you along?"

"No, Mama. Your fervent desire is spell enough. If you could . . . well, say a little prayer for me?"

I smiled. I was no Yankel and did not have the power to raise blue fire with the force of my calling to God. But the simplest prayers are often the strongest; I asked the Almighty to watch over Leo and bless his ways.

"Go in peace, little imp," I said. "Watch out for sorcerers' wards, werewolves, and the valkyrie."

He shrugged, winked at me, and shot into the sky. He quickly disappeared, like a star falling upward. It was going to be a long night, waiting for him.

And yet I did not have to wait long. I had taken the first watch and he surprised me by landing on the ground in front of me. "Oh, Mama, is he a nasty one," he trilled, without bothering to say hello.

Raziel was standing watch, too. I was glad it was not a Hashomer who stood with me, for I knew how deeply Leopold's sudden appearance would disturb most of them. "Hello, Leo," I said, my voice kept to a low whisper. "Tell it."

"He is a brutish bastard, and his wife is even worse. She has already come in and has announced to everyone that she is the queen of Poland. He hates her, all right, but he hates the Poles and Jews even worse."

"Well, he's a good Nazi," I said. "That's what he's supposed to do."

"He enjoys it though," Leo said, crouching at my feet like a little hairless lion, a naked tailless cat with a bristly mustache. "So: hates wife, Jews, Poles, and Police Chief Krueger, whoever that is."

That was interesting, and I mentally filed away that information. "What does he love, though, Leo? A man's love reveals his secrets. And we are looking for any weakness in his defenses."

Leo shrugged; despite his origins, he did not know or understand all that much about mankind and daily life. "Well, chess."

Raziel leaned forward, suddenly alert. "What?"

"The man is crazy about chess, thinks it is a metaphor for the universe or something. He is fond of his children. . . ."

My stomach did a slow, sick flip. "He has children?" For some reason this information sickened me, I suppose because it gave me some reason to regret his assassination.

"Oh yes, five children. Five! The youngest is just a baby still."

Five. Even though I was still on sentry duty, the news made me sit down to catch my breath.

"Pfft." Leopold was not impressed. "They've been setting Jewish children on fire in synagogues for the last two weeks. Some people need killing, Mama—it's the nicest thing you could do for his little poppets."

I thought of my own dead father and begged to differ, but I said nothing aloud.

"This is war," Raziel said as gently as he could. "He wants to kill every man, woman, and child he can get under his control, Magda."

The world would be a better place without such a one as Hans Frank in it, but killing him was going to exact a price from me. Still I could not delude myself that this man, devoted slave to Adolf Hitler, was incapable of any evil my sister had foretold.

"Chess," I mused. I reached down and scratched Leopold's long, pointy ears in thanks. "Time for our first move."

✳ 15 ✳

When morning came I took the refugees' lorry into Kraków to meet with Viktor at Hashomer headquarters. We needed to put our pawns, knights, and rooks on the board.

I rode with a small band of Hashomer, a load of refugee children, and Raziel, bouncing in the back of the truck. I tried to paste a serene, angelic expression on my face, but Raziel knew me too well to believe I actually met my fate with equanimity.

We spoke in Hungarian, which gave us a little privacy in the middle of that crowd of soldiers and frightened Polish schoolchildren. "He is the same as the wizard Staff that I killed," I said. "I know. But it is one thing to fight for your own life, another to plot the death of a human being in cold blood."

Raziel sighed. "If you have an enemy, it is better to know him well." I could tell he thought of Asmodel. "Hans Frank has come to kill you if he can."

"I wish I could take the long view," I said. I tried to tell myself I was tough enough to survive losing Raziel, or even Gisele. I wanted to become as unyielding in my ambitions as Asmodel. But I knew better.

Raziel hesitated. "Time means something different to me, perhaps," he said, his body moving with a sinuous grace as the truck bumped along the country roads. "But love is the prime mover. Magduska, God is love, and love will lead you through the valley of the shadow and back out again."

"Sometimes love is too beautiful to drag into the shadow of death," I said, with a sigh I couldn't help. I resisted the urge to stroke the back of his hand, because we were with so many other people, and also because I would bounce right out of the lorry if I let go.

Instead, I considered the next move in our deadly game.

My German was the best. At the meeting, that was the excuse we gave to Levin and the Communists in the end; Viktor, poor man, did what he could to minimize the fact of my magic to his rationalist comrades. But they weren't fooled. We all just pretended.

Together, we concocted a plan that, we hoped, would not only lead to the assassination of Herr Frank, but also, before we were done, would destroy his reputation.

For his part, Levin hid my Jewishness from the professors who organized our trap. It made our collaboration rather less complicated. He explained I was a Hungarian patriot who sought to aid Poland in her distress. I suspect the Poles knew better, or at least suspected, but we all played our parts flawlessly, the better to fight our common and detested enemy.

It had been my father, a shrewd man who lived by his wits in a magical, dangerous world, who had taught me as a child to play chess. That thought comforted me as Chana gussied me up in whatever finery she could scrounge—it would not do to meet the governor-general looking like a scullery maid or a wood hob.

"You are a princess from a fairy tale," she murmured in her homey Yiddish as she pinned a pretty little salmon pink netted cloche in my hair.

I thought of the Grimm tales I used to read, with their legions of imprisoned and murdered princesses, and I sighed. "I hope I'm more like Judith with Holofernes."

Chana, a devout woman, beamed at me, and held out a pair of real silk stockings to wear. "A woman of valor . . ."

I sighed again; those verses in Proverbs had been written by the great King Solomon, he who had succumbed to the lord of demons before he fell. "Chana," I began, and trailed off; the lump in my throat was suddenly too big to speak around.

Chana looked up sharply; she had heard the change in my voice. "Remember your Sh'ma," she said, steel in her voice. "And don't be afraid."

Despite the kindness in Chana's voice, my gut clenched. The Sh'ma was the prayer observant Jews recited in the moments before their deaths. Chana wanted me to be ready to die the proper way.

But the Sh'ma is also the prayer I use to strengthen my power of summoning, though Chana had no way of knowing that. I planned to remember the Sh'ma long before my life's end.

"Your daughter Ruzka is a lucky girl," I managed to say, my voice husky. "Her mama is a lioness."

Chana enfolded me in her meaty arms; I let her mother me, but not for longer than a moment. I had grown unused to mothering.

I pulled away from her embrace and cleared my throat. "Let's go down; the car is waiting." I insisted that Viktor serve as my driver; with his long, lanky figure and his icy blue eyes he looked less Jewish than the other Hashomer men.

I never found out how in heaven the Hashomer had organized the sleek, beetle-black Mercedes limousine; it looked suspiciously like the car in which the Nazi governor himself had arrived in Kraków.

We pulled out of the alley behind the pharmacist on Miodowa Street, and the Mercedes clattered over the cobblestones, not to Wawel but to the Literary Café by the university.

Governor-General Frank could not resist the enigmatic invitation of the Baroness Erszebet Bathory, of the Hungarian Carpathians, to meet him for chess and conversation in the glorious language of the Fatherland, High German.

The summer before, I had done more than my share of conversing in German while battling Nazi wizards, casting for Bavarian country witches, and confronting the sent specter of Adolf Hitler himself. After much practice under fire, I now spoke German tolerably well.

"Do you think he said yes to the chess or to the baroness?" I asked the back of Viktor's head as the car lurched out of the Jewish quarter of Kraków.

"A bit of both," Viktor said, after a pause. "The combination was obviously tempting. The governor has entered a firestorm, the place is not even pacified yet."

"Any port in a storm then, even a Hungarian noblewoman with a vampire's pedigree."

"That only added to her mysterious appeal, Magda."

Too quickly, we arrived at the café, just after sunset. I checked my lipstick and hairdo in the compact I carried: the effect was, I hoped, charmingly careless. I wanted to look the part of a frivolous, pleasure-seeking noblewoman who got a perverse little thrill from meeting the new governor alone, without his overbearing, recently pregnant wife.

Viktor shifted in his seat to face me. "I will be in the alley," he said, his voice low and urgent. "When you are done, get out fast."

"If I'm not out fast, get away yourself," I said. When he began to protest, I raised one gloved hand to stop him. "This is no time or place for chivalry, Viktor. Get out alive and we will meet again."

He tipped his cap to me, a devoted servant to his lady. "You are being watched," he murmured, then said something in Polish I didn't understand as the passenger door swung open.

It was Karol, the university professor (and enthusiastic Fascist) who had arranged our meeting during chess night at the Literary Café. "Fräulein," he said affably in German, as he reached for my hand to kiss. "Welcome to Kraków."

His German was wooden and Polish accented. My spirits rose: my German was better than that. I looked down my nose at him, copying my employer Bathory's distant, cordial politesse. "Charmed, I am sure, Professor," I said, my lips pursed, my voice high and breathless. "Has the honorable governor already arrived? I am oh so very sorry for the delay."

"No, Baroness, but we have had word he is on his way."

I hid my dismay with a slow, sweet smile. I had hoped to surprise him as he sat; this way, he and his entourage would have the advantage of the front door should matters go sour immediately.

"Excellent," I said. "I hope you have a big, fine chessboard. I considered bringing my own, but it is antique and a gift from my dear, beloved father."

The professor bent to kiss my hand again. I did not know which disgusted me more, his servile obsequiousness to me or his ill-disguised joy at meeting the German ruler of his conquered city.

"I have a number of suitable sets, my dear baroness. And we have set out some refreshments in honor of your meeting with Governor-General Frank."

"I hope you have not invited half the university to crowd the poor man, Herr Professor. I promised our governor-general that the meeting would be discreet."

The expression froze on the professor's face; I could see the hard clenching of his thin jaw. "Of course, Madame Baroness," he said, his voice sounding stiff and formal. "I would not presume to intrude."

"Very well," I replied, favoring him with a tight-lipped, vaporous, and aristocratic little smile. We passed over the marble threshold and into the café.

I was used to the grand, gilded cafés of Budapest, with vaulted ceilings and marble everywhere, so this sober, more modest establishment perversely disappointed me. I wanted the governor to meet his end surrounded by the most decadent, meaningless trappings of his ultimately impotent power. But I would have to make do with this merely handsome place.

The professor installed me in a narrow back room, with dark wood paneling and antlers on the wall, in imitation of a Prussian hunting lodge, I suppose. He offered me pastry and coffee, which I refused as prettily as I could. A quick scan of the room revealed a back door as well as a front; whether it led to the kitchen, a closed-up storeroom, or a WC I could not tell.

I sat with my back to the wall so that I could see the governor and his entourage as they arrived. If things got bad enough I figured I could escape into death, hopefully to return again—but death was no easy escape to make.

A great commotion at the door distracted me from my thoughts, and I almost knocked over the chess pieces arranged for me by the professor. I rose to my feet, tried to keep my knees from knocking together, and forced myself to remain in character: demure, and excited, in a dainty, ladylike way.

I looked up from the chess pieces to see the governor-general, Hans Frank, filling up the alcove with his bulk and that of his great entourage. He was not a large man, but his bombastic lawyer's ego filled the entire café and sucked every molecule of life and joy out of it with his presence. He strutted into the room, drunk on his own importance, his exalted place in history as the ruler of the conquered Polish slave people, and he surrounded himself with sycophants and bootlickers, individuals who reflected his greatness back upon him like subservient mirrors.

It was bad luck that day. I had hoped to lure Frank to a more discreet and clandestine meeting, a potential seduction that would have left more leeway for an escape. But he not only had his assistants with him, he also had with him the dreadful leader of the Gestapo, Krueger. And he had the same honor guard of werewolves protecting his person as were with him the day he had arrived.

I feared the werewolves would sniff me out. I was in grave danger indeed; I had taken the precaution of raising a glamour over my features, to confuse and dazzle any mortal that gazed upon my face. But I feared the curs would find out my magic by smell.

I made a great show of smiling and welcoming them, as if the café were my personal domain. "Welcome, dear gentlemen, welcome!"

Hans Frank's fat jowls jiggled as he leaned forward and muttered pleasantries in a German marked by a strong Bavarian accent. His rival and associate Krueger stood unsmiling to his right, unwilling to acknowledge me in any way. His stony silence was most unnerving.

The werewolves clustered around Frank, fur bristling. The one standing nearest to me looked up warily at me, blinking hard as he scanned my face. Stupidly, I had not thought to mask my scent, but Chana had powdered and perfumed me as part of her ladylike attentions. Her feminine wiles had saved me.

The werewolf sneezed and shook his big ugly head. Apparently Chana's rose-scented perfume did not appeal to him, and it had also confused him enough to hide my identity, at least for the moment.

The werewolves had worried me, but I understood immediately that Krueger was the most dangerous. He glared at the locket around my neck, the one in which Asmodel was imprisoned. I knew it looked out of place on the neck of a baroness, but it could not be helped.

"Cheap little trinket, isn't it," I said with a simper. "My English governess gave it to me when I was a tiny child."

"You speak English?" Krueger growled.

"Oh, no, I was a dreadful student, couldn't keep all those strange words in my head. 'Jitterbug'—ha ha!"

Krueger wasn't amused, but at least, I could see, he now underestimated me. With a bored sigh, he dismissed me as a brainless socialite. He rudely shoved past Frank to get to the big oak bar that curved along the back wall. "I want a drink," he barked at the terrified, pale-as-milk bartender, the only man with a grain of sense in the entire place.

"Please, sit, sit," I purred at the governor-general. "Next to me. I trust you are comfortable in the Wawel?"

He bent to kiss my hands. "Dear lady, it is a marvelous castle. A Teutonic stronghold worthy of the Führer himself."

"Splendid. I am so glad. I was excited to hear you love chess. So did my late papa. I could not resist the temptation of inviting you, and was thrilled you would venture out to meet me."

He smirked, and with a great manly show motioned for me to take my seat. He was in full uniform, his hat jammed low on his sweaty forehead, his gut straining against the belted, double-breasted jacket of his dress uniform.

I sank into my seat, barricaded behind a phalanx of white chess pieces. Frank, with great ceremony, removed his hat and lowered his ample behind on the chair opposite mine. The wolves crowded around, their yellow eyes darting around the low-ceilinged little room, looking for danger.

"Shall we play, Hans?" I asked, lingering over the words as if I was aware of my boldness in making the proposition.

Frank hesitated; the silence was full of menace. Then he

forgave me my impertinence. "Certainly, fräulein," he said, ignoring my nobility the way I had not acknowledged his title of governor-general.

My smile widened. "You move first. You are the black."

Hans Frank's style of play revealed his character. He played with an unsubtle brutality, aggressive from the first move, without finesse or calculation. His virtue was his lack of cunning: his drive to conquer was undisguised.

I was not very good at chess; for me, the game was a sentimental Ouija board that I used to conjure memories of my father, lost to death forever. I defended myself against more effective players as long as I could; I sometimes won in spite of myself, for I quickly lulled all but rank beginners into complacency.

Besides, this time I was terribly distracted; I was watching Krueger put away shot after shot of Jägermeister and wondered if he was well shellacked after so much liquor or somehow impervious to it. Despite this, I had a stroke of luck and by accident threatened Frank's queen.

He saw the danger before I did. "My queen is in peril," he muttered, and our gazes locked over the pieces. "One queen holds a dagger to the other."

I held his gaze, and he froze. "Hans," I crooned under my breath, like a black widow spider weaving a web of sound. "The queen is more powerful, yes. But you should see to your king. When you lose your king, oh black king, you lose the game altogether."

He tried to respond, found to his immense surprise that he could not. "Farewell, butcher," I muttered under my breath in Hungarian, and with all my power I squeezed.

His eyes bulged, but I held him fast, and I squeezed and squeezed until his soul flickered out and he sat dead at the table.

I worked his lungs like a bellows long after he was dead, propped up his lifeless body until my strength began to waver. "Why, Governor," I said as loudly as I could, but breathless. "It is your move."

The werewolf sitting at my feet lifted his muzzle from his paws and growled to himself. "Governor?" I said again, and then I let him slump forward onto the chessboard, and I screamed.

The room exploded into pandemonium. Krueger leapt forward, brandishing his pistol, snarling filthy curses in German as he yanked the dead governor-general backward in his chair. The Nazi's dead eyes bulged outward as he stared into nothingness. No matter what happened now, at least the murderous Nazi bastard would kill children no more.

Krueger kicked the nearest werewolf savagely in the face. "Stupid dog!" he screamed, his voice hysterical and high-pitched like a woman's. "He died and you just sit there!"

Before I could throw out a ward and expose myself by openly manifesting my magic, Krueger himself transformed into a wolf and attacked, with disorienting and breathtaking speed. Only an alpha dog could transform at will, and only the leader of a great pack could transform without the light of the moon or another, earthly sorcery to assist him.

The other werewolf, Krueger's deputy, got to me first. He knocked my chair backward, smashing it apart under his enormous weight.

I screamed again, the sound half choked by the force of his horrible jaws clamped around my throat. "Stop it, dog," I ordered, and I had the presence of mind to say it in German. And I grabbed his jaw with my hands, augmented my physical strength with just a touch of magic. If things had not happened so suddenly, the wolf would likely have sensed that magical muscle. But Krueger flickered back into human form, grabbed the wolf by the scruff of the neck, and smashed him on the top of his head with the butt of his pistol.

"You stupid ass—get off of her!" he ordered, and dragged the wolf backward. Whining, the cur obeyed, and I sat up, marveling at the Nazi's strength in his human form, and his ability to change without hesitation or apparent pain.

"You are lucky you didn't rip out her throat. This bitch may be a magical, some sort of spy," Krueger said. "I have silver bullets in my gun. Obey your orders!"

The werewolf slunk to Krueger's feet, his haunches bent low, tail tucked between his legs. I looked up at Krueger, and his pistol was now trained on my face. "You are coming with me, fräulein."

I had no false identification, nothing. I was worse than dead.

✳ 16 ✳

A shiny black vehicle pulled up to the curb outside the Literary Café. I considered attacking them all at once on the street, knowing my chances of survival were lower by far in the Gestapo jails and the already infamous torture rooms, but I was hoping Viktor got away, and I believed it was wise, even still, to cloak my identity as long as possible.

Without ceremony they shoved me into the Black Maria. The doors slammed shut, and the engine rumbled to life. It pulled away from the curb and lurched over the cobblestones, presumably on the way to Gestapo headquarters.

Krueger was waiting.

I had known I probably would not escape the trap we had set to catch Hans Frank. But despite my resolve, a dreadful panic seized me as the black van took me away. I thought I saw Viktor on the road in the borrowed Mercedes; perhaps my scuffle with the wolves had given him enough time to escape.

That half-imagined glimpse of Viktor, free, gave me a glimmer of hope. But otherwise I was gripped by a terrible fear, fear of what the Gestapo would do to me, what they could make me do. I remembered Asmodel's prophecy from inside the paprika tin, my death at Ravensbruck. Was this capture what he had foreseen?

My mind strayed to the man I had just killed, the strutting lawyer with the five children and shrewish wife. I had no remorse about killing him. None. I had asked Gisele to look into his future, and she had called him the Butcher of Poland. The man had already earned the title. Had he but the opportunity, he would have murdered millions. This was no case of condemning a man for what he was, without the benefit of a trial. He deserved to die.

I had decided to kill Krueger too if I could. But the man was vicious, and smart enough not to let his guard down around me even though I kept up my pretense of clueless innocence.

My fear was not so much that they would kill me: I had died before and knew how to get back. I was terrified of somehow betraying the Hashomer and Raziel, and even more afraid they would discover the ancient demon bespelled inside Gisele's old, dented locket. They could not get him out without me to spell him out, but I was afraid of what they could do to force me.

The Black Maria slammed to a stop, and the rear doors swung open. Rough hands grabbed me and yanked me out, the wolves now growling, making a big show of their fangs and desire to attack.

Krueger waited at the top of a short flight of wooden stairs. He grabbed me by the forearm and I gave a little cry of pain.

"This way, fräulein," he said, his eyes glowing with an unholy glee. My suspicions had been correct: the man enjoyed inflicting pain, was excited by the things he planned to do to me.

Unknowingly Krueger gave me a gift; my heart went cold with fury at this sadistic bastard and his unbridled power over innocent people.

I was no innocent, not any longer. I would not hesitate to kill Krueger if I could. He kept his gun out and pointed to my temple, so trying any quick magic was not an option: I would be dead before I could whisper the most rudimentary spell of protection.

"I do not know your game." He loomed over me, his breath sour as he spit the words into my face. "But I will have it out of you. Baroness, my ass."

"No, there is no game, sir. Of course I am a baroness," I protested weakly. I had decided that keeping up the pretense would buy me a little more time while they ferreted out the truth. "You may call my uncle's house in Budapest and see for yourself! His assistant, Eva Farkas, is his chatelaine until he returns from business in Berlin."

As a werewolf, Krueger was not privy to internal vampire quarrels: not even Hitler would be admitted to the Vampirrat in Berlin. Unlike the werewolves, the vampires might swear an alliance with a mortal, but never cede their sovereignty. I had some hope that Eva, quick-witted as she was, could devise some ruse to keep me alive.

In the meantime they locked me overnight in a cement room with no windows and a drain built into the floor. I stared at that drain for quite a while, thinking of the showers at the women's bathhouse on Margaret Island, which I used to visit in Budapest with my mother. Now, the drain reminded me of an abattoir.

There were no chairs, and only a single lightbulb swinging from its socket and a wire that disappeared into the ceiling. The room smelled of mold and something else, something fetid and awful that I was determined not to identify.

As the hours dragged on, I fingered the dented locket hanging around my neck. Asmodel was my last resort, my emergency weapon held in reserve, my glass ampoule of cyanide, too. Despite the solemn oath I had sworn to Gisele, I chewed my nails off one by one and itched to set the demon free.

But no magic could serve me here. I could call upon Leopold and send him to warn Raziel, but they undoubtedly already knew my fate, and the last thing I wanted was for Raziel to die trying to rescue me.

So I unclasped the thin gold chain around my neck, nestled the locket in the palm of my hand. I took a shaky breath to center myself, my lips began to form the syllables of the ancient demon's name . . .

. . . and with a great clatter, the locks were thrown open and Krueger himself came through the door of my prison.

I quickly replaced the locket, and forced myself to look into his eyes without flinching, without hope or despair. Krueger had his suspicions about me, but I would go to my death playing the part of a ditzy Christian noblewoman with nothing dangerous to hide. If Krueger killed me before he found out my true identity and mission, my friends could perhaps escape my fate. And I had my own ways of cheating death.

He nodded curtly at me and without a word he whipped out his pistol and pointed it between my eyes. "Baroness," he said with a snarl, "you will come with me. I will escort you myself."

I edged along the wall to the now-ajar door of the cell, and I backed away, stumbling in the sudden daylight of the hallway outside. I tried to sneak my sight into his mind, but he slapped me hard across the face and I smashed into the far wall, seeing nothing but stars.

"Don't try your dirty magic on me, you little bitch. I am wise to you. Once I figure you out, I will dispose of you. But not before. I swear to you, fräulein. I will not let you go until I have squeezed every last drop of information out."

He pointed the way down the hall and I stumbled ahead, half expecting him to empty a clip of bullets into the back of my head. I blinked hard to clear my mind, the life force surging through my limbs like blue electric fire. We reached the end of the hallway and Krueger unbolted the huge iron-reinforced wooden door.

We entered a busy room that was part of the ordinary world, with young men and women in crisp uniforms bustling about, carrying papers and laughing to each other. Just another day at the office, simply buried in paperwork. Good thing it was a Friday.

The morning sunlight hurt my eyes and I blinked hard to keep from being dazzled. I wiped the tears from the corners of my eyes and kept going, as if I were climbing a mountain instead of crossing a carpeted office.

Krueger waved his pistol at the threshold of his office. "Pass over, fräulein," he said, voice low.

As I stepped across the cheap carpeting, a sharp pain shot through me, a blue-hot terrible electric shock. I could not keep from him a low, barely restrained little cry.

Krueger snorted through his nose. "You won't be trying your magical shit in here, fräulein. The place is warded against filth like you. Sit down."

He shoved me into a heavy, splintery chair and, shaky, I grate-fully sank into it. The fact I sat in his front office and not in a basement dungeon filled with torture equipment gave me a faint but steady hope, like starlight. It was not much comfort, but at that point, it was all I had, except the dubious protection of the demon Asmodel.

"You will tell me why you killed Hans Frank," Krueger said from the doorway, without any preamble.

I swallowed hard. I had to make it out of this room alive, and I had to do it with my secrets intact. Too many people would die if my nerve broke, if Krueger indeed squeezed my precious secrets out of me.

"My dear sir," I managed to say in choppy, formal German. "The death of Governor Frank has shattered my future, I assure you. I have nothing more to say. His poor wife, his poor chil-dren." And I dabbed at the corners of my eyes with my bare fingers, having no hanky available to make my show of dainty grief more credible.

"You lie, you bitch," he snarled again. He stepped all the way into the room, slammed the door with a great show of fury, and shook me by the shoulders until my teeth rattled in my head.

"You are a spy!" he roared. "And somebody sent you to do this horrible deed. Who? I want the names, all of them. Who was it? The Communists? The Jew Communists? The Polish Army? Who?"

"I don't know what you are talking about!" I roared right back. "I am a baroness, you dirty dog!"

The sudden silence curdled, grew ugly. Krueger got very still, then he walked easily around the big, ugly desk and squat chair at the far end of the room, near the only window. A Nazi flag waved on a tiny flagpole on the desk near the big leather blotter.

I wouldn't meet his gaze. I only stared at the tiny bloodred flag as he hissed low, as he crouched over the blotter like a wolf about to spring.

"We're not here to talk about me, fräulein. Oh no. I assure you that you and your associates made a dreadful error murdering poor Hans. The fool was earnest and he was bloody-minded, but he was a loyal dog, one who waited on his master's bidding.

"But I am no dog. I am a wolf, fräulein. I am a vicious, un-civilized cur, the leader of one of the greatest packs in all the protectorate of Poland. And I will enjoy hunting the scum out of Poland. Especially foreign scum like you. I have no compunc-tion, none, about killing those who offend my kind. I lust for the kill. I will kill Jews, faggots, cripples, priests, Gypsies at a rate ten times that of that fat little fucker Hans Frank."

He leaned back in his chair and studied me as I avoided looking at him. "Killing Frank was your first mistake, fräulein. Your next one will be holding out on me for another moment, because you will suffer dreadful torments here, only to give me the information anyway in the end."

I shut my lips tight and willed myself to be still. I stared at the Nazi flag so hard and with such fury that the swastika in the middle began to smoke and blacken.

"Stop it!" Krueger snarled from across the desk. "I will shove the flag down your throat if you dare to desecrate it."

I raised my eyes to meet his. "There is nothing I can do to desecrate something already so filthy and evil."

Well, that had blown my cover, for sure. But it was worth it, to see Krueger so thoroughly lose his control. I could smell the scent of his fear under his towering rage. At the heart of every werewolf is a dog, no matter how nasty his fangs and his howl. He knows he must answer to someone above, and if he is an alpha he knows that if his hold upon his underlings slackens, he is walking dead.

He flashed into wolf form—I realized now that he transformed unwillingly when his passion overtook him, like a nervous tic he could not control. And that heedless rage was dangerous, and could lead him to destruction. Believe me, I know.

I thought of my death, my refuge in the next world, and I held my ground in the face of his insane snarls and growls, the snapping of his jaws mere centimeters from my face. Once, not long before, the prospect of my own suffering and death might have frightened me into attempting an escape or some kind of clever subterfuge.

But I knew my limits better, and my strengths. I could not fool such a creature, adept as he was in dominating those of lesser caste in the werewolf hierarchy. Krueger was used to having the upper hand, and wielding that advantage to inflict the maximum punishment.

Someone like me—someone who did not exist in his power structure at all—could fit into only one of two categories, threat or prey. And I had just demonstrated I would no longer pretend to be Krueger's prey.

The foul wards in the room hampered my ability to inflict spellcraft on him, to destroy him with magic. But I could torment him with my strengths, however caged they were, and I could tempt him to destroy himself with the effort he expended to torture and eliminate me from the world.

He returned to his human form with a visible effort and an

anguished snarl. "Fräulein," he said, all out of breath, as if I were the one interrogating him, "you will pay for your impertinence. By the time I am through with you, you will curse the day you were born."

He grabbed me by the hair and yanked me to my feet. I remained quiet, studying my enemy as he shook me like a rag doll. He wanted to kill me without any further fuss, I could smell it. He lusted for the kill, just as he had said. But his Nazi superiors, looming in the back of his conscious mind, restrained the wolf in him from ruling him.

I would have preferred to have died by the wolf, not the man. It would have been a cleaner death. But Krueger had lied earlier, to himself and to me. He was not ruled by his wolf. Krueger was now ruled by his Nazi masters. And though he did not admit it even to himself, his submission to the Nazi regime robbed him of his powers as a free pack leader.

I knew I would die at his human hands, in the service of a mortal human leader. And I knew that even that counted as a grim kind of victory.

He tossed me back into the same cell, smacking me hard across the face as if to mark me. "Choke on your blood, bitch," he snarled, his voice so thick with the wolf as to be all but unrecognizable. "Think on who you would die to protect, and know I will have them in my power by the end of this day."

He slammed the door with these charming parting words, and I sank to the cold cement floor, in exhaustion as well as relief. I had managed to survive my first social engagement with my captor, but I had the sinking feeling that he would take a cruel revenge on me for this dubious triumph.

Within minutes my fears were justified. I heard a low, soft banging on the exposed pipes stretching over my head across the ceiling. After a moment, I recognized the rhythm of the beautiful "Blue Danube" waltz:

Dah dah dah de dah—DUM DUM, dum dum . . .

And my heart sank. That little tune pierced my heart more painfully than anything Krueger had done, for that was the tune that Viktor liked to tease me with, his way of bringing me into the fold with the Polish partisans. Every time he hummed "The Blue Danube," he made light of my Hungarian roots, made them something pretty and funny, of little consequence and nothing to worry about.

In this filthy Nazi hellhole, the cheerful little tune all but broke my heart. I looked up and saw in the dim, flickering light of the single bulb that the exposed pipe snaked along the wall near where I lay on the floor in a ball. I crawled to the place where the pipe disappeared into the wall, and I used my bare knuckles to rap back the tune. I had heard Viktor, I knew it was him.

I tentatively tried to send a message to him telepathically, but a horrific headache put a stop to that. I imagined it was not just the interrogation rooms of this facility but also the prison cells that had been warded against the use of spellcraft. For now, I had only the resources that Viktor did: my humanity, my refusal to give Krueger the satisfaction of taking my pride from me, and my wits.

I leaned my head against the pipe, and to my surprise, heard Viktor's voice in my ear, as clear as if we spoke by telephone.

"Are you there? Speak with your lips against the pipe—it will carry the vibrations to me."

"A shame, my friend. You are here."

"You didn't think I could get away from the Literary, did you? Not when they figured out Frank was dead."

I felt an absurd little surge of pride, lying on the filthy floor of the Gestapo headquarters in Kraków. "Yes, Frank is dead."

"Let us not speak of this." I understood what Viktor meant. It would be simplicity itself to listen in upon our open conversation over the exposed pipe. Anyone along the entire row of cells could put their ear to the cold, rusty metal and hear anything we said.

"This is very important," Viktor said, and the steely command in his voice brought me back to my senses. Instead of the horrible miasma of dread in which I had been lost, I became alert and fully self-possessed once more.

"You must not show fear. No matter what they do to you, no matter what they say, no matter who they show to you, do not give them the satisfaction of your fear. They feed on fear like vampires, they drink it like a delicacy. And the more fear you feed them, the more they will want."

"I know. Thank you."

"You still have something they want even more. Information. They will not kill you as long as you have it, not on purpose."

I did not agree. I had heard of the horrible deaths visited upon partisans in Germany and other places in the Reich. If I could not escape somehow from this place, I expected to meet my end in the main square of Kraków, strung up and tortured publicly to generate the mass fear that Krueger craved.

But still, Viktor's words made my courage surge within me. He, like me, had been captured and imprisoned. Unlike me, he had no magical resources upon which to draw. And yet he remained magnificent in the face of torture and death. It was as if the fulfillment of his most terrible nightmares absolved him of the need to suffer under the yoke of his fears any longer. Gone was the hesitant, deskbound Hashomer leader I had met that first day above the pharmacist's shop in Kraków. Now Viktor was a lion. I knew I might break, but I was certain that Viktor would not. He had resolved to die with honor.

"You must not allow your guilt to get the better of you," Viktor went on. "The Gestapo will play upon your loves, your weaknesses, to break you. Don't let them."

I thought of Raziel and Gisele and caught my breath. It was bad enough knowing that Viktor had been captured in the dragnet they had thrown over the city to catch those who knew me. If they ensnared either of those whom I loved the most in the world, I recognized that the leverage would shift from me to Krueger.

I was weak, I allowed the images of Raziel and Gisele to fill my mind. And though the thought of them comforted me and gave me resolve, they also burned through the anger that had masked my terror. I curled up tighter, as if I could protect my heart as well as my guts from Krueger's blows and kicks.

Asmodel burned the skin over my heart. He fed on my fear too, grew stronger as my energy was focused on Krueger and not him. Yankel had done a masterful job trapping him in his locket-prison, more securely than Krueger had imprisoned me, but I wasn't sure that Asmodel would stay put in the event of my death.

I could hide the locket in the cell and hope I returned each time from my sessions with Krueger. Or I could die the partisan's death I was sure Krueger planned for me, and leave the locket to disappear into obscurity, the way *The Book of Raziel* had vanished countless centuries ago.

Sometimes magical objects are most effectively hidden in plain sight. And so I decided to keep the locket with me, for as long as they would let me. In order to make it more likely I could keep the locket, I stuffed it inside my brassiere, where it was no longer visible. If they took my clothes, I would have to find a better hiding place. But that was not yet, and part of me was convinced I would be dead before they worked around to such niceties as changing me over into prisoner's garb. Krueger's questioning held an awful urgency.

"Krueger doesn't want to find out if Frank was killed," Viktor said. I held my breath and worried that someone else, some Nazi bastard, listened to us, but Viktor, heedless, went on. "Krueger benefits more from Frank's death, natural or not, than anybody else. And if Frank was in fact murdered, it will cause complications for the new governor. Krueger, of course."

That meant the information Krueger wanted had nothing to do with Frank. That was where he had started, but he was only using it as a lever to pry out of me what he really wanted.

But what could he want besides the facts of Frank's death? Asmodel abruptly burned hotter against the side of my breast, and I suddenly understood. It was my witchery itself that enraged and frightened him, not the circumstances of his predecessor's squalid end.

Krueger must not get my magic out of me. And above all he must not discover the fact of Asmodel's existence, let alone the fact that I held him on my person.

It was terribly dangerous, but it was the only decent option I had left. With a sigh, I accepted it: I was going to have to die.

And despite the fact I had done it more than once before, that did not make it an easier prospect to contemplate. Dying is hard every single time you do it.

"My friend," I said, unwilling to say Viktor's name aloud in this dangerous place, "I want to say good-bye and thank you. I will not survive my next session with Krueger. You give me the courage to meet my end knowing that you fight on, and I will speak well of you in the world to come."

"You mustn't talk like that," he said. I realized that Viktor didn't understand I could truly, and not just metaphorically, return from the dead—we had never discussed the full scope of my abilities. And I could not tell him now.

"It is simply the truth, my dear," I replied, my voice steady even as the tears flowed from my eyes and over the exposed pipe. "I will be dead by this time tomorrow. I want you to know that I will not break. I will give Krueger nothing, and this is why I must die."

"Then courage, my girl," he said, his voice now a little hard to hear through the pipe. "We will stand together here, and that is a victory over the Nazis all by itself."

Brave, noble words, but I would have preferred to see as our victory Krueger dead and the Nazis forced out of Poland. But wishing did not work magic.

I waited for Krueger to come back, but now I did not wait alone. That rusty pipe had become a conduit for my courage, from Viktor to me and back again. And if the Gestapo had meant for us to talk, they were stupid to allow it, for it had a great effect upon what was to follow.

✳ 17 ✳

"We have Raziel," Krueger began, a big smile on his vulpine face.

I refused to give him the satisfaction of allowing the sudden painful shock of his words to register on my face. Instead, I shrugged and focused on getting the grit out from under my left thumbnail. "Do you? Why should I care?"

He laughed then, a low, blood-curdling sound. I had resolved to die early and with as little interaction as possible, but it now occurred to me that, just as I had information useful to Krueger, the Gestapo chief had information useful to me as well.

"Raziel is your boyfriend, is he not? A fellow Hungarian, a partisan . . . a Jew?"

"What nonsense," I said, willing with all my might to affect a bored, careless tone. "I don't know any Jews."

"Still pretending to be a baroness, fräulein." And Krueger laughed again, sounding genuinely amused this time.

"If you are trying to endear yourself to me, Krueger, you are failing," I said. I leaned back in my chair, stretched my aching back, and sighed as I studied the grubby, water-stained ceiling.

Krueger lit a cigarette, and I watched a thin wisp of smoke reach upward like a ghostly hand. "You have no identification," he said, affable now. "You have nothing but the truth to save you."

"You lie, Krueger. Nothing will save me, and we both know it. You might as well string me up in the public square and have done with it. But I am sure the Hungarian government will not appreciate the appalling treatment I have received."

"Clearly your night on the cement floor has made you cranky, fräulein."

"If you intended to frighten me, Krueger, you have failed. And such actions as yours have unforeseen repercussions."

My words hung in the air like the cigarette smoke, and Krueger said nothing to dispel them.

"I will give you one last chance, fräulein, because there is something of the truth wrapped inside your web of lies. There is something noble in you, something not Jewish, something I would have admired in a human being, not a verminous piece of filth such as yourself. Tell me the truth, and I will kill you humanely."

"If there is something you admire in me, Krueger, it is the part that would refuse the humane death of a farm animal. If you will kill me, rip out my throat like another wolf. But stop your babbling. Your cowardice wearies me."

I had intended to provoke him beyond the restraint of his

reason, but he maintained control, though with some difficulty. I quite deliberately shifted my focus from the dirty ceiling to his desk, the scorched Nazi flag, and then to his face.

A slow tic worked under his left eye, and his lips were clenched around the smoldering cigarette. "Your eyes are bloodshot," I remarked. "I imagine you slept worse than me. And why would that be?"

When our eyes met, I refused to lower my gaze. I was now ready to die as a tactic in our war. I wanted him to kill me. Only then would I have the final upper hand over him, haunt his nightmares until I could kill him in turn.

I wanted him to suffer.

His Adam's apple jumped as he swallowed, and his nostrils flared briefly with the effort not to look away. I knew with complete conviction that I unnerved him.

Before he killed me, I intended to break him, make him useless to his Nazi masters. My shadow would darken his every moment after my death, he would doubt his every act. In truth he would become a golem of my malign intentions.

"You never answered my question," I said. I did not have to pretend my self-possession: the prospect of my death gave me a somber power.

He growled, though he did manage to maintain his human form this time. "I am not the one being interrogated here," he said, his voice so thick with anger the German clotted deep in his throat.

"I told you yesterday, you will get nothing worthwhile out of me."

"But the fact remains, fräulein, we still have Raziel. You can lie to me about your connection to this man, but we have him."

He stubbed out the remains of his cigarette in a marble ash-tray at his left elbow, and for the first time since I had entered his domain he smiled. "I shan't bother using more persuasive methods on you, fräulein. For whatever reason, you prove too blockheaded for the usual methods we use here. But your friend, the one you claim not to know—I believe he will prove more pliant."

For the first time since Krueger had ushered me back into his office that morning, he had gained the upper hand over me. But I refused to admit it. "This Raziel is nothing to me. You say he is a Jew? Poor man. I have important people back in Hungary who will seek to avenge me. What does a poor wretch like this Raziel have? Truly, death is a welcome escape to one such as this."

His smile widened, and his teeth abruptly looked longer and more yellow. The wolf wanted to come out, and the man only held him at bay with a supreme effort now. "You speak of him like a beast of prey. As if you were a werewolf yourself. Fräulein, you are a curious specimen, aren't you."

"I couldn't say."

"I'm beginning to think you want to die."

I said nothing.

"You want me to kill you, you taunt my wolf and expect me to do your will simply because I am a hunter born." He shook his head and the smile on his lips grew unpleasant. "Fräulein, I did not rise to the top of my pack, to the top of the Nazi hierar-chy in the protectorate of Poland, by allowing a creature of lesser power to dictate my actions."

Words alone would not get me what I needed. I rose from my chair and took a half step toward the desk. "You assume my power is less. Even here, you may be wrong."

I stopped before my body actually touched his desk, and this wolf in human guise and I appraised each other. His smile floated away, and I finally had the measure of Herr Krueger, saw him complete.

"Fear rules you, Krueger. You can kill me, but that won't keep you from staring awake all night, waiting for the one who will rise up to take your place, just as you took Frank's place."

I thought of Viktor, knew his position was similar. All of us—wolf, witch, mortal man—were willing to die to achieve our greater ends. That made us all equals of a sort.

I had to force Krueger's hand, or we would stand at an impasse until he was done torturing me or Raziel. Neither one of us would break.

I raised my hands, and began the long invocation of the Bane of Concubines, not a curse concocted by the daughters of Lazarus, but a deadly spell nevertheless, one I knew I could wield.

The pain began as soon as I lifted my palms up with intention. The wards in the building against malign magics like mine dug into my flesh like barbed wire, and my eyes watered with the pain.

The foul magic of the Nazis contended with mine. For the first time, I sensed a direction to the wrongness, a flow like a toxic river. It seemed to come from the north.

But I only held tighter to my spell, and as with the Nazi flag before, the intensity of my fury overwhelmed the wards. Krueger's long, skinny face paled, and he leapt from his seat, as if it suddenly had gotten too hot for him.

He grabbed at his throat as my spell snaked around him and squeezed. I could barely speak the words of the spell aloud, but I didn't need volume to make the intention manifest.

He knew I was forcing him. He knew I wanted to avoid the spectacle of him torturing Raziel to get the truth out of me, but none of that mattered now. If he didn't take direct, physical action against me, my spell was going to take hold, and I would take Krueger with me, right out of his office and into the next world.

With a choked snarl, he shifted into wolf form and lunged for my throat. My magic had succeeded in goading him, where my contempt and resolution hadn't.

His jaws locked over my throat and I fell backward, toppling over the chair behind me. He bit deep, bit clean. I had gotten my wish: he killed me as if I were another wolf. A backhanded compliment, but most sincere.

So I disappeared into death, my own dark domain. And as I fled, I resolved to use whatever sorcery I had to free Raziel before it was too late. I was willing to commit any evil to save him.

As deaths went, my death at the wolf Krueger's fangs was not the worst. The sensations of ripping, bleeding, the lungs filling with blood, were truly awful, but the gift of Krueger's death was that it was so fast. And a fast death was exhilarating.

I shot up to the second Heaven, place of newly dead souls, with my pride and determination intact. But my triumph faded when I recalled that, for the first time, Raziel could not welcome me to his former domain, now shorn of Raziel's presence, bereft of his spirit, benighted.

Instead, my mother, Tekla, materialized out of the swirling mists, as though she had expected me. "You're late," she said, an edge of irritation creeping into her voice. "Always wool-gathering."

I stifled a sigh. My mother, a formidable witch indeed, never forgave me for refusing to learn her craft and our family's unique tradition. And the fact that I had already admitted she was right didn't mean she would forgive me even here, beyond the grave.

Sadness made my mother shrewish, and I knew she did not mean to wound me with her scolding. My mother was like a mother bear cuffing her cub.

My mother and I usually ended up disappointing each other, but that didn't make me love her any less. "A blessing to see you, Mama," I said, keeping my love for her to myself. "But I must get back, and quickly. Raziel is in mortal danger now, and he has no magic to protect him."

She arched an eyebrow. "Like your father."

The pain twisted like an astral knife plunged into my heart. "Yes. Like Papa."

A steady buzzing distracted me from my mother's sourpuss. Leo, freed from the confines of my mind, sailed happily around my astral body, glowing like a firefly. "My good deed is again done, Mama," he sang. "I am here, to serve you."

"This is an imp, Leopold," I said lamely, by way of introduction.

"Tekla, Tekla!" Leo sang, bouncing like a balloon at the end of a string.

"We've already had the pleasure," my mother said with a sigh.

"Thank you again, Leo," I said. "May I still call upon you? You surely owe me nothing."

He floated cross-legged in the air above our heads, his face mock serious. "I am at your service as always, Mama mine. I am growing twenty lifetimes at a time because of you. It's either help you, or get born as an earthworm twenty times. This is better."

"In that case, fly quickly to Raziel in the prison where I died. Squeeze through the wards if you can, and tell him I am coming."

With a nod and a wave, my baby imp disappeared to do my bidding.

"You won't stay dead, will you," my mother said. "Sweetheart, do you want the express train to Gehenna?"

"I don't care," I protested. "And why not? I will return, and figure out how to call a demon army too."

"Oh, for goodness' sake," my mother muttered.

"Why not, Mamika? You're the one who used to tell me the tales. The Witch of Ein Dor was the mother of Abner, the general of David's army. She summoned demons to the court of Solomon. She was a Lazarus. So why can't we compel demons to make war against evil?"

"Why not? Didn't you understand the point of all those stories? Oh, Magdalena, what did I do to deserve a daughter like you?" She sighed and buried her ghostly face in her translucent hands.

Her words stung, but I would rather have died another thousand times than admit it. "You must have done something really horrible," I said instead, and I laughed.

"I've been watching you from the next world, Magdalena. You've been conjuring demons, and consorting with vampires, and generally overestimating your abilities."

She expected me to protest, and I did not disappoint her.

"Mama, it's no time for hiding my light to ensure that I go to Heaven. Hitler is worse than Satan himself, and he is intent on taking over the entire world. How could you expect me to stand by and let him?"

This last finally coaxed a laugh out of my earnest, careworn old mother. "By the warts on the nose on the Witch of Ein Dor! You are a vexing child, aren't you. Has it ever occurred to you that events such as Hitler's invasion of Poland may somehow be beyond your control?"

Her words hit me like a blow, but I refused to go down. "Everybody says something like that, and all in their nose, sounding like a distinguished professor. And, Mamika, that is how horrible people like Hitler get away with it!"

I don't know why, but this last argument stopped her cold. She hovered, silent, next to me, and I realized with awe that I had just had the last word on the subject.

But I was wrong to believe that I had won the argument. "I can't stand it anymore. Fine. I am coming with you," my mother said, her voice prim, her expression stormy. Was it guilt?

If anything, persuading Tekla caused me deeper unease than simply fighting her. "How can you come back?" I asked her. "Your body has returned to the earth." I didn't mean to be a smart aleck about it; I honestly didn't understand.

Unfortunately, and as usual, my mother took my question in the least charitable light possible. "Listen, disrespectful girl. I was the one who did right to stay in the afterworld."

"To stay with Papa," I said with a little sigh I could not conceal. My papa, whom I adored beyond all reason, was a mortal man with no magic. And, alas, he was gone, truly gone.

Before I could say anything more, a strange, astral wind

whipped the gray clouds of the second Heaven into a churning black froth. The wind howled, desolate, and it occurred to me how much the place had suffered for the lack of Raziel's presence. Instead of a safe haven, the second Heaven was now a vacuum, a celestial battlefield. What harm had I done, tempting Raziel to descend to Earth?

A creature emerged from the wind: one with huge needle teeth, long grasping claws, and glowing red eyes. This was a demon of the lower realms, and yet it hunted souls on the celestial plane. The world—even the world beyond—indeed was coming undone.

The demon rose onto her hind legs: her teats, in two long rows like a sow's, swung freely down the length of her long bony body. "Ooh, a baby," she crooned, leaning toward me. "A lost little baby soul. Delicioussss . . ."

A baleful shriek jerked my attention to the demon's left. I expected to see more of them, attracted by the scent of my terror and helplessness as a lost spirit of the afterworld.

But I was shocked to see that it was my mother who was making such an awful ruckus. I could not understand the words she spat with fury in some ancient forgotten language, Sumerian perhaps, or Phoenician.

If I was shocked by her vehemence, I was positively amazed by my mother's magic. She worked magic, my mother did, in the place of death itself, in defiance of everything I had ever thought I had known about the Lazarus witches' creed and our supposed limitations. I gawked, overcome more by her than by the demons that now gathered like starving stray dogs all around us.

The first one, with the teats, did not give up easily.

"Tekklllaaa ... ," she crooned, and my astral skin crawled. My mother's spell had revealed her true name, and one's name in the possession of your enemies could be a fatal weapon, wielded against you.

My mother raised her hands into the mist, her high forehead and wild eyes in sharp relief against the stormy gray of the clouds. Her long reddish hair streamed out behind her, as if we fought deep under a churning ocean.

"*Astarte aggarat ... ,*" my mother said, her mouth filled with the words, as hard as stones. She spat them out at our enemies, and they struck hard. The teats-demon fell backward, screaming, and other creatures rose out of the mists and tore her demonic spirit to shreds, gushing astral blood.

My mother grabbed my arm as I stood there, gaping. "Return!" she ordered me. "Recite the spell of return, quick, before they are done tearing her apart."

"What about you, Mama?" I hesitated. "That was ... magnificent." I had never seen my mother work magic during her lifetime, and the spectacle had healed something in me that I had never before realized was broken.

"Yes, yes, but you need to go. Get out of here! Summon me for your army when it is time. I will not resist your crazy schemes any longer."

My mind reeled with my mother's promise, but I had no time to revel in it. The demonfeast became positively frantic and I knew they would soon be upon us again.

"I can handle them," my mother said. "Go—descend!"

The spell was simple, the way familiar. I recited the spell of return, the only one my mother had ever taught me that I actually learned, however unwillingly. I folded into a needle of light and shot back into my bleeding body, back into this world of ecstasy and pain.

But even as I fled, I wondered at the mystery of Tekla Lazarus, and why she would only consent to wield her magic, so masterfully, now that she was dead.

And even as I returned, I wondered how I could yet save Raziel, who still resided in the land of the living.

✳ 18 ✳

Cold. Cold and miserable and damp. They had dumped my body in the freezing cement basement, and I returned to life only to find that a mortal hand was clasped around the locket with Asmodel in it, in the process of ripping it away from my neck.

"Go into shit," I hissed in Hungarian, and it worked as well as a spell. The offending hand withdrew, together with the human being caught in the process of looting a dead body, and the corpse-robber's footfalls echoed away.

I was flat on my back on a cold, cement floor. The smell was extraordinarily bad; the light dim and reddish. In the last few months, I had become adept at dying and coming back, and I was glad of my expertise, for the circumstances in which I had returned this time were indeed grim.

Apparently Krueger's slashing fangs had not severed my

vocal cords, for I could still whisper a spell aloud, and that helped what came next to transpire more easily. I wove a spell of healing like a lace scarf, and wrapped it around my throat. Warm caresses of words knitted my flesh back together, healed my throat more with every beat of my resurrected heart.

With a sigh, I pulled myself upright, made sure Asmodel was still inside the locket and the locket was still securely attached to the chain Gisele had fastened around my neck. I listened hard; the would-be locket-stealer was gone.

I glanced around the cold, dank cellar and stiffened in shock. Viktor's lifeless face stared back at me from the floor, his brilliant blue eyes now empty, not a meter's length away from my own aching, but once more living body.

I searched for his soul, but he had gone, I prayed to a more hospitable corner of the second Heaven than I had just returned from. Perhaps his guardian angel was waiting for him there, for certainly Viktor Mandelstam had earned his place in the next world, a place of glory and of peace.

With a trembling hand, I reached out and closed his eyelids. His face was swollen and purpled with bruises, and his left ear looked like a cauliflower head, someone had boxed it so terribly. Poor Viktor. At least his sufferings were over, and I was sure he had borne them like a hero until they were at an end.

My body stiffened again as if stricken with Viktor's wounds. What a terrible end, what a devastating death. Without Viktor, the Hashomer would have to find some way to knit itself together, just as my flesh had to heal somehow, despite the punishment it had taken.

I forced myself to focus on life, and not on Viktor's body, so close to me, so empty of his essence. I sent my witch's sight throughout the building, angrily brushing aside the wards and accepting the pain as so many bothersome bee stings, the wards guarding the knowledge I sought: whether Raziel remained alive, or if he too had met Viktor's fate.

In the uppermost cell of the building, I found his soul steady and strong, clear and serene as always. Fear weighed heavily upon his shoulders, and he was hungry, thirsty, and weary. But he was alive. And they had not yet broken him.

With a low curse I hauled myself to my feet. I had no shoes on, but fortunately I still had on my baroness's blue dress. I squinted against the weak light as I searched for a window.

Now I had to be careful, despite the fact that I had cheated death yet again. It was too late for me to do anything to help Viktor—he had died alone, with no one to help him or hear his cries as they broke his body. But Raziel still lived. I had to find a way to release him from this terrible prison.

I was pretty sure I could escape this place myself. But if I left, was I condemning Raziel? I had only a minute to decide, a few moments to weigh my lousy choices.

If I stayed, what could I do? The wards in the prison were strong. My magic could penetrate them but I would soon be overcome by the pain and weakness inflicted by them. I could try to break him free using only my mortal efforts, but I could not prevail against an armed Gestapo and SS werewolves gathered in their place of strength.

No. I hated to leave Raziel here, in this awful place, but my best chance of saving him would be from a position of relative safety. With a heavy heart, I resolved to leave him behind and find a way to rescue Raziel from outside.

I took one more moment to send to him, despite the claws of

dark sorcery slashing at me as I did so. I whispered to him, "Do not fear," as he had whispered to me so many times. And I fervently hoped that my benediction raised his spirits the way his angelic ministrations had always uplifted mine.

With a wrench I withdrew my second sight from him, where he huddled in the corner of his cell, alone but for my message. Leaving him there hurt worse than the slashing pain of the wards, but we both had jobs to do.

"I will never be a princess," I whispered to myself, remembering my sister's motto, and I smiled so as not to cry. I returned my attention to the casement window I had located above my head. No bars across it: the dead do not break out of prison . . . well, so the Nazis thought!

With an elbow, I poked out the glass of the window, and held my breath at the tinkle of broken glass.

Outside, it was night, and no one was on the street. I hauled myself up and through the window, and away, unsteady on the cobblestone pavement, but free.

Once I made sure I wasn't being followed, I went like a shot for the Hashomer headquarters in Kazimierz. I let myself in and, shaking, called Chana's brother Asher on the telephone, knowing that our time as a fighting force in Kraków was at an end. Viktor had died with honor, but in a very real way, the Hashomer of Kraków had died along with him.

I had bad news to convey, and I wanted to do it quickly and in person. Asher contacted Levin, the Communist leader, but he told me the Polish nationalists had all gone to the salt mines in Wieliczka.

He said nothing about Raziel.

Mina was the first one through the door, and she took one look at me and my blood-soaked dress, and fainted dead away on the threshold. When Chana, Asher, and Levin arrived together a few moments later, they found me hovering over her limp body.

Chana screamed and Levin grabbed me and threw me into the office. Asher scooped up the unconscious girl and they slammed and locked the door.

"What did you do to her?" Levin roared.

"Nothing," I said, my throat still raw where Krueger had torn it.

"Poor thing fainted," Chana said in a quavery voice. She slapped ineffectually at Mina's hollow, gray cheeks. The girl looked more dead than me.

"Then what happened?" Levin narrowed his eyes and stared at me.

At this point, I was beyond caring what Levin thought. "Hans Frank is dead; we can claim his death for our cause. But we were detained. I escaped. But Viktor . . ."

The three of them stared at me, thunderstruck, while Mina started crying from where she lay curled up on the floor.

"The wrong one died," Levin spat. "I warned him not to interfere with Frank. But you seduced him, you with your magic and your lies."

I let him go on, I even let him strike me. Levin's grief and fury were shadowed with something else, something even darker, and I could not hunt out the secret of it and fight him all at once.

Unfortunately Asher pulled him off me, and the shadow over Levin's shoulder receded. Again from the north. I wiped at my face with the back of my hand: my nose was bleeding.

I stanched the flow with a whispered spell and rose to my full height, infused with my own grief and fury. Even Chana backed away in horror from the sight of me, and Mina, fully conscious now, whimpered from the floor.

"You know they have Raziel. But you never said how they got him."

No one answered me, and a terrible realization rose in my mind. "How?" My voice grew softer, filled with menace.

"He volunteered, Raziel did," Mina said from the floor. "The Nazis contacted us directly."

I knew what she was thinking: that Viktor or I had broken and given the Hashomer to the Nazis. "Viktor didn't break," I said, my voice a bit gentler now. Mina had adored Viktor.

"We thought they had killed you, too," she went on.

"Well, not exactly, yes? And I didn't break, either. I don't understand why Raziel volunteered. Why did you not just run?"

Levin's face was suddenly blank, a mask. Like an automaton, he spoke without a trace of emotion, as if his soul had been switched off. "We received the call a few days ago. They demanded another partisan or they would come in and kill us all. They promised to return Viktor in exchange for a volunteer and some information."

"And you just let Raziel go?" I could not believe it. "You thought for even a moment that Raziel volunteering himself would give you anything at all? You believed them?"

The rage boiled in me, my palms now itched to throw a spell

at Levin's big fat head. Only the thought that Raziel would not want me to do it stayed my hand.

"Raziel wanted to go," Chana said. Now she was crying too. "He said it would buy us some time."

Oh, Raziel. So brave, so willing to believe the best of people. For his sake, I scanned Levin again instead of denouncing him as a traitor.

No, he was not a collaborator, nor a Nazi spy. He desperately wanted the Germans out of Poland.

But the Russians . . .

"What do you know about the Soviets, Levin?" I said, my voice a half whisper. "What are they doing with their psychotronics, their science of magic?"

He startled, his lips moved, but no sound came out.

"Come, Levin, I put no spell on you," I said, my voice louder now. "Spit it out. The Soviets, the north. What do you know?"

Tears began to spill down Levin's rounded, red face. "The Russians, they have a technology, from the Institute for Brain Research . . ." But he stopped himself.

"The Russians are our enemy, too," I whispered.

Waves of grief poured from Levin; I could sense the Soviet-Nazi pact was more than he could bear. "You must choose, Levin. Your ideology or your people."

Chana's voice was soft but implacable. "We can trust Levin. Like we trust you. I've known Levin all my life. He is Jewish too, you know."

She paused. "We have known him longer than you, Magda. And yesterday the Nazis called again. What can we do? We can't leave the children behind."

Chana's soft words were like water wearing away stone. I could not deny the partisans' impossible position. It was only a matter of time until we were scattered or killed.

I trembled with the effort of restraining my magic. "Surrender me, then. I will do as Raziel did. Buy time, so you can get away."

I waved away their protestations. They could help me no more, and Levin was a broken man. If I was going to save Raziel, I was going to have to do it myself, somehow. Even if it meant destroying the Gestapo headquarters from within.

I went alone, in broad daylight, to surrender myself to the German authorities. As in a nightmare, the gray, squat building loomed huge, and I walked through the front door, back into Krueger's place of power.

It was awful. But the look on Krueger's face when he saw me once again gave me no small consolation.

"Yes, it's me," I said. We sat in his airless office, and Chana had absurdly insisted on a fresh dress before they sent me over, so I looked, if anything, better than a few days before. My throat by now had healed.

Krueger's eyes bulged from their sockets, exactly as Hans Frank's had the afternoon I killed him. He scrubbed at his mouth with his knuckles. "It is not possible."

"And yet I am here. Do I terrify, my dear Herr Krueger?" I could not help but laugh.

I expected horrible torments to result from my cheekiness, but Krueger looked distracted, sickly, defeated, as if he had been injected with some obscure but cunning poison. He seemed to have lost his appetite for torture.

Krueger only sent me back into my dungeon with hardly a word, and I spent a long night whispering into the pipe. No answer. I sent to Raziel, but I could no longer find him.

That long night of isolation brought me closer to the breaking point than anything else that Krueger had done. My traitor mind insisted that Raziel had been tortured to death. And all they would have to do was show me his broken body and I would unleash Asmodel and break my promise to Gisele. I would take all of them with me to the next world, and Asmodel himself I would compel to torment Raziel's killers for all eternity.

It would make me a greater monster than Krueger. But I didn't care.

After I endured an eternity of self-inflicted torment, daylight broke. There was no window in my cell, but I could sense the sun, much in the way that vampires do.

It was only then that I remembered to pray. I asked for forgiveness, I asked for strength, and I asked for courage. And finally, I asked the angel Albion directly to intercede for Raziel, no matter where he now was.

I expected some kind of answer to my prayers. But I was completely unprepared for the reply I received by the end of this crucible of a day.

A different man retrieved me from the cell that afternoon. He was a member of the Gestapo, but very young, and visibly afraid of me. He opened the huge metal door and swung it open on its creaky hinges, and said not a word.

He motioned for me to follow and I did, marveling that he did not tie my hands, or brandish a gun in my face. As we ascended through the snaking hallways to the chief's office, I considered making a break for it, but I could feel the foul wards still reaching through the walls and wires of the place. If I ran without spell-casting I would be shot dead before taking a dozen steps.

My Gestapo escort pointed me to Krueger's by now familiar office door. He rapped hard twice, and Krueger called out something muffled and unintelligible in reply. The young man reached for the doorknob and pushed the door open.

Krueger sat as usual behind his squat, ugly desk. The burned-up Nazi flag was gone. And the man sitting in the leather chair opposite Krueger's desk was none other than my employer, the notorious vampire Gabor Bathory. The last I had heard of him, the other Budapest vampires had abandoned him for dead, a traitor to the Nazi cause.

And beside him, bruised and bloody, sat Raziel himself. I was struck speechless.

"Dear little Baroness Bathory," Bathory said, acid in his voice. I shot Raziel a quick glance, amazed to see him alive, and it took everything I had left to maintain my composure without letting the mask drop from my face.

I thought fast. "Uncle Gabor!" I exclaimed. I did not miss a beat. My voice sounded squeaky and unsteady, but hopefully Krueger would attribute all that to a baroness's shock at being unjustly imprisoned. "I hope you explained to them who I am! Who I *certainly* am."

Somehow, my original, flimsy ruse had carried the day. A tiny smile played over the vampire's thin curved lips. His melancholy, bloodshot eyes looked up at me, and I recklessly met the vampire's gaze.

"Why yes, my little chicken. I explained to the nice gentleman here how impertinent it is of you to call yourself a baroness. I am most certainly not expired, and you have not acquired the honorific by either inheritance or marriage. You are a scandal, Erszebet. A scandal."

He arched a sardonic eyebrow, and it was all I could do not to applaud his bravura performance. I tried to look abashed and embarrassed. "Forgive me, Uncle. I'm always getting into scrapes."

He shrugged eloquently and gazed at Krueger. "The follies of youth will make you wise, my dear."

He and I spoke Hungarian, and the police chief allowed it, studying our faces to see if we did, in fact, know each other.

I heard a low murmur behind me, and I half turned. A skinny man with a droopy mustache repeated our words in German to Krueger, and he nodded and scratched at his chin. "Have you no papers?" he said to me again, without shaking me or screaming this time.

I shrugged. "I was a Romanian national until recently. Now our estates will become Hungarian again. I am not accustomed to explaining myself to anyone other than my uncle, who is my benefactor and guardian."

"Why are you in Kraków?"

I shot Bathory a glance. "I am sorry, Uncle. It was a boy." I paused and looked at Raziel again, my heart full to bursting. "This boy."

He smacked the flat of his hand on the top of the desk, and I jumped. "Not again, Erszebet! I will chain you to the ankle of the Mother Superior if you will not mind me!"

I bit my lip and glared at the ground. "I am not a child, Uncle."

"This is the prince, I presume."

"Why, yes. He flew me in his private plane, Uncle. We were off to Italy next, but then the Germans came to town. I was delighted, delighted!"

My fake smile curdled when I saw the look on Krueger's face. He did not for a minute believe I was a renegade baroness; for some reason he was forced to accept this absurd fairy tale as true.

I looked over to see that Bathory's face was now even whiter than usual, from the effort of our charade. "What has become of your dashing prince, with his private plane?"

I swallowed hard, glanced again at the silent form of my beloved, and I remembered my final sight of Antonio, ripped apart by Asmodel's depredations.

But I spoke of Raziel. "My prince has taken a terrible fall. And all because of me." I did not have to fake the lump in my throat, or the tears welling in my eyes.

"Well, I suppose you will come home with me, little chicken. Perhaps you have finally learned to listen. And we will return the prince to his people as well."

I dashed the tears from my eyes. "I am a little fool, Uncle." In this at least, I earnestly spoke the truth.

The three of us turned to face Krueger, who shifted uncomfortably in his chair. We all stared at one another for a while, and I was amazed that of the four of us, it was Krueger who looked most uncomfortable and eager to see our confrontation at an end.

"Are they free to leave, Herr Chief?" Bathory finally asked in German.

"Preliminary reports are that Governor Frank died of . . .

well, appears to have died of natural causes. Bad luck for you, Baroness, to have met him as he died."

"Please, Baroness Bathory no more," Bathory said, with a hint of severity in his voice. "Through her mother's line, not mine." He sighed, evidently impatient with the ignorance of commoners such as the police chief.

"I would detain you regardless," Krueger said, the edge of something nasty creeping into his voice. "But it seems that I am to become governor-general in Hans Frank's place."

Ah, my murder of his predecessor had directly benefited him. Surely he would not want to uncover evidence of foul play in Frank's death, lest he be viewed as a potential suspect. That was how widely known their mutual hatred was, in Kraków.

But his hard, expressionless face revealed no insecurities. "I have no more reason to detain you, fräulein. Your uncle has come to vouch for you—come all the way from Berlin." He studied my face for any signs of shock or surprise, but I would not oblige him. "It appears he has a privileged position with the Nazi Party. Your uncle's papers are impeccable. So is his reputation."

I had nothing to say, only numbly wobbled on my feet.

After a short pause, he swung the door open again. "You are free to leave. But, miss . . ."

He blocked the doorway with his body. I gulped hard. "Yes?"

He was silent for a moment, and then said, "I detest the game of chess, for a number of reasons. I want you out of Kraków immediately. Back to Hungary with you, with no more nonsense."

I tried for a watery smile. "Now you sound like my uncle, Herr Governor."

He did not return the smile. "Go. Before I change my mind."

Bathory jammed an enormous straw hat on his head, drew

his hunting jacket close to his neck, and brandished an enor-mous umbrella furled in his sunburned right hand. "Let us go, children," he muttered, his voice finally sounding fully ag-grieved. "And we will do our best to forget your crazy escapade, yes?"

"Of course, Uncle," I murmured, and I linked my arm in his. Arm in arm, the three of us left that horrible, evil place, and swept into the street, where a car was waiting.

Even though Bathory had opened the umbrella to shield him-self from the late afternoon sun, he hissed in pain. I bundled him into the back of the Mercedes and blocked him from the slanting rays of sunlight filtering in through the back windows.

It was Janos in the driver's seat. "Go," I whispered urgently, and he sped off with a screech of tires over the cobblestones.

✳ 19 ✳

Despite my best efforts to cover up Bathory with the blankets in the backseat, his face and hands got terribly burned by the sunlight.

"You saved my life," I said as we sped along, to distract him from his burned cheeks and knuckles. "And Raziel's life."

"For you at least, that is no big deal," he replied with a low chuckle.

I gaped at him in wonder. "My dear count, how did you get to Kraków to save me at all?"

"Never mind for the moment." His attention turned to Raziel. "Sir, do you need a doctor?"

"No," Raziel said, his voice faint and faraway. "Only rest."

I had much to say to Raziel, things I'd never thought I would get to say to him in this world. But I could not say them yet, not in front of Bathory. So I only squeezed one of his hands between my own. The touch of his fingers on mine was a more eloquent testament to life than anything I could have said.

In any case, before I had the luxury of being alone with Raziel again I had to talk business with my former employer. I leaned back, contemplated the dove gray felted ceiling of the enormous Mercedes. "Take us to the Cyganeria Café, Janos. On Szpitalna Street, with the arched doorway. Do you know the place?"

The driver nodded and sped up even as Raziel protested. "You must be joking," he said, and I knew why. The Cyganeria was the local Nazi hangout.

"Hear me out, darling. I am starving, famished. I am sure Bathory will not stay here, and I have much I have to say to him. Janos will drop us there and park in the back, like Viktor did for the Literary."

Raziel groaned, rolled his eyes heavenward. "And that worked out so wonderfully last time."

I turned to Bathory. "Do vampires have their own special café here, like the Istanbul in Budapest? We could meet there instead."

Bathory delicately picked at the skin that was starting to peel off the backs of his hands. "No, my dear. Poland is a devout country, and the vampires here are few and live underground, the wretches. Most of them live in Warsaw, but they are a quiet lot, and keep themselves hidden. This Nazi café should be fine for our purposes."

Janos unerringly navigated the winding cobblestone streets through the city's center, and eventually pulled up in front of the Cyganeria Café. With a great flourish he opened the back door so Bathory and I could emerge. Even in the dusk, the punishing sun beat down on Bathory and I hurried him over the threshold.

Raziel, exhausted nearly to death, waited for us in the car, where Janos remained, ready to speed away in case of trouble. The fact that Raziel allowed me to convince him to rest filled me with a terrible foreboding. What had Krueger done to him?

The Cyganeria depressed me even more. There was not a magical to be seen, and the place was stuffed full of Nazis and their opportunistic Polish girlfriends. My German and Bathory's indelible elegance made up for his sunburn and my disheveled state. The surly waiter put us at a tiny table hidden in an alcove. We would speak Hungarian and the veiled truth, here in the belly of the Nazi beast.

Bathory ordered coffee and prune cake in his impeccable formal German, and we were left alone. I feasted my eyes upon him, my beloved employer, who I had feared was finished.

"You've returned from the afterworld like a Lazarus," I said, and I could not keep the tremor out of my voice.

"Not quite. In the end, they did not in fact stake me."

The coffee arrived, and Bathory put in his three lumps of sugar, while I left my coffee by my elbow. In this crowded day, full of death and miracles, Bathory's reemergence stood head and shoulders above all the rest of it.

"How did you get away? The last I had heard, you were condemned by the Vampirrat."

Bathory looked up from his coffee, his sad-looking eyes taking on a predatory aspect. "Yes, I have my enemies among the MittelEuropa Vampirrat. But they were overruled."

"Overruled? But by whom? How?"

He smiled then, careful to keep his fangs covered by his lips.

"The Nazi High Command itself requested, quite pointedly, that they set me free. They in fact claimed me for one of their own."

His answer dumbfounded me. "The Nazis? But you were hauled into the council for treason to the Reich. Are you sure?"

"To a certainty, little chicken. The Arrow Cross in Budapest urgently demanded my release." He smiled again, knowing the effect his words would have on me.

"The Arrow Cross!" I could not believe it. The Arrow Cross was the dominant Fascist party in Hungary, and in their viciousness and anti-Semitism almost outdid even their big brothers in the Reich. They were no friends of Bathory.

Bathory's lips twitched under his Magyar mustache, and he took a long, foamy sip of hot coffee. I reached for mine, and slugged it down black, hardly tasting the metallic bitterness as the coffee burned my tongue.

He returned his coffee cup to the saucer with exaggerated precision. "Why yes, the Arrow Cross. Martin Szalasi is a turned werewolf, and his girlfriend alerted them all to the miscarriage of justice taking place in Berlin. With the correct application of cash, the proper parties were mollified and I was free to fly—here to Kraków directly, in order to save a certain reckless employee of mine."

My head swam with the news. "Martin Szalasi is a mad dog, not even a werewolf."

"True, but he seeks to curry favor with the Nazis in Germany. And all the money he offered the Arrow Cross raised his standing quite a bit."

"It was the girlfriend?"

"Yes. She was the one who convinced Martin I was worth saving. A great asset to his country and all of that. His girlfriend apparently is a great admirer of mine from the north country. A lovely young Hungarian patriot named Eva Farkas."

I all but fell out of my chair. Now I understood what Gisele had hinted at in Viktor's office, about Eva becoming a spy. "Eva plays a dangerous game," I finally managed to squeak out. I had always pointed out to her that her blond, blue-eyed self could melt into the Christian world and simply disappear. Now, it seemed she had taken my observation to heart, but had resolved to do much more than vanish.

"Dangerous game, yes, but Eva is a brilliant player." He leaned forward and lowered his voice still more. "Eva worked as a courier for me, as you know. But her talents were too fine to waste in simply delivering messages. She is deep undercover with the Arrow Cross, working for the Zionists and for me, too. All of us play a dangerous game, little chicken."

Bathory's eyes twinkled as he drank his coffee and stared at me. "The money came from Knox, by the way. I understand that this money came with strings, and I am happy for him to pull them. You are here with Churchill's sanction. Well, so am I."

Now my worry swung from Bathory to Raziel to Eva, like a compass that had lost its true north. Eva had placed herself in a ridiculous amount of danger, becoming the decorative flower of a vicious beast like Martin Szalasi. Being a turned werewolf was the least of the trouble with him; the Arrow Cross were crazed, mindless killers.

"Fear not, dear heart," Bathory said. "Eva saved me, I will save her in turn, though she is so resourceful I do not think she will need me to intervene. I fly for Budapest tonight." He poked at the prune cake with a fork. "This stuff is downright shriveled. Here, have some if you wish."

Even famished as I was, my mouth was too dry to swallow it. "You will watch over Eva? Swear to me?"

"More than that, little chicken. I will watch over all her in-numerable babies." That last made me gasp: he knew every-thing, even down to the network we had arranged to spirit the children out of Poland.

"Bless you, my darling count."

"Not so fast. I would be remiss, my dear, if I did not inquire into your own circumstances." His expression grew shrewd, and I busied myself with my napkin, wiping at my mouth and suddenly intensely conscious of my unwashed state, unbrushed hair, and my chewed-off, disreputable-looking fingernails.

He leaned forward, gathered my bare fingers into his bony, nimble hands. "What are you doing here at all, my dear? Anto-nio is dead. Apparently *The Book of Raziel* is useless without a wizard to wield it—and you have neutralized both wizard and demon."

My mind reeled under the onslaught of his questions. The last thing I wanted was to face the answers. Instead, I dwelt on the dangers Eva faced in Budapest. "You must get Eva out of Hungary altogether. She is in terrible danger."

"She is using her talents in the most profitable way. Are you?"

With a gentle squeeze, Bathory released my fingers, and I leaned back, filled with doubts I could not conquer.

"The situation here is dire, Count," I said under my breath. I took a furtive glance around, but the hearty Germans, and the jolly looking Polish girls with their terrified eyes, were too busy trying to impress each other to notice the messy Hungarian girl and her sickly looking uncle in the alcove.

"It is dangerous everywhere, my dear," he agreed. "However,

Budapest is your native place, where you speak the language, can readily identify your friends and foes, and where you can do a great deal of good. But here?"

He arched an eyebrow and shrugged his narrow, bony shoulders. "What are you doing here?"

"Do you not feel the pull of your kiss?" I asked with some surprise. "Gisele is here. Did you not know? I could not let her throw herself into the volcano like some kind of virgin sacrifice. And I bade farewell to the governor-general a few days ago. That is certainly something."

He tried to meet my gaze, but this time I avoided looking into his eyes. I was immune to his vampire's thrall, but I had a harder time resisting the lure of his common sense. I had argued the same to Gisele not that long ago.

"Little chicken," he murmured, "that sadistic swine from the Gestapo will be replacing Frank. If anything, he will be more decisive and vicious than the man who . . . died."

Even in our relative invisibility, Bathory was not willing to say aloud what he understood was true: I had killed Hans Frank myself. "If you and your comrades claim this as a victory, they will deny it and still come after you. If you don't, well, what difference at all have you made, really."

Miserable, I shut my eyes and swallowed hard. But the truth stuck like a thorn in my throat.

I forced myself to open my eyes and look straight at Bathory, with the direct gaze he almost never had to confront. "Dear Count," I said, "We are going to lose, no matter what we do: we have no tanks, we have no artillery. I can raise an army of the dead, of demons, but what is our military objective? What can we count as a victory?

"We've already lost the battle here. But if we crush Hitler in Warsaw, we will win the war."

Bathory laughed aloud, a sound I ordinarily loved but which now cut me like broken glass. "I used to worry you would play your talents too small, my dear. I will no longer count that as a concern of mine."

He stroked his whiskers with the tips of his fingers. "From what I understand, without *The Book of Raziel*, your powers will only extend so far, yes?"

I nodded, impressed by his command of the facts. "I have no time to hunt for the Book. The original does still exist but I have not found it. The Nazis have the one re-created by the wizard Staff, and I fear they will learn to bend it to serve their purposes. I must fight with the weapons I already have. You know well, perfection is not of this world."

"You may fight a supernatural war, my dear. But in the end, the werewolves will prove your match."

"The Polish Army is quite valiant. And they fight to save their country."

"They are valiant, yes, but they are also crazy and suicidal. They would do better to flee like cowards and live to see another day, a winnable battle. So would you."

His unspoken rebuke—that I too was crazy and suicidal—hung in the air between us, a silent specter I chose to ignore. "I have done all I can in Kraków. I am going to press forward to Warsaw now, and fight with the Polish Home Army."

"You are assuming they want you and your talents and your comrades, my dear. All indications are that they do not."

It was true: early reports indicated the Home Army had violently rejected overtures by the socialist Zionists, by the local

earth spirits, and by the magicals among the Gypsies. They
wanted to fight an honorable war, soldier against soldier. Bathory was right: the officers, many of them, were crazy, glory-
seeking fools.

"I understand their fear of us," I said. "For all our grand
proclamations of solidarity, we could be Communists or even
Nazi spies, for all they know."

Bathory drained the last of his coffee. "This café wearies me.
It looks dark enough outside—time for me to say farewell, my
little star. I implore you to return to Budapest, where you are
wanted. I fly for Budapest this very night."

"Beware the Budapest Vampirrat," I warned him.

"The Vampirrat should beware of me. And of my loyal lieutenant, the renowned witch Magdalena Lazarus."

We were a formidable duo; Bathory was right. But I still had
my own fate to follow. "I cannot foretell when or if I will return
to resume my service, sir. Gisele would be the one for making
that prediction. But I kiss your hands for all that you have done,
for saving Raziel, most of all."

He stared at me long and low, and I was shocked to see the
old vampire overcome with emotion. In his own way, Bathory
was no less an idealistic fool than the Poles. Despite the rise of
the horrible Arrow Cross, despite the more genteel Fascism of
our own dear leader, Miklós Horthy, Bathory still believed with
every fiber of his being in the singular greatness of the Magyar
people, of the nation-state of Hungary. And he was willing to
ignore a great deal of ugliness in order to keep believing.

All of us believed in something or other. It was better for my
purposes that Bathory maintain his illusions. "I miss Budapest
desperately," I said, and at least in this I told only the truth. But

the Budapest I loved was already gone forever. "I must make my stand here, regardless. Please believe me, Count. Our battle is still the same."

He sighed and bent to kiss my hand in farewell. "You would be the queen of my kingdom if only you would accept your place. I fly for Budapest, little chicken. May your Grandmama Witch watch over you and keep you."

He rose, bowed formally to me, as a young courtier would have bowed to Empress Maria Teresa, and he bent to kiss my fingers once more. And then my dear Count Bathory disappeared into the night to face his enemies in Budapest.

Janos dropped Raziel and me at the edge of town and sped away with not a word of farewell. Without Viktor's lorry, it was a short walk to the Wieliczka salt mine about ten kilometers east of Kraków, in the village of Wieliczka. Raziel himself had been told by the other partisans how to find it, since it was the final place of haven. A Catholic priest and hundreds of miners had barricaded themselves inside, the partisans said, and it was my hope that Gisele had made her way there.

Raziel and I stood together in the starry night before we started walking. Despite the bruises and the weariness in Raziel's eyes, he had never looked so beautiful. There was so much to say, it didn't make sense to even try to say it.

As we walked, the locket burned. My skin had developed a little locket-shaped brown patch over my heart, where the locket rested and Asmodel still struggled. Long after midnight, when we had stopped for the night to rest and hide, I caught

Raziel staring at the locket, and he moved it aside to kiss the burned place and to fall asleep with his lips resting on that spot above my heart.

I couldn't yet bear to ask him what had happened in Krueger's prison, not if he did not want to tell me. Both of us were in silent agreement to instead celebrate the fact we both miraculously still walked the earth. Hidden in shadows, we kissed and kissed until we fell into exhausted sleep. And we woke before dawn and rested in each other's arms before setting off.

We traveled by day, dangerous as that was, because Raziel and I feared the creatures of the night still more. Werewolves now roamed the countryside of Poland without restriction; the silver bullets the farmers kept in reserve were too precious to shoot, and the Nazi authorities encouraged the lycanthropes to attack.

I had once seen Raziel kill over a dozen wolves as an angel, using nothing more than the words of the Almighty. But now, angel no more, Raziel watched over me with his wits alone. And may God help me, I loved him even more this way.

I feared for him still. Men die. But Raziel himself felt no fear now. I knew that not because he told me—we barely spoke on our way to Wieliczka—but because he slept so well that final night, blissfully pressed against my body, his skin warm and scratchy, his body smelling of pine needles, musk, and cinnamon.

I did not want the journey to end, but it did. We made it to the salt mine. And there our troubles truly began.

✳ 20 ✳

The entrance to the mine looked nothing like I had even vaguely expected. I imagined rough, rustic caves off in the wilderness somewhere, but we found the entrance to the Wieliczka salt mines framed by a large curved gate leading to a trim factory building with a huge double door facing a parking lot. The place looked closed, though the metal gate to the front drive stood ajar. The first indication of trouble was this openness, the lack of posted sentries.

I made straight for the front entrance, but Raziel held me back. "No, you'll be dead before you make it to the door," he said.

Instead we crawled through the underbrush to the edge of the parking lot and watched. Weird little fairy lights danced at the threshold of the mines, like blue fireflies.

"The earth spirits are guarding the door, do you see?" Raziel said. "They've taken a side, the miners' side, and they are guarding their hiding place."

Things had gotten desperate indeed if the ancient spirits of the mine had taken notice. Usually they ignored the furious buzzing of human affairs, knowing that things usually weren't as bad as they seemed in the short term and even the worst things soon faded away.

I sent my witch's sight to find them, and I saw them now, outlined in blue, blind-looking women with long straight hair and interlocking arms blocking the way into the mine. Salt is a natural barrier to magicals, one of the reasons the Poles had chosen this place to hide, but these ancient ladies came up from the veins of the earth intermixed with the salt, and they were as lean and tough as hounds. Their magic was older than mine, and it rose up from the very earth we stood upon. I could not defeat them, and I did not want to; I only wanted to identify Raziel and me as their allies.

So I plucked at their airy souls like harp strings, gently, so they vibrated, careful not to cause even the slightest pain. "Sh'ma," I called softly, birdsong at morning, quietly as I could. "Sh'ma!"

I saw the spirit in the center turn. Her face grew stern; I did not know her language and she did not bother making much of a distinction among human beings. All she cared about was that her humans were locked inside and the enemies outside the threshold had to be stopped. From four they became six, then seven, then a dozen, and their thin, translucent bodies pressed together to block the door.

Earth magic, ancient and low-lying, was alien and hostile to mine, which was based in fire. Raziel had no magic in him at all, but apparently the fire that blazed within the Hebrew words profoundly troubled these earth spirits.

The ground itself began to crumble. Quickly I sent to my sister, called to her, soul to soul. I could not send words to Gisele through that earthen barrier, but I could play upon her soul like a heartstring, and I prayed she would recognize that touch as mine.

Before I could know for sure, the earth spirits, enraged, rushed us en masse. I threw a ward of protection between us, made it visible, flashing with fire so that they were forewarned.

They veered away, and a shower of sparks rose between us as their magic clashed against mine. I held my palms out to strengthen my intention, put my energy into the wall I had hastily constructed.

I could not speak to these ancient spirits, could not explain we were allies. My wards could not withstand the overwhelming force of their massed assault, but there was nowhere for Raziel and me to retreat.

Cracks appeared in the asphalt of the parking lot under our feet. A blue-lit hand reached up and grabbed Raziel around the ankle.

I blasted witchfire down the crack, but Raziel grunted in pain and I knew I was too late. Raziel tried to yank his leg away, but even his tremendous strength was not enough to dislodge the hand.

I drew closer and he grabbed me around the waist. I began to recite the Ninety-first Psalm—Yankel had taught it to me in Hebrew. Raziel said it with me, and the words sent down a shower of sparks.

The first hand disappeared, but a fresh one shot out to take its place. The ground trembled beneath us, so strongly that I almost lost my balance.

The door behind the spirits swung open and Gisele, thank goodness, ran between them, her face glowing in the fading light. She reached through my wards—there was nothing that could keep my little sister away from me—and threw her arms around me and Raziel.

With a clap of blue lightning the earth spirits withdrew and disappeared. The three of us stood outside the slightly open door, and I dropped my aching arms around her chubby shoulders and squeezed.

"Come—quick!" she said, her husky little voice a restorative potion. She pulled us through the door and slammed it behind us.

I had not expected the mines to be so cold. We descended a creaky wooden stairway that spiraled down, down, down into the damp veins of salt. Hundreds of steps, and we ran all the way down. Most of the mine was illuminated, but we passed through a long, dark corridor before we stopped in a lighted alcove to take a breath.

We had no time for a tender family reunion.

"It's been terrible," she said, and it was so cold I could see the plume of her breath. "Governor-General Krueger has decided to make an example of us. Instead of sending the regular army, he keeps sending the wolves."

"How can they get in? The earth spirits guard you."

"We are under siege here. It is good you came when you did.

Soldiers patrol for mortals at dawn and the wolves come by night. The farmers have tried to bring us food but they cannot get close to us . . . the ones who've tried were murdered right outside so we could see."

"A siege can last a long time, regardless," I began. But then I saw the desolation on Gisele's face.

"You do not know," she whispered.

My heart began to pound against my ribs. "Tell me."

"Warsaw has fallen. The Soviets have invaded on the side of the Nazis. Hitler and Stalin have carved up Poland. We are not much more than grass trampled under their feet now."

I thought of Levin. "Where are the Hashomer? The other partisans?" I asked.

Gisele looked away and sighed. "Most of them are here. But Levin is dead. He killed himself after we got the news about the Russians."

No wonder the secret knowledge had torn him apart. Levin was a Communist, but he was also a Pole.

We had no time to mourn his death. "All is not lost. It cannot be," I said. My heart pounded louder. "Thousands of children got smuggled out of here, into Budapest. That is not nothing!"

"But we are still too late."

"Not for them!" I had never seen my sister so bitter.

Gisele's laugh shattered like salt crystals under our feet. "You think the werewolves hunting us like rabbits care about Hitler? You think the demon cares about who he uses to accomplish his ends?"

She closed in on me, grabbed me by my shoulders. And my sweet little mouse roared in my face like a lion. "My nightmares have invaded the world."

I swallowed again, gasped for air. "Defeat is not my problem, little star."

Gisele's eyes filled again with tears, and she didn't look away, even as the tears spilled onto her cheeks. "Then what? What do we do?"

"I look into the abyss and don't look away. You do, too, my darling. I see that our cause is lost, the war is lost. The only weapon I have left is hanging trapped around my neck."

A gentle, reproving voice rose from behind us. "Oy, children, stop fighting."

With Yankel's words, despair's spell was broken. I turned, and saw that the little potbellied watchmaker held his arms out wide. And like a child I hurled myself into his embrace and held him close.

I cried then, I will confess. But crying was too much of a luxury, as big an indulgence as despair. Grief was a peacetime diversion, and we had to put our despair away until the war was over.

I told them about Hans Frank and the prison, I told them everything. Raziel said nothing, but I had never seen his expression so grim. When I was done, we stood together in the sudden cold silence.

"Give Asmodel to Yankel," Raziel said. "The demon is too great a temptation. And Yankel can master him and use him against the Nazis. It is time to try."

The human weakness in Raziel's voice cut me like a razor blade. Raziel's spirit was steady, but his exhausted body held pain.

"You're right, my darling. His wickedness calls to mine." I unclasped the chain and passed it to the old man I trusted like a second father.

His eyebrows bunched together as he contemplated the little, dented old locket resting in his palm. "Poor, tormented soul," he said. I wasn't sure if he meant Asmodel or me.

He looked up at Raziel. "His very presence is like a stab in the heart, *nu*?" He said it in Hebrew first, and then in Yiddish so I could understand.

"Don't trouble yourself," Yankel said to me. "You are a special torment to Asmodel, such a nice, pretty, smart girl. But I can't forget where you come from, *mamele*. You've been strong. But you have the dark magic in you that the demon wants. I'll keep him. Don't worry, you did good."

The locket disappeared into Yankel's vest pocket, and I sighed with relief. "Good-bye albatross," I said in Hungarian, and Gisele, despite her sadness and despair, laughed, a haunting sound like chimes.

Yankel turned to Raziel and spoke with him in Hebrew for a good five minutes. I wiped at my eyes and tried my best not to care that I couldn't understand them.

At the end of his torrent of words, Yankel turned to me with a crooked little smile on his face. "*Mamele*, you don't need a demon watching over you. You got your big man here, Raziel HaMelech. I will take the cursed one off your hands. I need to talk to the priest about this locket now, so we don't have any misunderstandings. We've had enough *tsouris* here without the adversary coming between us."

Before I could ask him to tell me more about the priest, he leaned in, kissed me between the eyebrows. "I bless you that you stay as good as Sarah and Leah, woman of valor. I go speak with Jan now." And Yankel winked and shuffled out of the room into the labyrinth of salt.

We watched them go, and I all but sank to the ground in weariness.

"Let's get you fed and bundled up before you go off and die again, Magduska!"

I looked at Gisele. "Food? But I thought you—"

"We are under siege, but we are not done yet." She reached up and squeezed my shoulder. "Poor sister, tempted by that awful demon. I don't know how you found the strength to keep that locket closed."

Raziel, Gisele, and I ate some bread and water in a mess hall carved out of salt. The walls, the floor, even the benches were carved out of gray, translucent blocks; the effect was quite modern, as if we dined in a cafeteria of the future made of some unknown, futuristic material.

The mess hall was full. Miners, mostly, but also ground trolls, dwarves, Gypsies, and regular families that had fled here for shelter.

"Kraków has gone back to normal, we hear, as if the war had never happened," Gisele said. And I knew what she meant. Most people wanted to live their lives in peace, and they went through the wildest contortions to keep everything in their lives in place, as much as they possibly could.

To do that, people like Gisele and me and the other people who hid in the salt mine had to become invisible. For to acknowledge the presence of hundreds of countrymen, trapped in the mine and slated for extermination by the conquerors of the city, would be to acknowledge their own normalcy as a faint, fading myth.

"Who leads these people?"

"The priest. He is a powerful Catholic priest, and he is

determined to stop the Nazi sorcerers. But he is a Catholic. Not all Catholics hate magic, but this priest does." Gisele leaned forward and whispered. "You can imagine what he thinks of the trolls and the Gypsies. He doesn't like us, so we try to stay out of his way. He dislikes the magicals far more than the Jews. He's been protecting the Jews from some of the miners, in fact, but if it weren't for Yankel, he would have turned us away altogether."

"This priest, he is a fighter?"

"He is old like Yankel, but he is fierce, and plans to defend this place to the death, even with all the women and children inside. Even the magicals. Though he doesn't like us, at least he understands we're on the same side. He knows as well as we do that there is nowhere else to run."

I had not come all this way to come under the dominion of a disapproving priest. I finished my bread and looked over the crowd one last time.

"This is like a prison, a friendly jail," I finally said. "I have no quarrel with the priest, but I am not going to stay penned up in here with the refugee children and learn my martyr catechism like a good little girl. Forget it."

Gisele sighed and shook her head. "I knew you would say something like that. But, my darling, it is terribly dangerous in Kraków, now that Poland is conquered."

I shrugged. "Sitting in this mess hall is worse than death. I did not come to Poland for this."

"That priest needs a witch," Raziel said, startling me. "He may not like it, but without magic, the priest and his people cannot hold out long against a full assault."

"But this particular priest believes my magic is of the devil."

I smiled. "He's right, of course! If I were a good girl, I'd be finishing my knitting on Dohány Street and going to sleep now so that I wouldn't have bags under my eyes in the morning."

Raziel did not relent, or smile. "It doesn't matter what the priest thinks. This is the largest pocket of resistance left in this corner of Poland. It falls upon us to fight."

His brave words warmed me. I looked at Raziel, and the sight of him, still ready to fight despite all that had already happened, gave me strength. "We need to talk to any Hashomer holed up in here. We need to stick together."

But we never got the chance to find the Hashomer.

A wind rustled around our ankles, and the little hairs at the nape of my neck rose in warning. The earth spirits rushed past us to escape something that had made it through the front doors of the mines.

I leapt to my feet, even before the sound of low howls reached, echoing, to my ears. "We're too late," I said, my voice trembling. "They've come for us."

✱ 21 ✱

If only I had had a day to get to know the place better, I might have been able to fight off the werewolves.

But as it was, the mine was a cold, magnificent labyrinth of ballrooms, fairy bowers, chapels, concert halls, and uncarved, curving tunnels of salt. I had time only to grab for Gisele's hand on one side, and Raziel's on the other, before all hell broke loose underground.

Salt had a strange effect on magic. It was poison to certain types of magicals, but it also provided a strong buffer against evil spirits. It did not blunt my magic, but channeled it into the spaces between the veins of salt in the mine. I could penetrate the barrier if I chose, but my magic flowed more easily, almost like water, in the spaces between.

I had lost my hesitation for summoning the dead to my side,

and I called to my mother and my children imps with a barely restrained panic. The killers descending upon us were swifter and more terrible than I had yet encountered in Poland, and considering the nasty specimens I had fought so far, that was a terrifying prospect indeed.

The ghosts rushed through the corridors of salt in a mighty rush, my mother at their head, leaving the air supercharged with lightning in their wake. My mother called upon the ghosts in Hebrew, her voice echoing through the translucent carvings and spires.

But they could not stop the wolves. Raziel let go of my hand and I yanked Gisele behind me just as the pack found us.

I expected Krueger himself, but the first wolf was a stranger to me. The leader's muzzle was wet with blood, and his grayish yellow fangs bristled from out of his hideous snout. He didn't bother saying anything, simply lunged for my throat, and I swatted him away with my wards, knowing they would keep him off of me.

Except this time my wards were useless—perhaps the foul magic emanating from the north had strengthened since Hitler's victory over Warsaw and his pact with the Soviets to divide Poland. The wolf tore through my spell of protection like through a spider's web and smashed into me. I fell backward and crashed to the ground under the wolf's weight.

The wolf sank his teeth into my right forearm, and I summoned his soul out of him with a yell of pain and rage. But his soul would not come. Stubborn, he worried at my arm and shook it like a rag, and my eyesight faded to a static-filled gray.

A huge, deafening gunshot exploded the world. Finally, the wolf's grip slackened. The smoky haze slowly dissipated to reveal his glazing-over yellow eyes, his jaws still locked on my arm.

Gisele had shot the wolf. Raziel jumped on its stiffening back and pried the beast's jaws off my forearm. The creature fell dead onto the floor, the back of its head blasted apart.

I gaped down at its carcass, as amazed by my magical impotence as by the creature's death. Another huge gunshot almost knocked me off my feet: Gisele's gun shot bullets that seemed big enough to dispatch an elephant.

Her screams snapped me back into unearthly focus. The smaller wolves circled her, growling, and my mother and a crowd of spirits sought to harry them.

I grabbed the silver carving knife I had used to cut my bread, and with a spell of augmentation I plunged the blade into the base of the nearest wolf's skull and yanked hard sideways to sever the spinal cord. The wolf fell, twitching, at my feet. With a huge tug I scraped the knife through the vertebrae and free.

Though my own arm was throbbing, I jumped on the back of the next wolf; it turned its long gray head to snap at my weakened arm, missing it by only a few centimeters.

Then Raziel was upon the wolves and with big slashes of the second knife he had grabbed off the table he killed two more. He staggered to the back wall while I grabbed Gisele and blinked at the acrid gunsmoke that burned my eyes.

"Gisi, where are you hurt?"

She kept shaking her head and sobbing, driving me half-frantic. "No, no, no . . . ," she sobbed.

I frisked her all over, looking for wounds. I found none.

"Not me, Magduska," she gasped. "Yankel."

I tucked her under my chin and slammed my eyelids closed. Her heart beat so hard she shook against my chest. I took deep, long breaths to steady my own pulse, and I sent my senses out to Yankel in the subterranean caverns, knowing to the bone that Raziel would protect me while I searched for him.

After only a half-dozen deep breaths, I found him and knew why Gisele had cried out. He had fought valiantly to protect his charges, but he was an old man. And he fought in a place that was fundamentally hostile to what he was, who he had been made to be.

I only realized I had started running when I stumbled and Gisele kept me from falling. Raziel covered us from behind; I could hear his breathing, ragged but still steady. If he was hurt too, it was not badly enough to slow us down.

My mind did not know the way; my feet carried me and I followed the footsteps. I expected the worst, knew my people had lost this battle underground.

My headlong rush checked as I stumbled upon a small mountain of bodies, SS men with their death's-head insignia standing out starkly on their bloodstained collars, dead miners sprawled across the floor, still clutching pickaxes and makeshift bayonets fixed on the ends of broom handles.

I forced my way to the epicenter and began to find the bodies of people I knew, people who had managed to survive the Nazis by seeking shelter with Yankel in the forest.

At the center of the enormous room, Yankel still sat up, propped by the body of a gigantic miner, an ordinary Pole who had died to defend the watchmaker of Kraków.

He gasped for air, his poor body shredded by shrapnel and the fangs of wolves. A mob of dead Nazis and wolves surrounded him. His prayers had held them at bay, but apparently he could not stop them forever.

"Come away," I whispered urgently.

"Too late," he gasped. "Take, Asmodel . . . to the Wolf's Lair," he said. "I could not unleash him in time. You must use him. You will know how. You will do it."

"But—if you—"

"*Mamele*," he said. "Do what you think is right."

He smiled, his face awash in blood. "Bless you, little girl, I am so thirsty," he said, speaking clearly for the first time, as if he had recovered himself. "Get me some water. Go."

I reached for his hands, but Raziel gently interposed himself between us. They spoke together in Hebrew, so softly I could hardly hear them, then Raziel reached out and closed Yankel's eyes with his fingertips.

"He is gone, Magduska. Come."

I heard a great roaring in my ears, and the room faded from red to gray and began to tilt. Raziel caught me before I toppled over.

A wave of nausea broke over me, and he shook me by the shoulders. "Come," he said again, his voice hard, and he pressed something sharp and sticky into my palm.

It was the locket with Asmodel still trapped inside, caked with Yankel's half-dried blood.

✳ 22 ✳

Raziel dragged me from that terrible place into another, an even deeper and colder region of the mine. "Yankel wants us to save the priest," he said, again and again until the words' meaning sunk into my mind.

"Magduska, try," Gisele said, and it was only then that I realized she had followed us all the way into the place of horrors where Yankel had died. "If Yankel wants you to use Asmodel, then do it. We have nothing else left."

That shamed me into recalling myself to life. "The priest will not approve of my methods," I said, and almost succumbed to a bout of crazy laughter. "I think Sir Priest would rather die than have his bacon saved by an ancient demon, wielded by a Jewish sorceress. *Nu?*"

"It doesn't matter," Raziel said, his voice cold and calm, merciless as a steel blade. "We need him. So do it, Magda."

I gave up arguing, being droll, or succumbing to hysteria. I'd try my best, fail, and die for good finally, and all this madness would soon, mercifully, cease. The knowledge of my impending death steeled me, and I cracked open the locket.

The two photographs inside were drenched in blood. I swallowed back the queasy bile in the back of my throat, and muttered to myself in Hungarian. "Okay, you ancient bastard," I said. "You will come to do my bidding, but you obey my rules, stay on my leash."

A rumble rose from the locket. "Asmodel," I said three times, pinning him with his name, "I command you to go forth and slay the slayers of the righteous one Yankel Horowitz the watchmaker. Go forth and kill with great slaughter all the members of the host that rose up against the Lord's own. The minute you are done, go back into this locket and wait. Go—now."

I sang the Bane of Concubines that the witch of Amsterdam had taught me months before, and that was enough to bind the demon while he did what he craved to do anyway. I did not need to follow him with my body; my witch's sight followed Asmodel as he assailed the Nazis and wolves from behind. They had nothing to match his awful power, nothing, and he ripped them limb from limb, dismembered and disemboweled them, killed them and enjoyed it, showing off to me, for he knew that I watched him wielding his powers of destruction.

The priest rose up in the doorway holding a giant crucifix and Asmodel bellowed with laughter. "The Christ has not come to save you today, old man, but Satan!" he roared.

"Shut up!" I ordered, and his voice cut off mid-taunt, but the damage had been done. The priest and his men barricaded themselves behind the door, and the brave old man threw a bottle of holy water straight at the demon's face.

It did nothing to hurt me: my sight was a sending only, and I had nothing to fear from holy water in any case. But vampires are burned by holy water, and demons are burned by it too, like an acid.

Asmodel bellowed in pain and clawed at his eyes with his great, bloodied talons. I yanked him back into the locket and stuffed him back in, felt little sympathy for the creature as he screamed and sobbed inside.

He would murder Nazis to taunt the priest and tempt me with the demonstration of his power, but not to save my beloved teacher from a horrible death. I expected nothing less from him, but his perfidy angered me anyway.

I looked up into Raziel's eyes. "He saved the priest," I said.

"No, you did it," he said, his voice tinged with both admiration and a careful gentleness. "You used the demon and did not get ruined. Yankel was right to trust you."

I shrugged, suddenly weary beyond all caring. "All that murder just strengthened him, Raziel. If I let him out again, I don't believe I will be able to stuff him back inside like I did. The priest doused him with holy water, and that threw Asmodel off guard, but next time I can't expect to be so lucky."

"If you think it will help," he said, "Asmodel can enter into me, take me. If you can control him better that way, I will submit to him."

My stomach turned to water at the thought of it, at the thought of loving Raziel with the demon coiled up inside him like a tapeworm. "No . . . no, my dear angel. That will not do the trick."

His hopeful expression faded, and he sighed. Suddenly I could feel my body again, and my arm hurt horribly.

"Please look at this arm," I said. "Did the wolf do a lot of damage?"

He immediately stretched out my stiffening arm to its full length. "It is not terrible," he said, a little too diplomatically.

I sighed and fought the dizziness that buzzed like mosquitoes in my ears. "The battle is over for now. I guess we won, some kind of victory. Let's go talk to the blasted priest and his men."

I clutched the locket inside my left fist as we limped arm in arm down to where the priest remained holed up with his men. Again, the bodies piled up tremendously near the center of the battle, by the barricaded door.

My mother's ghost waited for us there, her arms crossed. I was too tired to care if she disapproved of me, or if I disappointed her. Strangely enough, my weariness freed me to simply love her, my fearsome and beautiful dead mother.

But Tekla had eyes only for Gisele. "Little fairy!" she exclaimed, and I recalled as she said it that this was her nickname for Gisele. Me, I was "mischief," or "pain in the ass." No matter now. I truly no longer cared that Gisele was her favorite. Gisele was my favorite, too.

Gisele drew close, and I was shocked to see her dry-eyed, my sentimental one. "Thank you, Mama mine, for saving Magduska! Bless you, bless you, may you fly straight to heaven for all your good deeds."

My mother shook her head; it was her lips that trembled, her eyes that sparkled with iridescent tears. "No, no . . . your father is safe in the seventh Heaven, poor man, but I have meddled too much now. I am more a troubled ghost than a spirit at peace, little one."

"Now that Yankel . . ." Gisele fought to keep her composure. "Yankel has passed into the next world—he is a great soul and he will speak for you, I promise, I swear it."

"Hush, don't harm yourself with careless words."

"Good-bye, Mama darling. Bless you, bless you."

They moved closer, opened their arms to embrace . . . and my mother's shade passed through Gisele's body, as insubstantial as a sunbeam, and she disappeared.

I glanced anxiously over at Gisele, but her eyes remained dry. "The way is clear now, don't you see?"

When I didn't answer she turned to me. "It is done. We did our best to stop all this from happening. It was not to be, Magduska darling, but we know we did everything we could. Now we save ourselves and everyone else that we can."

"But how? Why?"

"It's just the right thing to do. And you, brilliant one, clever one, will figure out all of the hows."

Standing ankle deep in dead Nazis I could only marvel at Gisele's folly and at my own. We were walking dead. Our rewards were not in the victory but in the battle itself.

I willed myself to ignore the carnage the demon had caused, and focused on the doorway in front of me. "I am not afraid to die," I said as I pressed forward to rap on the priest's barricaded door. "I am just afraid of losing you, too."

"We have lost already, Magduska. Nobody can take our defeat away from us. It gives us a strange kind of strength, to lose. Do you see it now?"

I sighed and held my shredded arm to my side. "I suppose that I do. The minute we decided to defy our killers, we won." That was Gisele's position, but I did not share it.

The priest let us in the door for Yankel's sake—he and his men still didn't like or trust us, but at least he respected us. He understood I had saved them, if his men did not. Upon his orders, they bandaged my wounds, washed us and gave us clean, new clothes, and gave us a small but deeply appreciated meal.

As before, I admired the man's unflinching position; it was so easy to live in a world of bright lines, of clear demarcation between right and wrong, good and evil. I envied that simple, righteous priest. The martyr, the great Jan Czajkowski . . . may he rest in peace in the Christian Heaven until the trumpet sounds.

"Now, you foreigners must leave," the priest declared. "Poles must fight here for Poland. May you go in the light of the Lord."

✳ 23 ✳

We traveled under cover of darkness until we reached Yankel's hut in the forest. A fallen angel; two lost Hungarian girls; and a primordial demon powerful enough to destroy all of Poland, trapped inside a cheap, dented locket.

By the time we got there, Gisele was stumbling with weariness. She vociferously insisted we all share the little cot, but she was asleep by the time her body became horizontal.

I took off my too-big miner's jacket and draped it over her exhausted, slumbering body. "Our work is not yet finished, my love," I said to Raziel, my voice little more than a weary croak.

"We must deal with Asmodel tonight? Are you certain?"

"I don't have the strength to hold him anymore, my love. Already his call is defeating me."

And it was true: his plaintive wails, blandishments, and

threats drowned out all the sounds of the night, the thread of my own thoughts, Raziel's words. Like a ringing in the ears, I could not block out the sound of Asmodel's beseeching voice. The tremendous pull now, to the north.

"It must end tonight, Raziel."

We stumbled outside the hut and closed the door. I whispered some basic wards, and Yankel's calm spirit had left a residue of peace and protection over the place. We let Gisele rest and slowly wandered to our old, moss-covered spot by the little brook.

The late September air was noticeably colder now. I took a grim satisfaction in noting that fact, in grasping the knowledge that Raziel and I still lived, that we still could fight our enemies another day.

I thought of poor Yankel, and Chana too, surely dead by now—I hoped Chana had had enough time to remember her Sh'ma. I sat down at the edge of the stream. The moonlight, cold and clear, danced upon the surface of the water, beautiful and untouchable.

"It can wait until tomorrow," Raziel said.

"No, it cannot, my love," I replied. "Every moment I wait, Asmodel gains the upper hand. He knows I need him. He knows I am not strong enough to prevail without him. He knows I want my lost Book, that he is the only other thing that comes close to it. And he knows that without *The Book of Raziel*, I am doomed, you are doomed, Gisele . . ."

My voice trailed off, and I sat and watched the water dancing over the stones.

"My poor girl," Raziel said. He sat down next to me and took my right hand into his lap; my left hand, my stronger, uninjured arm, kept custody of Asmodel wrapped inside the ball of my fist.

Raziel's simple kindness disarmed me, but I would not surrender to it. "No, this is the path I chose, and this is where it led. You warned me, the Witch of Ein Dor warned me."

Raziel stroked my bruised and bloodied knuckles with his patient fingertips. "What choice did you really have, Magduska?"

I clenched the locket tighter in my other hand and waited for my pulse to stop racing. I bade good-bye to my grief for Viktor, for Chana, for Yankel, and let them float away along the surface of the stream.

I did not know what to do with Asmodel. If letting the demon possess me would end the war in our favor, I was willing to do it. If I had to die for good, I was willing—death itself held few terrors for me, though I had learned to love my life.

But I now saw how Asmodel's actions turned in the hand, a sword cursed with a malign spell. Yankel had tried to teach me before it was too late, but better late than never, as they say.

Every time Asmodel had gotten loose, our situation had gotten markedly worse—I thought of Antonio's horrible death, the demon's sadistic attack on the Nazis themselves, too late to save Yankel. And now Gisele, along with me and Raziel, had been gently, but firmly, banished from the salt mines and the Poles hiding inside.

Asmodel was our only hope. But it was a false hope.

One-handed, I clumsily worked the clasp of the locket free and forced it open. Yankel's blood flaked into the palm of my hand. Underneath, the pictures had warped and darkened: on one side, Gisele as a girl of twelve, formally posed in a photographer's studio, hair curled and tied back with ribbon.

On the other, a picture of my beloved father, his eyes already full of grief and weighted with the worries that would kill him less than a year later. His stiff collar pinched his neck, his mustache drooped, and his sad smile spoke of monstrosities and screaming injustices still to come.

I brushed my father's picture with my thumb, and startled violently when the image began to move and speak. "My darling, why have you locked me away from you?"

My heart all but stopped beating, and I almost dropped the locket altogether. I blinked back tears, swallowed away the huge lump in my throat, and pressed my lips together hard to keep from saying anything.

I knew it was the demon speaking and moving, not my beloved, dead father, forever beyond my reach. But I so wanted it to be my father speaking I was tempted to pretend.

But no. The demon was using the illusion of my father's image to reach to me, any way that he could. I was intent on using Asmodel's powers to serve my purposes, and Asmodel was just as determined to use me to serve his own ambitions. I could not give an inch, I could not waver; under no circumstances could I let my guard down for so much as an instant.

"I know it's you, Asmodel. We need to have a bit of a chat."

My father's smile widened, and a glimmer of hope shone in his eyes, though the father I knew had seen his hopes crushed before he died. "A . . . chat." The smile grew a little hard. "It is so difficult for me to speak, stuffed inside this tiny locket, crushed. Let me stretch my arms, mortal girl."

"I am afraid not."

My father's smile disappeared, and a fine sheen of sweat began to shine on his high, smooth forehead. "Then, really, what is there to talk about, Magdalena Lazarus?"

The sweat began to stand out on my own skin; when Asmodel spoke my name, a clear, sharp pain pierced me in the stomach like an enormous needle.

"Fine, then." And I made to close the locket; I wasn't bluffing, either.

"Wait! Stop."

I slowly opened the locket again, looked down at my beloved father's face. He leered at me, a huge, horrid smile, and when his lips parted, I saw his teeth were broken, stained, and sharp. It was Asmodel, not Papa, I knew, I kept telling myself, but I looked away anyway.

I stared into the shadows playing in the near darkness, and I held on to my determination like an amulet, like a magic stone. "Poland is lost. Stalin has invaded from the east."

Silence from the locket, then a long, slow chuckle that turned my blood to water. "He kept his promise. Excellent. Do you see, dear heart? You cannot stop a thing. The Almighty has chosen to scrub you from the face of the Earth, like a stain of rust on an otherwise clean steel blade."

"You are correct, Asmodel. I cannot defy the One who made the entire world."

The locket fell silent, and I dared to look at it, balanced with the chain between my fingers. I remembered reaching up, up when I was young, admiring the locket in my stubby baby fingers, turning it to catch the light. To my little eyes, that locket was the most beautiful treasure in all the world. For in those days it had a picture of my grandmama inside. My mother had kept her own memories trapped inside in those days, before everything had fallen to pieces.

I waited for Asmodel to speak again. His cunning was legendary; he had tricked King Solomon into letting him free in the days before the Great Temple was built, and the wise king had paid the price by going mad and losing his throne for long years. I had no hope of outwitting such a one; my only chance was to see where our interests perhaps coincided.

Asmodel finally broke our silent deadlock with a sneeze—my magic often has that effect on those I work it upon. "You want Hitler dead though, of course, little Jewess."

I hated the term but ignored the feather ruffle of my irritation. "That would slow down the Wehrmacht, wouldn't it, my jolly demonic friend."

Asmodel growled; like all creatures of darkness, he hated the light that jokes shed on even the grimmest circumstances. Even my limp, silly, unfunny jokes. Perhaps especially those. "Hitler wants your sister dead."

"He does," I readily agreed.

"No one can snuff out his life except for me, Asmodel, the ancient one, the lord of all discord."

"No," I said with a little laugh. "You cannot kill him yourself, you creature of air. Not without Divine sanction. And for some mysterious reason I will never comprehend, the Almighty wants this horrible man to walk the Earth."

"The Lord is a vengeful God," Asmodel crooned, a note of sympathy vibrating in his surprisingly mellifluous voice. "He chastises your people, punishes you for your many sins."

Not long ago I would have fallen for that line, but now I just sighed and laughed again, a quiet, sad little laugh. "No, Gisele is without sin. Yankel was without sin. I cannot presume to understand what the Almighty is up to with all this misfortune."

My lack of rage made him sneeze again, or maybe he struggled a little too hard against his magical bonds. "Who cares?" he finally said, snuffling the words through another sneeze. "Why bother talking to me at all if you intend to become a saint at this late date?"

"Hitler is your creature," I said.

The sudden silence was heavy, filled with tension so electric I thought the nearest tree might ignite.

"Hitler is his own creature," Asmodel said, his words careful, his voice now smooth and courteous. "He made his own choices, his wizard called upon me most respectfully. Hitler invited me into his soul, to strengthen his powers. He chooses all."

"So if I chose to let you in, I could choose to evict you again at any time?"

Again, silence. Asmodel was used to doing the tempting. I waited for his reply. The only thing I had left was time, a whole night's worth, stretching into forever, a universe of darkness. If nothing else, my clash of wits with Asmodel gave me something to do in the teeth of my despair. A way to crochet a little hope out of nothing.

"If—if you did invite me," Asmodel said, his voice now filled with admiration and regard, "your power would completely obliterate both Hitler and Stalin. Neither man possesses any magic of his own—but you . . ."

My eyes strayed to the locket. My father's portrait beamed up at me, his face full of desperate longing, tears standing in his enormous, sad eyes.

I held the locket a little tighter in my fingers and I waited.

The silence was more eloquent than anything I could think of to say.

I coughed a little and realized I had been holding my breath, and then I shook myself free of my desires—despair was a better state of mind when consulting with a demon. Ambition led straight to presumption and from there to hubris.

"Let me in," he whispered. "We can turn aside Hitler's army together. And turn aside the Almighty's harsh decree."

"But I thought Hitler was the tool of God."

Again, the silence. Honesty, the bedrock honesty that rejected all false mirages of hope, insulated me against the demon's many charms, but for how long? How long before Asmodel would awaken my desire to strike?

"Your desire to strike comes from the Almighty Himself," Asmodel said, reading my thoughts. "He gave you will, the will to act, the will to change the world. Why would the Creator Himself give you such a will, such magnificent powers, and then forbid you to use them?"

I had, of course, asked myself the very question on many a dark night since I had first called upon the Witch of Ein Dor and set off on my ill-fated quest for *The Book of Raziel*.

I did not believe Asmodel's prescience came from any black sorcery or special window into my soul. I knew that once, long ago, Asmodel must have asked himself the same question. And his answers led inexorably to the locket, to me, to his imprisonment in the depths of a Polish forest in the war of 1939.

"Come forth," I said. And faithfully, Asmodel appeared. Beautiful again, naked again, kneeling at my feet. Infinitely dangerous.

"Beautiful deceiver," I said with a sigh. "It is just no use. I know I am too weak a vessel to keep you contained. I am no Witch of Ein Dor, I am no mighty King Solomon. I am no Yankel Horowitz, watchmaker of Kraków."

I reached down and stroked the blond glory of the demon's hair where it fanned over the high, noble forehead and his straight, neat eyebrows. "My soul is like a candle flame, Asmodel. You cannot touch it, you cannot smear it with dirt. That spark comes from the One above, it belongs to Him and to Him it will return, no matter how much sin I commit down here, whether with you or with Raziel, in the name of helping my sister or defeating our enemy."

Asmodel took a sudden sharp breath, as if something I said had mortally wounded him. "But why did the One above give you these gifts, then? Why?"

"It is not my job to know, Asmodel. You ask questions that will haunt me to the end of my days, questions I have no answers for. I will not stand aside and do nothing, but I will not act knowing that I make things worse."

I leaned forward and kissed the demon on the lips, a chaste kiss, but one that lasted a moment longer than it should have. "Asmodel, I am not strong enough to use you as a weapon. This kiss seals our kinship, for I question what you question."

I glanced up and saw that Raziel was patiently waiting for what I had to say—but the heel of his hand still rested, ready, on the hilt of his silver knife from the mines. He was ready to die and face eternal damnation to save me, yet again.

My smile widened as I returned my attention to Asmodel. "Our path together ends here, old demon. I will let you go now. I give up. There is no other way."

Raziel gasped, and I did not dare to look at him. Instead I

kept my level gaze on Asmodel. "You are a beautiful illusion, Asmodel, but no less false for that. The Garden is guarded by angels with fiery swords, and they won't let me in again, not even for you. In fact, I believe that you are the one barring the way, yourself."

Quick as a cat, Asmodel sprang to his feet. I held up a hand to stay his flight: not my untouched left hand, but my battered, bruised right one, the vulnerable one, the one that regardless still held the locus of my power.

"I will set you free, Asmodel, but you may not harm a single hair on the head of any true friend of mine, any of my ancestors, blood relations, or descendents, you may not harm Raziel, Leopold, or any other creature of the air who has ever offered me any sort of kindness. You may not touch me, track me, or search for me. My very name is a bane to you."

He smiled at me and I knew I was right to concede my defeat. I could not use his power; the idea I could was itself a danger and a delusion. I could not stamp out evil, or banish it from this mad, bad world—it was folly to even try. No, all I could do was choose the good myself—and if I couldn't do that, at least try to reach for the good. That was my job. The rest, I finally accepted, was all beyond my control.

Asmodel rose into the air, hovered above me like a dark, confounding cloud. And though he had prevailed over me, and though he sought my destruction and the death of everything I had ever loved, anything of good in my world, a sick little part of me loved his mad insistence that the world could somehow change and become perfectible.

He leaned down out of the dark cloud and kissed me, a dark,

savage kiss that hurt like the sharp bite of a horsefly. "You have bound me, pretty witch. But that is not enough to stop me."

He shot into the air with no further farewell, glittered like a falling star, and he disappeared.

"He is going straight back to Hitler," Raziel observed. His voice was calm, but when I turned to look at him, his knife was still unsheathed—though I wondered if silver was any bane to a creature of air like a demon.

"He goes north," I said. "I don't know more than that."

Raziel snorted in surprise. "You do not know of the Wolf's Lair, Hitler's eastern base of operation? The Hashomer told me a little of it before I went to face the wolf, Krueger. And . . . Krueger saw fit to tell me more. Krueger must have gone north by now himself."

I thought of the Soviets and sighed. Krueger must have been called north to the Wolf's Lair once the Soviet attack on Poland became imminent. No wonder he had been so scattered and defeated the day he had released me to Bathory's tender mercies. Krueger had been forced to leave his seat of power in Kraków to become just another bodyguard of the Führer. I knew my enemy now, and Krueger despised subservience, secretly even to his master, Adolf Hitler.

I could bear to keep silent no longer, not after this encounter with Asmodel had torn me apart. "What did Herr Krueger do to you, my love?"

"Not much. Only made me watch as he worked Viktor over. I knew I would be next."

I curled up on the ground, completely exhausted now. His voice never wavered. "Wolf's Lair is to the north, in Prussia, in the forests just north of the town of Gierloz. The seat of the great Eastern Werewolf Pack, and Hitler's headquarters in the east."

"So Asmodel too goes north. Where the foul magic resides."

My nemesis had gained his freedom, and only now did I realize how much energy it had taken to hold him. Now, freed from the need to hold him captive, I could focus upon the object of my affections, my beloved, my soul mate Raziel. At least for a precious few moments.

"Yankel wanted you to take Asmodel to the Wolf's Lair, not just let him go. You mustn't give up," he said.

"What makes you think I gave up?"

He blinked hard, scrubbed at the bristles on his chin before he answered. "Well, you kissed the demon good-bye and all but wished him luck and a fair journey."

A laugh rumbled low in my belly. "Asmodel hates that he loves me. Wants me for his own."

"I don't believe Asmodel is capable of love, not any longer. But you told Asmodel you gave up."

I winked slowly at Raziel, forced myself to smile despite our desperate circumstances. "Do you not realize? I was lying."

With my witch's sight I watched Asmodel run north to the Wolf's Lair, and my painfully beating heart pinned me to the earth as if it were an enormous lead weight. I had not seen the last of the ancient demon. In that, Raziel was right.

✳ 24 ✳

"I lied to Asmodel about giving up, but I don't know quite what to do now," I continued.

I lied now, too. I knew exactly what I had to do. I just wasn't quite sure how to do it.

When I looked into Raziel's eyes, he stared back steadily. "Why did you come?" I asked him, the same question that Bathory had recently asked me. My own voice sounded calm, conversational. When you've lost everything in your world, indeed the entire world itself, when staying alive was more of a liability than a workable plan, remaining calm was not so difficult.

"Come to Poland? Come to Earth? We have spoken of this before, Magduska." He sounded impatient, annoyed that I asked him to speak of himself rather than to consider how to make the most of the fact that he was still alive.

"I need to hear it, one last time."

He looked sharply up at me, his eyes narrowing. "I came because I could no longer stand Heaven, my love. I could not stand safety, I could not stand neutrality, I could not stand celestial distance from those I have come to adore. You do not have to be perfect for me, Magduska. God knows I am not perfect for you. I came to act, to choose."

I could not accept the future with calm finality. I had too much Asmodel in me. The vision of what I would do next superimposed itself over Raziel's words with a sudden, searing clarity. It was not complicated, what I was going to do now. But it was going to be the most difficult thing I had ever done.

And both Raziel and Gisele would suffer for it.

"Please, you must tell Gisele good-bye for me, my love."

"Good-bye? Haven't you said good-bye to that girl too many times already?"

"But she cannot go the places I must, now." And neither can you, dear Raziel. "Asmodel is the only advantage we have left," I continued aloud, listening to the wind listlessly rustling the leaves over our heads.

Raziel's laugh was short and hard, a loving caress. He reached for my hand in the silvery darkness. "Asmodel? He is racing to the Wolf's Lair. Perhaps we are better off without such advantages."

The demon of the future still hovered over us. I would not let it possess me, as Hitler would surely allow Asmodel to enter him once more.

"I need your help, Raziel," I said, my voice still calm and quiet, the serene dispassion of the angels, of the demons.

"I have come to help you. That is why I am here, in the end," he said, his voice now choked with his love, a love too heavy and rough to stay afloat in the second Heaven.

"Yankel was right. I need to hunt Asmodel, follow him to Hitler as a policeman uses a bloodhound. The way we followed him to Gisele the day we came to this place, this Poland, in the name of love. And then I must call my mother and the vengeful spirits to my side. I cannot compel them without *The Book of Raziel*, it is true. But these spirits will come willingly. They came to me in Wieliczka."

"Without the Book, my love, the spirits cannot do much damage, however willingly they come, and however desperately they want to help you too. This is why I fell. They, mortal souls, do not have that choice."

He spoke the truth. But that still did not change what I had to do. "My mother can work fearful magic against other air spirits, from beyond this world. I do not understand it, and I don't know what price she has paid for the gift. But it doesn't matter anymore. All that matters is that we stop Hitler from winning this war. Because once Asmodel finds the gemstone Book, the Sapphire Heaven, there is nothing more I can do to stop the Nazis, and with the power of both Asmodel and the Book behind them, they could conquer all the world."

"Asmodel seeks destruction, not conquest," Raziel said, but his voice wavered. He wasn't sure.

"Either way, millions would die. I have to stop them both. It's over for Gisi and me, hopefully not for you, my darling. The time has come for me to sell my soul for as much as I can get."

He stared at me, eyes wild, and I wondered if he yet understood what I had resolved to do. I interlaced my fingers tighter with Raziel's, pulled him closer to me. "You know what must happen now, my love. And every minute we hesitate, Asmodel gets farther away, has more of a chance to find Hitler and protect himself against me."

His eyes widened in shock. He knew. "No, Magda. Don't do this."

"No, it is you who must do it, my love."

We looked into each other's eyes, so deeply I all but felt my soul slip from its moorings inside my body and join Raziel inside of his own. "I can't chase him in this form," I whispered.

He kissed me, to stop my words. The sensation of his lips against mine was so vivid, so precious; but I had to leave his kisses behind. "I need you to do it," I murmured, my lips still pressed against his. "It needs to be clean. So if I can come back, I'll have a body to return to. A bullet wound takes too long to repair. But a knife, of silver, would be perfect."

Tears slid down Raziel's cheeks. He grabbed me by my shoulders, kissed me harder. Our tongues touched, so gently, and his fingers trailed up the sides of my neck and plunged into my hair. He kissed me again and again, kissed me breathless, as if he could kiss my soul on its way, without violence.

But we both knew I could not follow Asmodel in the path of love, the path Raziel and I walked together. Love was not enough to save me, or to stop Asmodel from completing what he had started, aligning himself with the monstrous genius of Hitler's struggle.

I drew the knife out of the sheath belted at Raziel's waist, reached for his hand and gently led it away from the back of my neck. I closed his fingers over the stubby handle, held both my hands over his tight, tense knuckles.

We kept kissing. I asked a terrible thing of my beloved, but I knew the mettle of my man, knew he could do what had to be done.

I kissed him back as hard as I could, a final kiss of farewell. And when the knife slammed beneath my ribs, I was so focused on loving Raziel I hardly even felt the pain of my death.

✳ 25 ✳

As before, I hunted the demon over the bleeding countryside of Poland. But unlike before, the darkness, not the light, drew Asmodel, and I hunted the demon in the guise of an air spirit, not a mortal woman.

I shot away from my corpse like a hound after a fox, even as I resisted the impulse to stay hovering over my dead body the way that ordinary spirits do, to make it easier for their angels to find them and to lead them to the second Heaven. I had to resist the spirits that would lead me away to the next world, where by all rights I belonged as a murdered human being. I had to stay hungry, a ghost; a demoness; a vengeful dybbuk—not a spirit searching for Heaven. Heaven would have to wait to exercise its judgment upon my wayward soul.

I had killing to do.

Only one backward glance did I allow myself before I disappeared into the night: to see Raziel guarding my body, covered in my blood, holding the dagger he had used to kill me. I trusted him body, heart, and soul, and on the slight chance that I could succeed in my goal without suffering some cosmic annihilation, I would attempt to rejoin Raziel in the world of the living.

I doubted I could work such wizardry again.

Asmodel surely could sense I hunted him. He could hear my spirit whisper like the wind over the half-harvested, rolling hills of wheat, a van Gogh painting of Hades. But he had sworn not to touch me, and I had bound him to his vow. Besides, Asmodel had more important adversaries to vanquish, and we both knew that I would hunt him to his destination.

I could not outrun the demon as he ran. But I could cast ahead, see to where Asmodel sought sanctuary.

The Wolf's Lair. Far to the north, east of Danzig, near the border with the Soviet Union, the ancestral home of the great Eastern Werewolf Pack had been given over to their newly elected pack leader supreme—the German Führer, Adolf Hitler. Hitler had entered Poland behind his huge army, and now hid within the impregnable stronghold of his allies, the werewolves. Every pack leader in the Reich and Eastern Europe had sworn fealty to him; now Krueger himself and his own enormous pack guarded their Führer tooth and claw, would gladly give their lives for the glory of protecting Hitler.

I followed Asmodel to this place, alone. And long we traveled. I did not have the luxury of time, the gift of my witchery stretched over the span of many days. And I did not have the power of my ancestral Book, *The Book of Raziel*, to augment my inherited powers enough to make a difference.

I would have to find another way, despite the odds. I could not let Asmodel reclaim his hold within Hitler's soul, or my sister's horrible visions would no longer be forestalled. But I had not lied. I did not possess enough strength to bend Asmodel to my will. My immediate future was hidden from me; I only knew that my ultimate fate was death, my own domain.

My mother's soul flickered next to mine. Out of the second Heaven, Tekla was vulnerable to the demonic spirits attracted to her power, to her solitary state. Neither she nor I were where we were supposed to be.

"Mother," I shrieked into the wind, "are you sure? I go to my doom, like the fool I am. You don't have to share my fate."

"Don't talk back to me," she replied, out of the wind that surrounded us. "This is my fight as well as yours. You won't go after the demon alone."

And with a cry, Tekla raised the dead. In our wake now followed a huge train of hungry ghosts, vengeful spirits, and imps—the ghosts of our ancestors, the people the Nazis had already murdered, all animated by the prospect of avenging their deaths and protecting their living relatives from the menace, the Nazi war machine that was chewing up Poland.

The legion of spirits was not yet fully manifested; it was no more than an angry blur hiding behind the veil separating the worlds. But they followed.

I said nothing. But I reached out and grabbed my mother's hand, and I squeezed her fingers, hard, and held on. Together we swooped north to the Wolf's Lair like an enormous swarm of bats.

6

I had expected a dark fortress, something grand and forbidding, ornate and feral, something like the soul of the wolf, Krueger. The Wolf's Lair was so much more than what I had imagined. It was a hundred times more awful.

Horrible as the SS werewolves seemed to me, I could still find their weaknesses and exploit them. But here in their place of power, a malign magic overlaid the blind fanatical loyalty of the werewolf people; the fortress I had envisioned indeed rose up like a granite peak within the pine forest where the Wolf's Lair was hidden. But the stronghold of the wolves thrust deep into the ground, like twisted, horrible roots, and tunneled into the very rock beneath the dirt, where the true power of the Wolf's Lair could be found.

To say the place was warded was to ignore the physical manifestation of that evil magic. The very wood, crowded with bizarre, terrible predators, had been twisted by the pull of the Wolf's Lair into something unnatural and horrible.

This was the source of the malign magic of the Budapest Vampirrat, the hideous wards of Krueger's headquarters in Kraków. It was Teutonic black magic—but it was augmented a thousand times by another power. I had felt that power for weeks now; it had eluded my detection even while taunting me with its presence.

And the source of that power, I was appalled to finally discover, was none other but the re-spelled *Book of Raziel*.

The shock of it all but burned my spirit away.

It was my fault. I had done this.

I was the one who had uncovered the handwritten, ancient copy hidden away in a warehouse in Amsterdam.

I was the one who had enabled the Nazi wizard Staff to reconstitute the Book. I hadn't killed him fast enough.

And now, my Book had been cannibalized by an alien, terrible magic, and it animated and strengthened my enemies. I sent my sight into the fortress, and a wave of nausea sent me reeling.

My mother's spirit drew closer. For once, her voice was gentle. "What is wrong?"

I could barely force out the words. "Can you not tell, Mamika? It is the Book. Re-spelled."

Tekla raised her sharp gaze and she stared keenly into the darkness. "The Russians," she said. "I don't know how they did it. . . ."

I could no longer form words past the tears. I dashed them angrily away with my fingers.

She didn't look at me. "It wasn't you," she muttered. "The wizard would have hunted down that scrap of Book sooner or later."

She kept squinting, searching the night. "This is Nazi magic," she finally said. "It feeds on the Book's power like a vampire. And it was the Soviets that created the machine to make it possible. It is not a sorcery—the Soviets hate our kind. It is more like an engine, one that sucks out the magic of the Book and diverts it to their own devices. And it is the Soviets who have built it. They must have given it to the Nazis, as part of their pact."

Finally, she turned to face me. "I don't know if any magic at all could break that Soviet technology."

"We still have to try. We've broken so many tenets of our creed already, haven't we?"

Tekla tilted her head and squinted at me. "The old path is fallen away," she said. "Sometimes to honor the spirit of the law, you must break it."

The trees groaned in the night, but the ghosts following me

and my mother had encountered far worse than the predators and the sorcery of this place. They had been murdered, their loved ones murdered, and my army no longer had anything to lose, not even Heaven. The next world did not prove to be an easy place for my people to settle; like me, restless, they returned to the scene of the crimes committed against them. My people, like me, could not help but seek to alter the events of this world, the world of the living.

They did not care how powerful was the evil magic of the north. Whatever our fate, we met it together. Better than a demonic army could ever be. And I was but one of this host.

We infiltrated the wood and perched among the trees, an undead flock of crows. "We can't get through this thicket, Mamika," I said.

"With magic," my mother said. "By spell you may do it, and we will follow."

"How is this possible? I am as dead as you. 'The dead can work no magic,' you used to say."

"The Lazarus creed tells you what you should not do, not what you are unable to do."

I stared at my mother, dumbstruck. She sounded just like Yankel Horowitz, speaking of kielbasa and golems.

She laughed, delighted by my bewilderment. "It is the same as when you killed the wizard Staff. You are a spirit of air, a daughter of women, not men. You can work your magic, child. It is a sin, but it is still possible. And in these circumstances, I don't even think it is a sin."

I let go of my mother's hand at last, drew away from her so I could take in the sight of her. Her hair flowed all around her like crimson smoke, and her eyes blazed in that hideous darkness. She had refrained from working magic in her lifetime. Well, she was making up for it now, for better or for worse.

I started by calling Leopold, my faithful imp, denizen of the realm of air. He appeared whiskers first, then haunches, then finally his lively face.

"Finally!" he said, with no formal salutations. "Waiting is such agony! Why have you not whipped those Nazi dogs already?"

I sighed at his enthusiasm, wished his ebullience was mine. "It's not so easy, Leopold darling. Want to try your hand at it?"

His face glowed, and not for the first time I wondered at his ultimate fate. He was my brainchild, after all, and I couldn't help fussing over him like a broody mother hen.

But I said nothing; what was the point? We were all there to breach the defenses of this half-submerged fortress and destroy Hitler and as many of his soldiers as we could, in hopes of breaking the German offensive before it was complete.

I had no more hope that such a victory would keep my sister's visions at bay. I only fought to give more innocent people the chance to get away from the war, go to Timbuktu or Zanzibar or any other safe place they could contrive. I was going to lose, but I still fought on the side of the angels.

"Now Leopold, gather up your brother imps," I said. "Get them organized in companies. If you can recruit spirits of the Earth to the cause, all the better."

Leopold rolled his eyes, in a wonderful imitation of an obnoxious child. "Mama! What spirit of Earth would bother noticing me? I will gather the spirits of the air. Of course." And with a parting snort, Leopold shot off into the sky, an imp charged with a great and noble mission.

That was the easy part. I knew Leopold's imps and lower devils were loyal—they loved to make mischief and tweak their betters, and here they had the added advantage of fighting for once on the side of the angels.

But what if I somehow succeeded in getting into the Wolf's Lair? How could I possibly prevail against Asmodel's power magnified by the wolves' and the corrupted magic of the forest itself?

I only resolved to try. "Double or nothing," I muttered under my breath, and then I began to intone the Lazarus family spell, the one my mother Tekla had taught me only unwillingly and after both of us were dead.

I wasn't strong enough to call them all to Earth—there were so many. "Call them with me, Mama! You always were a better witch than me, with more magic. Mama, please."

She looked up, her eyes sparkling with ghostly tears, even as her smile widened. "Finally, finally, you pain-in-the-ass child, you show me some proper respect."

I bit my lip and shrugged. Anything I tried to say would only come out wrong, anyhow. She sighed, and we both let the secrets of our complicated love affair go unspoken.

But then my mother's eyes widened, and some fresh horror now made her gasp. "Little fairy," she whispered, and the astral hairs along my arms all rose in formation, like a miniature army.

"Oh no," I said, "Gisele . . ."

It was true. The vampire's kiss had bound Gisele more closely to Bathory than I had realized. She had called to him, and unbelievably, Gisele had gotten Janos to drive the car from Kraków far to the north, to the very edge of the forest where we had gathered. She had brought Raziel, and even my body, wrapped in Yankel's good tablecloth. I could see my body stretched out on the backseat, and Gisele and Raziel standing by the car's rear bumper. Janos, poor creature, stayed inside, engine still running.

It gave me a strange, yearning, almost unbearable feeling, seeing my dead body. I again felt the pull to wait, to be led to the next world.

"How did you find me, mouse?" I yelled across the veil between the living and dead. "You came so far. Hundreds of kilometers!"

Her face was as still as a painting. And the awful tension inside of Gisele was finally gone. "It is not so far as you have traveled. Raziel told me, he asked me to help. And I've learned that just having visions isn't enough, Magduska. I've got to act on what I know, or my visions will destroy me. Besides, we don't want you storming the lair all alone."

She paused, and took in the sight of the vanguard of thousands of ghosts gathered with us at the forest's edge.

"Alone is not my current trouble, Gisi," I said. "Stay back, this battle is not for you, my love."

"But it is for me," Raziel said. He had Gisele's gun wedged into his belt, and the knife that had killed me, cleaned and sheathed once again. His coat pocket bulged with other weapons I could not see. "You will not go in there without me."

He knew it meant his death; we both knew it. But I had no time, and no right, to protest. "Quickly, Mamika. I need your magic now."

"Magic, ridiculous," she murmured, even as she raised her arms high for the opening benediction. "You work more magic than I ever did. The witch of Amsterdam taught you well."

I never loved my mother more than I did in this moment. "But you were wise enough to forbear."

She shrugged, then laughed. "Wisdom is overrated." And with an astonishing boom, the air around us rushed with a sudden press of uncountable thousands of souls now manifest. My mother closed her eyes, raised her voice to sing spells I had never heard before.

The deed was done almost before I realized she had decided to act. She and I stood together in a teeming sea of souls. I was amazed to see Raziel staring slack-jawed with wonder.

I indicated Raziel with a quick tilt of my chin. "Mama, if you can shock the angels, you know you have just done something amazing."

She did not respond—she was working far too hard—but her face lit up with the delicate joy that had entranced my father into loving her and marrying her, despite the fact she was a witch and therefore unsuitable and dangerous.

Her voice rose in a beautiful, infernal harmony, and the thousands of souls began to sing with her. I have never heard such haunting, soul-piercing voices, and as they sang, the souls manifested more and more into the shapes they had taken in life. We were surrounded by the songs of ghosts.

It was as if I were a fairy queen reviewing her gossamer court in a spring progress. The people swirling in the air all around us in the clearing wore medieval caftans, Hasidic wool, jazz suits and wide Oxford bag pants from the 1920s. They came alone, or paired with lovers, or in great laughing groups of friends, reunited in death.

I had determined for them to come, indeed was prepared to summon them myself if I had to. But the sight of them mesmerized me, and saddened me, and frightened me.

My mother stood in the midst of this whirling cavalcade of

unquiet spirits, and my eyes kept looking to her most of all. Because though these ghostly ladies and gentlemen amazed and entranced me, it was my infuriating, intoxicating mother whom I loved.

She glanced my way and flicked her hand at me. "Go on, lazy! You will catch flies, standing there with your mouth hanging open." A tiny smile of satisfaction played over her face, and she turned away, still working her dazzling magic.

Leopold had the imps; my mother had the ghosts. I trembled to think of the demons. I looked across the clearing to where Raziel still stood, holding the gun clenched in his hands. He had convinced Gisele to go back inside the idling auto, and she looked through the window at me, her palms pressed against the glass.

The wind kicked up by the ghosts whistled in the long clumps of grasses poking up between the thin birch trees, the leaves trembling and rustling over our heads.

I would not try to stop my Raziel from following me into darkness and death. Neither would I let him go alone. Because of Yankel, I knew how to raise golems, and now I called the mud up from between the roots of the trees. I used the Kabbalistic rituals he had taught me to breathe life into those mud men arranged in rows.

True magic required containment. I never understood the value of my limits until I stood in midair, a kind of demoness yet graced with my family's magic. I had learned by now to accept myself, broken and imperfect. And my limitations themselves invested my magic with strength.

Raziel now led a column of some two hundred golems, raised from the tainted mud of the forests north of Gierloz. It was time to breach the defenses of the Wolf's Lair.

✳ 26 ✳

In a flash, I knew how to do it. "Sh'ma," I began, and the army behind me echoed after me, "Sh'ma," with the ghosts filling in the silence afterward with the susurrations of uncountable Hebrew prayers, a rushing river of words.

I called the Book itself to me. *The Book of Raziel* has no soul but it was made for me, it called to my blood and soul. I had never in all this time thought to call the Book the way I summoned souls, the way the Book called to me. Even imprisoned and twisted by its captors, the power of the Book returned my call.

The air rumbled, and a screaming roar ripped the magical wards surrounding the lair like an enormous, invisible electrified fence. I whispered to the Book, and its power escaped the prison the Soviets had built for it. Our host pressed forward,

Raziel and the golems following behind. The trees hummed with the Book's power.

Though I had breached the wards of the lair, the wood was thick with corrupted magic. Even as a ghost, I found it hard to stay, assailed by the stench of it and by a steadily growing fear.

Where were the sentries? It was far too easy for us to breach the defenses of such a grim fortress. The ghosts kept their prayers running in an unceasing flow, and their words trailed behind us up to Heaven in a golden cloud. But their prayers alone could not explain our relatively easy progress.

We soon came upon a real wire fence, like the factories of death that Gisele had foreseen. The ghosts and I passed through, but the golems, Raziel at their head, hesitated outside the fence. He cried to them in Hebrew, and the Hebrew letters on their foreheads glowed like miners' lamps in the darkness.

In orderly rows, they tramped forward into the fence, and the rows drawing up from behind pressed the golems into the dull wire. The sheer weight of their muddy bodies crushed the fence, and their hundreds now marched through the gap in the fence that they had made.

The earth beneath us trembled with the pounding of wolf paws. My heart leapt at the sound of it. Finally, the battle would be joined. "The wolves, Raziel," I shouted. "Fight them, you and the golems."

Everything depended on my getting to Asmodel and Hitler. Speed and surprise were more important than anything else, and I had to get to them before it was too late.

Asmodel was too much for me, but Hitler . . . even if he had willingly become a host to the demon, Hitler was still a mortal man. No matter what the wards around him, I would attack him with everything I had.

But the wolves now stood in my way. Krueger himself led his pack in defense of their pack leader supreme. He and his wolves were ready to die to protect the Glorious Reich. I was eager to oblige him. My hands burned with magical energy, aching to strike.

I gathered my power, wove the curse into my words. The wolves, hearing my voice in the clearing, sprang forward to attack.

I inserted Krueger's name into the malefaction and I hurled it at him. The magic burned, a ball of blue fire, and it exploded in Krueger's lupine face, blinding him and singeing the fur on his face and neck.

"Krueger! Creature of Hitler, come, come!" I drew him forward, and snarling and whining, half blinded he came, his claws digging deep furrows in the dirt. The moon shone overhead, bathing us all in her cold, silver light.

He bent at my feet, and his wolves held back, snarling, unsure of what to do. And there we stood, in something of a standoff. As long as I kept Krueger pinned, his soldiers stayed back; but they would not retreat.

All of these thoughts, buzzing in my head like a swarm of enraged bees, stayed my hand from drawing out Krueger's soul then and there. Instead, I twisted his neck, to a point just short of strangulation, and I forced his muzzle into the dirt.

"Yield to me," I gasped. "I am your better. Admit it—or I kill you like a dog. Now!"

Krueger struggled for air, found none. He gave a strangled

little cough. His eyes rolled, then steadied. For a moment we stared into each other's eyes, and I sensed his rage and terror as if it were my own.

"I yield," he gasped through the foam that had formed over his jaw. I released the choke hold a fraction. He sighed and said more loudly, "I yield. You are my master."

My mind strayed to wondering at the odd magic that allowed a wolf to speak German, and in that moment I completely lost my advantage. Before I could react, the entire pack swarmed over Krueger's body. His own pack ripped out his throat for a traitor, and in a vicious blur they tore the very fur off of his body. Krueger died a speedy and wretched death at my astral feet, and all that was left of him when they were done was a shredded pile of gray fur and bloody meat.

In the next moment, the pack turned on us, and I swept them back with an arching spray of witchfire. They drew back, yelping, their faces scorched.

I called upon the golems. I could not compel them to appear, as they had no souls and retained their primitive animation only through the magic of the Hebrew alphabet. But I could call to them in the holy speech and so I did.

"Sh'ma!" I yelled, using the holy prayer as a locus for my summoning. The golems crashed through the low underbrush and they advanced on the Nazi dogs, muddy arms outstretched as if they were mummies. The wolves sank their teeth into their limbs but only got a mouthful of crumbling dirt for their trouble, and one or two of them were crushed to death under the immense weight of four or five golems collapsing over their skulls and burying them with their disintegrating, pebbly bodies.

We lost a lot of golems, with not a lot of effect. Only three wolves down, including Krueger, still nearly a dozen wolves left, all with great slashing yellow fangs, all of them eager to rip out Raziel's throat.

Running was not a possibility. I gathered my strength and prepared to go after them again. But before I could press forward, a blur to my left ran ahead, bellowing in Hebrew, drawing the golems forward to flank him. It was Raziel, holding the silver knife out and swinging it like a wild man of the forest.

The wolves were wary, suspecting a trick. Raziel leapt for the nearest one and landed on its back, twisting its tail to drive it mad. "Come, you dirty dogs!" he shouted in Hungarian. "I kill you now!"

The wolf he rode twisted around to snap at Raziel's leg. With incredible speed Raziel pulled the pin on a grenade from his pocket, shoved it down the wolf's gullet, and jumped free.

Raziel staggered backward, instinctively we covered our heads, and a moment later the grenade detonated, splattering wolf guts everywhere. I looked up to see Raziel covered in blood, still wielding the knife.

Before any of us could react he leapt onto the next wolf's back, yanked its throat back and expertly slit its throat. All of us, wolf, ghost, and human, gaped at that feat—that tough, gray fur was supposedly immune to the bite of iron or steel. But not silver.

A great spume of blood sprayed from the wolf's neck, and he turned to snap at Raziel's arm even as he died. Raziel yanked his arm free and, covered in wolf blood, he brandished the knife, laughing like a madman.

He frightened even the ghosts nearly as badly as he did the wolves, and all of us drew back. The remaining wolves growled and Raziel lunged for them again.

He had called their bluff and they turned and fled into the forest depths, howling for their dead comrades.

Our tormenter, Viktor's killer, Krueger, the second governor-general of the Protectorate of Poland, was dead. It wasn't nearly enough.

We swarmed forward now and found the fortress at the center of the compound, half buried in the feculent dirt of the lair. The very worms under our feet were infected by the malign magic here.

I blasted the front doors with a ball of blue witchfire and we hurled ourselves into the breach. But even as I flew through the massive, now-shattered doorway, I still worried.

Raziel echoed my fears. "That was much too easy," he called to me, where I floated at the level of his shoulder a few meters ahead of him.

"They want us to come," I said. "It must be a trap. Go back, Raziel, you and the golems. Trample the fence, open the place to the forest."

Even as he ran, Raziel shook his head. "No," he said, sounding like a true Lazarus now. "I am coming with you to fight until the end. It is time to finish this."

In this terrible place of judgment I was grateful neither of us faced this final trial alone.

✳ 27 ✳

We swept forward, and one by one I shattered the wards of each sector of the lair. Our horde of unquiet spirits screamed and roared as we neared the center of the compound. No matter what happened to us, the lair would be useless as a stronghold when we were done.

We came to an enormous central hall, half buried like the entrance to an enormous wolf's den. This was a place of malevolence, where Teutonic and satanic rites were practiced. Hitler had taken a wolf lodge, a refuge for the pack, and invested it with horrible evil. Built it into a huge bunker that could house two thousand men.

And the wolves had willingly sworn fealty to this perversion.

A great host of Nazis sat on chairs set in rows in the central hall. They were all waiting for us, as Romans waited for entertainment in the Colosseum.

Hitler sat on a throne on a dais above this small, select army, his mouth lightly covered with frothy drool. His eyes were dull, and glowed faintly red. Asmodel had already taken up residence inside.

My spirits sank. I was too late.

He gripped the armrests and leered at me, seeing me with Asmodel's demonic vision. "You have done most magnificently, fräulein," Hitler said in his own voice. Asmodel was permitting him to speak.

The ghostly mob behind me churned with anger. Their energy augmented my power. I drew forward, and stood alone before the enemy of my people, the enemy of all that was good and true on Earth.

It was the first time I had met Adolf Hitler face-to-face. Asmodel had come upon my summons to Budapest in Hitler's guise, but he was only a sending, not the physical man. But now I spoke to the mortal man who had already caused so much misery and destruction.

"You will now die," I said in German.

Hitler threw his head back and laughed and laughed derisively. This laughter echoed and screamed through the army of Nazis in the great hall.

"You cannot touch me," Hitler said. "You are not the first to try. It is my destiny to prevail over you."

He had his own version of a prophecy to believe in. "Destiny is not set in stone. No prophecy foretold this moment."

His smile faded. I stared into his eyes, saw Asmodel staring back at me. He snarled in an ancient language, but he could not touch me. I had bound Asmodel with his own vows.

But Asmodel didn't have to touch me to hurt me. "*Schutz-staffel!*" he screamed. "*Macht schnell!*"

A squad of men dressed in black SS uniforms fanned out in formation from behind the throne and attacked—not me, they couldn't really touch me. Instead they attacked Raziel directly. The golems formed a ring around him, and killed dozens and dozens of the men, but more kept coming.

The battle turned into a melee. When the men in chairs saw that the SS could not take Raziel alone, they rose on Hitler's screamed command and attacked. All the mortal men saw was a single man, Raziel, and two hundred unarmed soldiers made of mud. He looked an easy target.

Raziel was not. The Germans were swarmed by ghosts, and though the ghosts could not take them physically, they could manifest and haunt them, terrify them. Each soldier was besieged by a ghost, blinding him with terrible images, moaning in his ears. The soldiers began to fall around us, not dead, but shrieking in fear and horror.

I called to Leo and the army of imps. "Now, Leo! Now!" A swarm of imps assailed the soldiers, and unlike the ghosts, these creatures could hurt their enemies. The room echoed with cries, gunshots, the cacophony of war.

Asmodel screamed through Hitler's mouth. A terrible miasma of evil shook the fortress to its foundations.

Unbelievably, the demon was working magic through Hitler's human body. According to legend, the rules of the world, such a thing was not supposed to be possible.

Someone like Hitler wasn't supposed to be possible, either. I had learned to be skeptical of mere legends. Perhaps the Soviet psychotronics had somehow granted Asmodel this unprecedented ability.

Asmodel's magic smelled of pus, of rot, of excrement. The stench of it filled the air, to the very rafters of the hall. I choked on the smell but stood my ground. Awful as Asmodel's demonic magic was, with the power of my own host behind me I now believed I could still best it.

I swept forward and hurled a huge ball of witchfire at the Führer. Hitler screamed again, this time in pain, and the throne toppled backward; the fire burned him from head to toe. Asmodel belched curses and doused the fire, but I had inflicted a physically lethal blow.

Hitler staggered to his feet, skin peeling off his face and exposed hands. He screamed again, a malefaction in German, but I dodged the curse and it instead landed on the nearest Nazi soldier behind me. He writhed in pain, fell to his hands and knees, and died, a charred, blackened carcass.

I gathered up another ball of witchfire. One more blast, and Hitler's body could stand no more abuse. Asmodel could not animate a corpse.

But everything around us abruptly stopped and I held my fire.

They had gotten Raziel, disarmed him, and held him fast. Three or four men dragged him forward and threw him at Hitler's feet.

He rose again, and they tackled him and hit and kicked him until he was still. My Raziel knelt at the feet of Adolf Hitler.

I drew forward, witchfire trained on the Führer. "Back," he snarled. "Or I will drink his blood right now."

I hesitated. Raziel was the source of my strength. But he was also my greatest weakness in this terrible battle to the death and beyond.

There the four of us stood, air spirit, Führer and the demon possessing him, and fallen angel. Centuries of enmity and strife had brought us to this moment, on an altar dedicated to evil. It was the moment of Asmodel's triumph over his eternal enemy: Raziel.

"You will be my sacrifice," Hitler hissed. And it was Hitler who spoke, not Asmodel. Hitler's evil was thick and opaque; the demon and his ancient rivalry all just a tool, a potion he ingested to work his evil on a more profound level. "Your Almighty will not save you now. Go on! Call to Him! See if He answers you!"

I swallowed hard. Raziel looked up slowly from where he crouched. "Sh'ma Israel," he began, in a low steady voice. The host of spirits echoed his words in unison, filling the great hall with Hebrew, arching out with great golden slashing wings of fire.

The Almighty did not answer him. But thousands of human voices did. The din was enormous.

"Stop it!" Asmodel snarled through Hitler's mouth. But it was too late to silence the voices from beyond the grave.

The prayer echoed in that vast hall and finally faded away. It could not save Raziel.

The SS men drew forward, grabbed him under his shoulders, and dragged him to his feet. I rushed to him, but Hitler held up a hand. "Stand back," he said. "He is in my power now. Make a move to stop this and I will torture him, I will cause him infinite suffering in this world and beyond."

I refused to obey him, but before I could take another step

forward, Hitler himself stepped off the dais, grabbed Raziel by the hair, and in a single movement slit his throat with his own silver knife.

I rushed the circle. But I had reached him too late.

Raziel was dead. Now I had nothing left to lose.

✳ 28 ✳

"You broke your vow somehow, you infernal bastard," I said to Asmodel.

He shrugged with Hitler's shoulders. "I didn't do it. Hitler did it. I only stood aside and let him."

Raziel's spirit shot to Heaven, through the roof, and my mother and the entire host of spirits saw him on his way. I let them all go, for their sakes as well as Raziel's. These ghosts had already been through enough and they had done all that they could. Raziel would lead them upward; that in truth was what my angel had been made to do.

But I was made of darker materials. I turned to Asmodel and Hitler, a huge ball of witchfire writhing between my palms. One last shot and the Führer would be burned to a crisp. As dead as Raziel. And my vengeance would have only just begun.

"Do it," he whispered through Hitler's lips, even as the Füh-rer's eyes widened in terror at the sight of me and my punishing fire. "Finish it now."

I trembled with my lust to do it, Raziel's body crumpled at my feet, his blood seeping into the horrible stone of the lair, al-ready soaked with uncountable oceans of sacrificial blood.

But I let the witchfire dissipate, the blue flames dissolving into wisps of smoke. "I have sworn my own vow," I whispered. "You are Hitler's master now, Asmodel. You are not mine. I will not do your bidding."

Hitler began to jitter and twitch like a marionette tangled in his strings. "Kill me!" Asmodel shrieked through Hitler's now-resisting vocal cords. Asmodel wanted Hitler dead.

Why?

I fought to think through my rage and grief. My beloved lay dead at my feet, on my account; so many people had died on my account, to further our desperate aims. To stop history itself from happening.

"Kill me," Hitler moaned and shrieked, his body now con-vulsing. He ripped at his shredded skin with his own fingers and screamed in pain, and I am ashamed to admit I enjoyed his suffering, I wanted to kill him for all that he had done, for all that Hitler aspired still to do.

"You want him dead, Asmodel," I snarled. "You do it. I will not serve your bidding."

"Stiff-necked fool," Asmodel snarled back. Hitler's famous mustache was now clotted with snot, drool, and blood. "You have the scourge of the world in your power. Your beloved is mur-dered at his hand. You cowardly little bitch."

I had had enough. I gathered the witchfire back into my

palms, but instead of blasting Hitler I smote the walls of the lair itself. The entire place shattered around us, the walls blasting apart, the humans, wolves, and chairs flying outward in a circle from the explosion.

Hitler and I alone stood in what was left. The watery light of dawn filtered down from Heaven. Day had come. Hitler still lived.

"I am no ghost, to fade by morning," I said.

"So kill me, bitch," Asmodel said. His words slurred through Hitler's twisted, unwilling lips.

"You tempt me, Asmodel," I replied. "It was far too easy to breach the defenses of this place. You wanted me to hunt you. You wanted me to find Hitler, to kill him. Why?"

We stared at each other for what seemed like forever. "Because then you would be mine," Asmodel said at last. "And we could finally re-create the Garden."

"This?" I looked around the twisted, stinking wreckage of the lair, now exposed to the light of day. "This is your Garden, Asmodel. You may tend to it yourself. I won't do your work for you."

I had often said I knew my limitations. This was the first moment I truly realized them, and accepted them. I was right to let Asmodel go; he destroyed and ruined everything he touched.

And he devoured Hitler, he raped him from the inside. Asmodel was a worse punishment of the Führer than any clean death I could devise. And killing Hitler would not stop the killing. Asmodel would simply pick up where Hitler left off, using me or any human being as host. Hitler or another would leap farther down the path of destruction that he had set in motion. A million Kruegers just waited for the chance.

And I could not stop Asmodel. Not by myself. I knew my limits, and that knowledge saved me.

I floated backward. "Tend your Garden," I whispered. Then, much more slowly, I ascended, following the silvery traces of Raziel's passing as he had risen.

I left the smoking ruins of the Wolf's Lair behind. Adolf Hitler, still willingly possessed, still consumed with hatred, stood alone in the ruins, burned and torn, surrounded by blood and death.

✳ 29 ✳

No Tekla, no Raziel greeted me in the afterworld. I was fair game for any demonic being that happened upon me; more than ever before I was a lost soul, wandering the intermediate plane between life and death.

I accepted my fate. Despite the fact that Hitler still lived, though terribly maimed, I knew I had made the least bad of all the bad choices I had been given to make. Killing Hitler would have led to worse destruction than leaving him alive, slowly murdered by his parasite, Asmodel.

Asmodel would try to keep him alive for as long as possible. But Asmodel destroyed everything he tried to possess. For Asmodel, poor Asmodel, did not know limits. He refused to bow his head to the greater plan of the world, and so he made a hell of every plane he occupied.

The gray nothingness stretched infinitely before me, and I wandered for some time, utterly alone, through puffy gray clouds. But I did not descend into the lower realms. I grieved, but I was at peace.

A flickering star grew larger and larger, glowing silver, then gold. I watched it come, and its beauty stopped my astral heart.

I hoped it was Raziel. But it wasn't.

It was Yankel Horowitz, the watchmaker of Kraków.

"Sweetheart, what are you doing wandering around here?" he said, in the language of angels.

I half laughed, half cried. "I don't know," I finally said.

"You want to follow me? You did enough, you know. You can come to the next world, relax. I'll help you find your way."

I hesitated. "Did you see Raziel?"

He shrugged and scratched his nose. "Raziel HaMelech? He's a bigger cheese than I'll ever be, pretty girl. I'm sure he's where he is supposed to be."

Yankel's kind solicitude broke my heart. I hugged him on the astral plane, and tears streamed down my face. "Bless you, holy man. You have better things to do than babysit me. I still have some work to do. Go to your reward, righteous one."

"No, I won't leave you lost up here." He put his fingers to his mouth and whistled, not a harsh wolf whistle but a gentle sound like a mourning dove.

The plane of nothingness was filled with the rustling of infinite, invisible wings. With a sudden burst of inspiration I called, "Albion! Albion!"

The angel of England appeared before us, first one wing, then another, brightening and brightening until the clouds surrounding us glowed with glory.

And in her care, looking somewhat abashed but none the worse for wear, were two handsome young men. One Viktor Mandelstam, and a certain fallen angel I knew, Raziel, the one who kept the secrets of God.

"I won't go back without you," I said with some urgency, before anyone else had the chance to speak or even say hello. "I can't live without you, Raziel."

"Don't play small, Miss Lazarus," Albion said in a prim voice, her angelic speech inflected with a lovely British accent.

"You sound just like my mother," I said. Sadness began to pull me downward, but Raziel slipped his hand into mine and pulled me back up.

"I mean it, my darling," I said, and I faced Raziel. "You are my soul mate. I understand now why my mother didn't come back to Earth after my father died and she followed him here."

"We don't always get to decide these things," Raziel began, but Albion raised a hand and stopped him.

"Peace, my brother," she said. "Unless you defy the One's decree, go forth and do what you must." Albion hesitated and looked around.

"Nobody said anything, and I'll see you on your way. So get out of here," she said quickly, in a low voice, looking so furtive and clandestine, another one of Churchill's spies, that I couldn't help but laugh.

I turned to face Viktor. "You were an angel to me in Kraków," I said. "Thank you from the bottom of my heart."

"You have nothing to thank me for," Viktor said. "Bless you. Raziel is with you now, so you need a new guardian angel up here. Yankel is going to ascend too high for that job, so . . ."

"I'll make sure he learns quickly," Albion interjected. "I have a feeling you are going to keep him very, very busy."

I swallowed the huge lump in my throat. What Viktor offered me from beyond was far greater than any words of thanks I could offer. I simply nodded, and Viktor smiled back. He would continue the fight from here, in the next world.

I squeezed Raziel's hand harder. "Are you ready, my darling?"

His smile was so bright it dazzled my eyes. "Ready for anything, Magduska. Life is calling."

"Okay, then, my love. Hold on tight. This is going to hurt."

I recited the Lazarus family spell, and both Raziel and I shot back to Earth in a needle of light. We left the angels behind in Heaven.

We were lucky. Or perhaps Albion had interceded more than she was strictly supposed to. Raziel's body had come to rest next to mine at the edge of the wood, next to Bathory's auto. A last golem had collapsed, carrying my love's dead weight, and the remains of his muddy body cushioned Raziel from the road. Gisele knelt next to our bodies, weeping not with grief but with the effort of her exhortations.

I shot into my body with a groan. The pain of the knife slash to my heart hurt like the devil. But before I turned to my own fatal wound I set to repairing Raziel's, because he had no magic to hold him in his body once he returned.

Even as I began healing the vivid slash to his throat Raziel came back to the living. With a groan, he tried to sit up, but Gisele touched his shoulder.

"Rest, dear angel, let Magda help you. That's right."

I whispered the rest of the spell, my teeth gritted against the pain. Once I saw Raziel would live, I started working on myself.

I was almost done when a shadow fell over my face. It was Janos, leaning forward, his molelike eyes squinting behind their heavy spectacles in the soft morning light.

"Miss," he said. "Miss. May I suggest you hurry?"

I blinked hard and whispered the final invocation. With a gasp I forced myself to my feet; I knew what Janos meant.

With Albion's help, Raziel and I had done the impossible, returned from the dead. But the four of us and Bathory's elegant, lonely automobile were surrounded by thousands and thousands of Nazis. Hitler was still in power, willingly possessed by the terrible, beautiful Asmodel. Our position was still precarious, to put it nicely.

"We smashed apart the lair," I said in a low gasp. "That will slow Hitler down a bit, at least. Let's get out of here before they get their bearings."

Janos's face fell. "So the evil man is still alive," he murmured, his composure for once shaken.

"Yes, he is, thank the Maker," I said. "He will be the instrument of the demon's destruction, in the end. And the demon will destroy him in turn."

"If that is a victory, miss," the driver said, "I tremble to contemplate defeat."

"I guess it all depends on your frame of reference," I said, tired to the bone. We got in, and Janos started to drive.

✳ 30 ✳

OCTOBER 22, 1939: 10 P.M.
CAFÉ ISTANBUL
BUDAPEST, HUNGARY

By Hand Delivery
To Magdalena Lazarus
c/o the vampire Bathory, chief vampire of Budapest

My dear Hungarian witch,
Brava, and brava again. I cannot call upon the angels
the way that you do, but whispering spirits tell me that
you have put quite a dent in the Nazi war machine.
Oh, the papers put about that Herr Hitler was burned
in a curious electrical fire, but I know the truth. He is
recovering, but from all reports the Führer will never
be the same.
    I am, to be frank about it, quite pleased. You have

bought Britain time, time to arm against the Hun.
Every extra day we gain before Hitler turns his ambi-
tions westward is another day to build munitions, call
upon our soldiers, prepare our fair island to defend
against Nazi attack.

And there is no honor amongst thieves. There are
rumors that Stalin and Hitler have already fallen out.
Stalin, too, buys time, but Hitler grows impatient al-
ready, I hear. This is an educated guess, but one that I
believe you will make good use of: Hitler will make a
break for the Caucasus oil fields, and sooner than I
had thought. Hitler needs oil to run his war machine,
however much you have dented it. Once he seeks to
invade the Caucasus, Hitler will enrage the Russian
Bear.

And you will be ready, dear Lady Lazarus, won't
you? Knox, who has delivered this letter for me, be-
lieves that what you seek is also in the Caucasus. And
he wanted you to know this fact, particularly.

Most important, know that your sister has arrived
safely to our shores, with the assistance of both Knox
and Bathory. She will stay at Chartwell until we have
found her a more suitable place. She is very quiet, and
very sweet, your little sister. But she is possessed of
your family's dark and terrible fire as well. She is not
such a dreamy little mouse as you described at our
dinner at Chartwell.

Please find enclosed a small token of my esteem. I
had Knox take the trouble of changing it from British
pounds to Hungarian pengős, as those will be more

useful to you. I would have sent you gold, but Knox
would not have been able to carry this much so easily.
　I bid you well, my dear. Your former employer has
reportedly been restored in Budapest, above his for-
mer position, so I am hopeful this letter finds you in
fine fettle.

> *With all good wishes,*
> *Your obt. servant,*
> *Sir Winston Churchill*

I sat in the Istanbul of an evening in late October, my beloved Raziel at my side. Only a faint scar now remained of the
terrible slash under his chin, but Raziel bore other scars, ones
that could not be seen. It had been a long and hellacious month,
getting out of Poland and back to Hungary once again.

It was like Heaven, or a dream. Once more I sat in the Istanbul Café, once more the rumballs, the heavy enameled coffee
cups, the gilded, Levantine opulence of the place. And holding
court in the middle of all of it, Bathory, restored to his rightful
spot in the center of the Hungarian universe.

Bathory read the letter to us in English and translated into
Hungarian as he went along. I stirred my coffee long after my
lump of sugar had melted away, and Raziel played with the
brim of his fedora, lost in thought as Churchill's words unspun
over our table at the Istanbul.

Bathory finished reading Churchill's missive, and folded up
the heavy, cream-colored paper and returned it to its envelope.
And I wondered at the strange miracle of befriending this Englishman, a man who worked no magic yet was possessed of so
much temporal power.

We sat in silence after Bathory had done. "So Knox has gone?" I finally asked.

"Of course," Bathory replied. "Hungary is distinctly unsafe at the moment for Knox. Not even I may protect him completely, here. Knox has nobody like Eva to speak for him, hidden in high places." And, terrifyingly, Bathory smiled.

"The letter says your position is restored, dear Count," I said. "What has the Vampirrat of Budapest to say of this?"

"Oh, them." Bathory's thin, bony fingers caressed the edges of the envelope. "I got rid of them."

Raziel and I exchanged a glance. I decided not to press the matter further.

"Now that I have heard what Mr. Churchill has had to say, I have a matter to discuss, dear sir," I said. "War still rages. For the moment, the Soviet Union is a fellow ally of the Reich."

I took a deep breath, and went ahead. "After hearing of Churchill's suspicions, I now wish to visit our friends, the carpet merchants."

"The Azeris, eh?" After reading Churchill's missive, Count Bathory was not all that surprised.

"Yes. I think that I will find there what they seek."

An Azeri rebel had come in supplication to Count Bathory the previous summer, hunting for a superweapon his people believed could free them from Soviet domination. I more than suspected they sought the gem of Raziel, the Sapphire Heaven.

"I believe it is in their land."

"In the Caucasus?" Bathory cocked an eyebrow at me. "In the oilfields?"

"In the Garden," Raziel said with a gasp, and I saw he understood the reason I staked our venture on a guess. The fertile lands of the Caucasus, I believed, were the physical locus of the ancient Garden of Eden. The gem of Raziel had returned to its source. Asmodel had unwittingly given me the idea.

And I believed I now had both the courage and the magic to hunt the Sapphire Heaven. The gem could not be sullied. It remained in its pure, original form. It was a prize beyond all measure.

"We are leaving in two days, as soon as I can change over Churchill's pengös," I said. I reached for Raziel's fingers and gently squeezed. "As long as you are ready to go, my love."

"But you have only just arrived," Bathory said. "Give yourself a rest, my little chicken."

"My enemies refuse to rest, dear count," I replied.

I studied the rim of the coffee cup by my elbow as I went on. "We have only two days in Budapest. But it's time enough for a short honeymoon." And I looked sidelong at Bathory and smiled.

Bathory roared with laughter, rose to his feet, and reached to kiss my hands, my cheeks, and he clapped Raziel on the shoulder with congratulations. Raziel, smart man, made sure not to look the vampire directly in the eyes.

"The finest hotel in Budapest for you, then," Count Bathory said. "The lieutenant of the chief vampire of Budapest should have no less."

I smiled at Bathory's words, but I could not take my eyes off Raziel. Against all odds and expectations, my angel sat here with me, without his wings, confounding both the future and the past.

Our defeat in Poland had set us free. I was ready to give myself to my fallen angel, heart and soul. And Raziel, my man, was ready to take me.

ABOUT THE AUTHOR

Michele Lang is the author of the historical urban fantasy novel *Lady Lazarus,* to which *Dark Victory* is the sequel. Like her protagonist Magda, Lang is of Hungarian-Jewish ancestry. She and her family live on the North Shore of Long Island, New York, where she is working on the final novel of the Lady Lazarus trilogy.